Romance THY Enemy

Romance Thy Enemy

KAYLA MCGRATH

Content includes graphic sex (oral, vaginal, and anal), family death (grandparent), loose themes of loss and grief, alcohol consumption, drug use (cocaine) from one dimensional side characters, allusions to offensive language from one dimensional side characters (slurs, fatphobia, etc.), discussion of cheating from a previous partner (not committed by the MCs), and mentions of strained family relationships from side characters.

Please also be aware of the author's note at the end of the book.

For Tess, who was there for me when I was so alone.

1816

CHAPTER ONE
Mina

Sweet wine turned sour on Mina's tongue when she heard her name paired with Graham's. She pulled the glass from her lips and pressed herself against the wall, turning an accidental eavesdropping into a deliberate eavesdropping.

When she went to the kitchen for refills of Pinot Gris for herself and Illiana, having her best friend and said best friend's fiancé discussing her was the last thing she expected.

Through the mostly open concept space of Emmett and Illiana's house, Mina could see the alcohol markers and coloring books waiting for her and Ana to return to them. But the hushed conversation at the foot of the stairs halted all that.

"You know they can't stand each other. I don't want to make them uncomfortable, my love," Ana was saying softly.

Meaning her and Graham—obviously.

There was no one else on the planet that she couldn't stand, and only one person who, in turn couldn't stand her.

"I know," Emmett answered, "but Chase and Patrick are in the middle of adopting and they have enough on their plate. Kieran flat out refuses to be a best man ever because so many people used him for his maturity and financial stability to fund their weddings, then dropped him as a friend afterward—which I can understand. Riley, he's my brother, but we just aren't close enough; and having that responsibility on top of kids is a lot. And if I chose Nate, well, that feels like twisting the knife after how he felt about you last summer." Emmett sighed and Mina wanted to sigh with him.

None of them would forget her cousin, Nate's unrequited ten-year-long crush on Illiana after only the briefest of impressions, but luckily, he'd been a great sport about the whole revelation. Still, anything related to Illiana seemed cruel.

"Graham is my only option—and if we're being honest, he is my first choice, all things considered."

Illiana ran her hand through her long blonde waves, her cheeks flushed from wine and frustration. "That's where I'm at too. As much as I adore your sister, Sloane knows how close I am with Mina, and she'd refuse because she knows I'm compromising. She'd tell me that Mina and Graham should set aside their differences for our wedding. Madeline would say the same. And Delilah is wonderful, but having your ex as—"

"Right, yeah," Emmett cut in, cheeks coloring beneath the olive hue of his complexion.

Wedding? Were they discussing…?

Oh no.

A pit yawned and dropped in Mina's stomach.

"So, I want Mina to be my Maid of Honor and you want Graham as your Best Man, but we probably can't. Is that where we're at?"

Emmett ducked his head and guilt rushed through Mina. This was all her fault. Their wedding hadn't even happened yet and she was ruining their special day. All because she and that stupid, tall, dark, and—no. Because she and Graham couldn't be in a room together without one of them biting out jabs and snide remarks.

"We *shouldn't,* is where we're at," was what Emmett said. "We'll figure out something, sweetheart."

Then Emmett kissed Ana's forehead and slipped back up the stairs, leaving them to resume their girl's night.

Mina tipped her head against the wall, her golden-brown curls shrouding her face in a thick curtain.

"*Fuck,*" she whispered.

How was she supposed to fix this? How was she going to make sure her best friend had her dream wedding in every way she deserved?

Waiting a couple minutes, Mina approached, finding Illiana coloring a cozy and bold-lined page with a cherry blossom shade marker. The entire palate of the page was shades of pink.

Mina handed Ana her glass while she took two large gulps from her own. Internally, she was steeling herself. Trying to rectify this mess she made. Swallowing hard, she sat down, her brain saturated in cheap wine, her mouth fuzzy with decreased inhibitions.

What could she say? She had a sudden change of heart? It was all a misunderstanding? They bonded over their mutual love of peanut butter cups?

Nothing was coming to mind—she couldn't rescue them from this ridiculous travesty.

Of course, they could be adults about it, but she didn't know if Graham was truly so capable. After all, he was the one who'd started this whole thing.

Twirling a yellow marker, Mina felt the alcohol fog in her brain loosen her tongue. Before she'd even processed what an impulsive part of her brain had decided, words were spilling from her lips.

"I'm secretly dating Graham."

What?

What. The. Fuck.

Illiana dropped her marker, her face a mask of shock. "*You're what?*"

Apparently, so secret neither of them had any clue.

That was absolutely not what she meant to say, but in some insane way, it was the perfect fallacy. Even so, panic wasn't reasonable, and the anxiety-riddled part of her brain was on full alert from the veritable Pandora's Box of shit she'd just unleashed.

There were so many holes in this plan. Graham could counter her with a single word and it would be over—and so much worse. She could simply backtrack and tell Ana she was joking, but she already felt like she was in too deep.

No, she had to commit to this. For Ana. She hated lying, and the guilt of lying to her best friend was agonizing, but this was an essential lie.

"I didn't know how to tell you," Mina began, taking another sip of wine. "But I'm pretty tipsy now, and I thought I may as well rip off the bandage. We..." she hesitated. "We wanted to wait before saying anything."

"Oh my god, Mina? What? How?" Illiana grasped both Mina's hands. "I want all the details." The glitter bright excitement in Ana's blue eyes took her off guard.

Had Ana been...hoping for this?

"Can I just check in with him to make sure he's ready to tell the boys too?" Mina asked shyly.

Internally, all she was thinking was: fuck, fuck, fuck, fuck, fuck.

"Oh, for sure!' Ana withdrew and waited with rapt anticipation.

Mina pulled out her phone and texted a number she'd only messaged a handful of times—due to necessary reasons only. The sparse text thread scattered with blue and gray messages were weeks, months, and years apart. That did little to sell her flimsy fib.

Emergency. Call me now.

Ten seconds later the phone was ringing in her hand.

Mina brandished the device in front of Ana. "Speak of the devil."

Using Graham's call as an excuse, she stepped out to collect herself and prepare to sell this ruse for the greater good. At the door, Mina hit answer and immediately started off the call.

"Hey, babe."

Mina was opening the back door, crossing into the late February night. Her breath puffed in white clouds against the dark, the chill air a pleasant balm on her flushed cheeks.

"Are you safe?" Graham's voice was slightly panicked. "Is there someone—?"

"I'm good, just drinking wine and coloring with Ana. Listen, I was thinking I could come over tonight and talk about some things."

There was a heavy silence on the other end.

"Are you well?" he finally managed. "You called me *'babe'.*"

"Yes, I am," she said firmly. Ignoring the second half of his response.

"Are you drunk?"

"Well, yes, but that's beside the point."

"Are you getting a migraine? Do you need me to help you with something?"

She hated that he knew that about her—that she was prone to debilitating migraines that sometimes left her bedridden. She forced herself to forget Canada Day last year when he took care of her during the annual pool party. Her hackles instantly went up in response, prickling at his too keen observance.

Inhaling sharply and examining the gold ovals of her nails, Mina shuttered her eyes. "I'm fine. But I need to talk to you. In person. Tonight."

"But you're safe?" he pressed.

She pinched the bridge of her nose. "I am safe."

"Okay, well I'll text you my address and I'll see you when you get here. I can call you a cab."

"I've got it," she snapped.

"All right. I'll see you soon, Jasmina."

And then he hung up.

Mina gritted her teeth. Graham was the only one who ever called her Jasmina, and it ground on her nerves—like sandpaper against myelin sheaths.

She was taking a moment outside, tasting the winter air, the crisp bite of frost, smelling the coils of smoke from wood-burning chimneys, the feel of the cold seeping into her bones. Mina called a taxi to be delivered immediately to ensure a solid exit strategy. After ending the phone call, she'd been left shaken—uncertain. Taking a couple more breaths, she reached for the door handle.

When Mina returned, Ana was waiting.

"So?" she asked, so full of energy, like an excited little bunny. All pink and soft and sweet. "Spill the details!"

Mina finished her glass of wine, replenishing her intoxication levels that the cold air had sobered. Setting the glass down with a delicate clink, the little flower charm spinning on the stem, she opened her mouth.

"It's new and it's…exciting. For a little while we wanted to keep it just us—especially with such a developed friend group—but now, I think we might be ready to be in the open."

"And that supposed hatred you held for him?" Ana queried.

"Water under the bridge."

"*Water under the bridge?*" Ana echoed. "Just like that?"

Headlights cut the night as Mina's taxi pulled into Emmett and Illiana's long driveway, the vehicle making a questionable ticking noise she could hear even from inside the house.

"Well," Mina began, scrambling. "It's a bit more than that, but it's a long story. Graham wanted me to come over tonight to talk and my cab is here. I can fill you and Mads in when we go for our walk?"

"You better," Illiana said, pointing her index finger menacingly. "This is big news, ma'am."

"I promise. Love you."

"Love you, too."

They hugged, then Mina grabbed her belongings and stuffed them into her bookish tote bag, shrugged on her olive puffer jacket, and headed for the door. Once she was in the cab, she rattled off Graham's address—1816 Prince Drive—and the car pulled away into the night and across town.

Rose Point wasn't large, but it was situated only twenty minutes outside of Victoria, which, being the capital city of British Columbia, quantified an inflated population—both within the city and the small town. However, even with that proximity, Rose Point was able to preserve that small town feel with the nearby city perks.

Overall, it was an ideal set up.

When they pulled up to Prince Drive, shock filled her.

It was her dream house.

Not just any dream house, but the dream house she drove by so often—out of her way, she may add—she'd lost count. How had she never realized it was his?

Graham's house was a gorgeous two storey restored Victorian with a hexagonal covered porch off to the right side, and gingerbread eaves decorated with white lacy detail—perfect against the muted green of the wooden siding. The front door was painted a bold and bright sage, the deck a worn walnut, the same color as the garage door off to the left of the house. On the opposite side was a currently, not bloomed cherry blossom tree, the branches skeletal in the winter night.

She loved it.

And she hated that she loved it.

Because it was his.

Graham wasn't supposed to have a nice house. He was supposed to have a shitty apartment with a mattress on the floor. That is what her nemesis's status should've dictated. He also shouldn't have a perfectly swept pathway up to the two stairs of his house, or a disgustingly quaint spot for a swing on the porch, illuminated by a golden light.

Mina breathed deeply, paid the driver, and got out. As she skipped up the stairs, the inside light flicked on and the door opened, revealing Graham in all his *Graham-ness*.

He was easily over six feet tall with tousled brown hair in a stylish fade, gemstone blue eyes, and features that should be illegal to possess. High cheekbones, full lips, a straight nose, a shadow of stubble. Stupid, tall, dark, and handsome.

His lean form rested in the doorway on high alert, his eyes roving over her entire frame, searching for anything of concern.

As soon as she reached the doorway, Mina inclined her chin and set her jaw.

"Are you going to invite me in?"

"What, are you a vampire now?" he asked in his stupidly hot rumbling voice.

She bit back a retort and spit out her confession.

"I need you to be my fake boyfriend."

CHAPTER TWO
Graham

I need you to be my fake boyfriend.

Those were the words repeating over and over in his head as he stared at Jasmina, the little thing full of resolve and determination. Her hazel eyes were hard as she stood in the cold, waiting for his response.

"Do you want to come in and explain?" he asked, despite his confusion. Completely forgoing his vampire quip.

He didn't hide his befuddlement well, but what he did hide well, however, was how flustered she had him. Graham had always been horribly attracted to her, but for whatever reason, Jasmina couldn't stand him—no matter what he did. Her constant rebuking at his attempts of friendship—or even extensions of olive branches, which were swatted away—had him answering in kind with petty verbal jabs. Especially, the one where he called her by her full given name.

And she'd called him babe.

She gave a curt nod as he stepped sideways and allowed her to pass into the warm interior of his house.

The foyer was full of rich wood, from the original hardwood floors to the L-shaped staircase and carved crown moulding. Ivory wallpaper done up in near-invisible forest scenes covered all the walls, while a semi-modern, brushed gold ceiling light offered a soft illumination.

Graham and Nate had spent hours fixing up the place after inheriting it from his maternal grandparents, the house having belonged to their parents before that. Unfortunately, the age—while offering plenty of character—came with plenty of issues, some of which were cosmetic, which he handled himself, but some that had required professionals.

"Can I take your coat?" he asked as Jasmina strode through the room, crossing to the woven rug on socked feet.

Jasmina was the definition of gorgeous. She had thickly lashed, green-gold eyes, smooth, umber skin with luscious curves that decorated the firm muscle of her slim build. Lips, that he always caught himself staring at, were full with a perfect cupid's bow, but the corners always turned down when she caught him looking.

He could see her eyeing up all the details in his home—the wooden, slightly gothic framed mirror, the botanical sketches, the wall sconces that match the ceiling light, the textured cushions on the bench—and he silently thanked his interior designer sister who'd helped him out with a woman's touch. Apparently, even though he was extremely observant, he still looked at everything with Man Eyes.

Jasmina fidgeted as she leaned against the entry table, twisting her hands together and avoiding eye contact. She didn't say anything, but she did remove her coat. Wordlessly, he took it and hung it on the hook by the front door—another matching piece—and awaited her explanation.

Graham started for the kitchen through the arched doorway and grabbed green grapes from the fridge and a pack of pre-sliced gouda and cheddar squares. From the pantry he found a box of crackers and dumped them in a bowl. When he turned around, Mina was there, standing at the island counter, discomfort lining her frame.

"You know," he said, putting the snacks on the counter and filling two water glasses, "this whole not explaining thing is doing wonders for recruiting me as your fake boyfriend."

She exhaled shakily and Graham instantly dropped the sarcasm. The fact his satire didn't have the regular effect on her was alarming.

"Jasmina," he said softly, putting a hand on her sleeved wrist. She looked up, eyes flashing with something fiery, then with a quick intake of breath, she began.

"I overheard Emmett and Ana talking tonight."

And then she just word vomited. It all came out in one steady stream—her wine-induced solution, her guilt, her well-intentioned lie, all of it. And with each word and every rationale, he mirrored it.

Graham was just as implicit in the problem between his best friend and fiancée as she was, and the more she spoke, the more he agreed with her motives. It was a solid idea, if not yet a solid plan, but he could work with that. She wasn't even finished talking yet, but he was already fully on board.

Sometime during her explanation she'd reached for the grapes and now she was unconsciously nibbling on the cheese and crackers. Graham was glad his provisions were comforting her—he found people were more at ease when there was appetizer-type or finger-foods available.

Graham didn't interrupt her, just listened intently and nodded when appropriate. He kept a neutral and attentive face, but inside he was positively freaking out.

This girl, who he'd had an unbearable attraction and irritation to was proposing a fake relationship. And not just a brief one—no, this plan would extend longer than she had probably accounted for.

"That's why I really need you to agree to this fake relationship," she finished as she reached for the last grape in the bowl.

"Okay," he replied, conviction lacing his tone.

"Okay?" she asked, lifting an arched brow.

Graham realized he'd been a bit hasty with his confirmation. He realized he should have drawn it out a little, made it seem like he wasn't so eager to accept. There was some hope in backtracking though.

"Okay, I'll do it." He raised a finger. "But we really need to work on our conversation skills."

"Our conversation skills seem just fine at this moment," she countered.

"This conversation is probably one of the only civil ones we've ever had. It's a matter of time before we're at each other's throats and sniping back and forth, and that's exactly what I mean. We need to put a stop to that—at least in public— for the duration of this agreement."

Mina's lips flattened into a hard line. "Are you sure you can do this?"

"Are you sure *you* can, Jasmina?" There was a playful edge to his words.

Jasmina glared in response.

"All right," he conceded. "How long are we doing this for?"

"Until the day after the wedding," she announced without hesitation.

Surprise stole through him. "You want to pretend for three months?"

"I don't want to ruin their wedding."

"And when we inevitably 'break-up'?"

"It will be mutual."

Graham let a beat of silence pass, watching her green-gold eyes analyze him with a professional air.

"If we do this, we need some ground rules. A contract, if you will," he pronounced.

The drawer jingled with oft-used utensils, screws, and forgotten Allen keys as he opened his junk drawer and found a notepad and pen. The gingham print border was sage and white, with a groovy font proclaiming "Good Vibes" printed across the top in green and teal.

Graham began in his decisive scrawl.

The participants of the fake dating exchange include one, Ms. Jasmina (Mina) Coulter and one, Mr. Graham Starling, until the mutually agreed upon end date of May 22.

The rules outlined are as follows:

(Note: These rules are subject to negotiation if both parties agree.)

"Don't you think this is a bit overly formal?" Jasmina asked, peering across the white marble countertops. "You're not even a lawyer." She paused, probably realizing she actually didn't know the answer. "Are you?"

Graham chuckled. "No, I'm a speech language pathologist."

"Really?" Her voice rose half an octave and her brows reached for her golden-brown hairline.

"You seem shocked."

"I just didn't think you were that…"

"Educated?" he guessed.

Blood suffused her cheeks and she took a sip of water to attempt to hide it. "Yeah. Sorry."

He shrugged. "You've disliked me for years; I'm not surprised you thought that."

"What's that supposed to mean? You think people who didn't go to university are inferior?"

"Woah," he rebuked, putting his hands up in surrender. "I said no such thing. Uneducated and people who haven't attended post-secondary schooling are just as valuable as those who have."

Jasmina watched him reproachfully, then deflated. "Sorry, I jumped to conclusions."

"None taken," he said placatingly. "But before we begin, we should establish how we got together."

She tapped her lip. "What were you doing Valentines Day?"

"Nothing. I was here."

"Does anyone know that?"

"I didn't advertise it and they didn't ask so I'm assuming no."

Jasmina flattened her palms on the island. "Then we ran into each other on Valentines Day. At..." He could see her clearly wracking her brain. "The grocery store."

Graham grinned and chimed in on the tale. "I found you in the frozen aisle grabbing mint chocolate chip icecream and peanut butter cups."

Clear shock seemed to color her face. A transparent, *'How does he know that's my favorite?'* written across her features.

"And you made a quip about me being all alone—all Jasmina bullshit—but asked if I was hungry because you had a pizza to pick up in fifteen minutes. Then you asked if I liked pepperoni and green peppers—"

This time it was his turn to be surprised she knew his preferred pizza toppings.

"And you said, *'yes, of course.'* So, I suggested we go sit by the ocean and eat the snacks and pizza together."

"In the middle of February?" she interrupted.

"The truck is very warm and the stars are stunning over the water."

"Ooh," she cooed and it did an odd thing to his heart. "Very romantic—I like it."

"I had hoped you would."

His heart beat unevenly. Yep, that was definitely his heart doing butterfly front-flips.

"And then…something just clicked," she finished softly.

"And then something just clicked," he echoed.

She extended her hand. "This is the agreement?"

"This is the deal."

And he shook her hand, trying to ignore the spark of electricity that passed between them when they touched.

CHAPTER THREE
Mina

"I still can't believe you didn't tell me about you and Graham."

Ana was griping to Mina, pale cheeks flushed with emotion and cold.

"We just wanted to keep it *us*. You know, until we decided if it was more of a sure thing," Mina defended, praying her dishonesty didn't bleed through her words.

"And is it?"

"That's what I want to know," Madeline interjected.

The three of them were walking the Ocean Walk on the coast of Rose Point, passing by the old lighthouse after work, hot drinks in hand—Ana had her usual matcha latte, Mina had a chai latte, and Mads had a lavender London fog. It was chilly, but it felt like winter was finally having its last bite before letting the questing fingers of spring take her turn.

"We had a discussion last night and it feels like it's heading that way," Mina said, but the lie tasted bitter. She was realizing rather quickly that being untruthful was against her nature and it was having a visceral reaction on her conscience. "It's just…it's still new. I don't want to jinx it."

"How did it even happen? Like, what changed suddenly?" Mads asked, sipping her latte. The tip of her nose was blushed with the cold, and it made her caramel eyes glitter.

Mina was internally grateful that her and Graham had devised this exact story last night. And so, she dove into the tale, shovel and all as she dug herself deeper into her lies.

Ana and Mads were entranced by the utter romance of it all, Ana grinning ear to ear.

"It's like a true, enemies-to-lovers story," she pronounced, blue eyes shining with pure delight. Like Mina, Illiana was an avid book reader, only she preferred contemporary romance to Mina's romantasy—despite all her attempts to persuade Ana to the dark side (fantasy, that was), her trials were for naught and she still preferred her real-life love stories than the ones with wings and shadows.

"We are not enemies-to-lovers," Mina answered laughingly.

They certainly better not be. This whole fake dating arrangement was a necessity. It was not a trope in a book that would have them falling in love—no. Absolutely not. This was not one of her books, this was her life.

"You say that now," Ana sing-songed, dancing a little in her pink workout set. As she walked and shimmied, her long, blonde ponytail swung with her graceful movement—which was courtesy of her ballet background that she unfortunately had to retire after an injury.

Mina glanced away and looked to the gray waves of the ocean, the winter-killed foliage bracketing the path they walked, their sneakers crunching on the ice-melting salt, her black joggers swishing against her thighs. The branches of the skinny trees around them were skeletal, pushing the bounds of their bark to burst with green buds of life that the next month was set to bring. January and February were always hard and dreary months, and it was March that always marked that slight uptick in mood and mental health—and Mina was desperate for the first sparks of weather-induced serotonin.

"It's your birthday party this weekend," Mina began, diverting away from the conversation regarding Graham. "Need me to bring anything?"

Illiana gave a small, scathing smile at the topic switch, but let it slide. "I think we have everything, but if you want some specific drink, then feel free to bring that."

Just then, Mina's phone buzzed, and when she checked it, she found Graham's name there. She pocketed it to deal with later.

It was at that point that conversation eased and topics slipped into the more casual ones—books, shows, mutual friends, upcoming plans, the like. The three of them walked and sipped, nursing their hot drinks inbetween their chilled fingers, laughing as clouds of breath puffed into the air. After forty-five minutes of walking, they'd completed their loops and all said their goodbyes before hopping in their respective cars.

Once Mina was in her silver RAV4, waiting for it to warm up, she looked at Graham's text.

If you're free tonight, can you come over so we can discuss the agreement? I'm making dinner.

Mina sighed and texted back a confirmation.

His response had come almost instantly.

You're the best girlfriend ever.

Mina rolled her eyes so hard she saw the back of her skull.

Steeling herself, Mina tossed her phone into the cupholder and curled her hands over the steering wheel, breathing through the brewing stress. Seconds later, the auge of anxiety lifted and she put the car into gear, and pulled out of the small lot.

The sun was setting quickly as she navigated the quaint streets of Rose Point, and though the risk of snow was low, it wasn't zero. It wasn't unusual to find snowflakes even into April—and it also wasn't unusual to endure heat waves as early as May. Weather on the west coast was finicky at best.

As she pulled onto Graham's street, she slowed and paused her audiobook as a new chapter began, readying herself for the new reality she'd created. Parking in the Victorian driveway was easy, but getting out of the car and onto said driveway was a bit more of a mental ordeal. She was trying very hard to psych herself up.

Her and Graham didn't like each other. And now they'd willingly signed themselves up to be in close proximity to each other several times a week for several months. At the best of times, they avoided each other at social events, but typically they annoyed each other. Though, at the worst of times they practically antagonized each other. Nothing cruel. Nothing dangerous. Just constant sniping and snatching opportunities to one-up the other.

Graham texted again.

Just walk in when you get here.

With a smiley face emoji.

It was unsettling.

Mina forced herself out of her car and made her way up to Graham's house. Inside, she found him at the stove stirring with a wooden spoon, the pan sizzling and filling the kitchen with the scent of rosemary, thyme, and garlic butter.

"Hey, you," he greeted with a disarming grin. "Hungry?"

"Yeah, actually," she said hesitatingly.

Graham's house was warm, the cozy crackling from a woodstove whispered from the living room. Mina found herself thawing—in more than one way—as she slid onto the island's low-backed bar stool.

"Good, I'm making herb chicken, mashed potatoes, and asparagus. Sound all right?"

Her mouth was already watering. "Sounds perfect."

"Great," he said, reaching for a notebook beside him. "While I cook, you go over this and try to memorize as much as possible." He slid it across the island, and she slapped a hand over the star-specked cover to catch it. "It's a bunch of basic info about me that you'd know as my girlfriend."

"We didn't establish that we were beyond dating."

He tossed her a droll look. "Natural progression, Jasmina."

"Fine. What kind of stuff should I know?"

"Open it up and find out. I've been working on one about you, too."

"You have?" she asked, raising a brow as she flipped the notebook open.

"Yeah, but I'll need you to go over it just to confirm a few things."

Organized, listed, and sectioned were clear details about Graham. The sort of information that a friend would know—and yes, certainly a girlfriend—but there was something about delivering a virtual manual of oneself to someone. Something raw and vulnerable. But also, to summarize a person into a few lined pages? She didn't like it. She rebelled against the softening of her heart.

A whole section dedicated to work had his job title, schedule, hours a day and a week, lunch break time, regular break times, work address, work number, his work number extension, his work cell, boss's name, important co-workers and their basic duties, years employed. Everything. It was meticulous. The personal life section had his morning routine, night routine, workout schedule, and all of that was separate from the family section.

"You made me a study guide?"

"And one for myself."

"I didn't realize I was getting homework with this," she quipped.

"Do you want to get caught?" he asked.

No.

Her look must have spoken her thoughts aloud because he nodded and continued, "On that note, we should make that rule number one. *'Don't get caught.'*"

"That seems reasonable."

Graham stepped away from the stove and scribbled the new rule on their Good Vibes notepad. After Rule #1, he kept writing.

Rule #2. There will be no dating of, sleeping with, or engaging romantically with anyone else of any gender during the time of this contract.

Rule #3. No unauthorized touches of either party around people or in public—to be described—or unconsented PDA.

"These are the obvious ones in my opinion. Have anything to add?" he asked.

"This is…a lot right now," she said, rubbing her temples as they throbbed. "I think a migraine is coming on."

"Food will probably help. Have you eaten enough today?"

Mina frowned in guilt. "No."

Graham didn't say anything, instead, he grabbed two Tylenol from a drawer and filled a glass of water. He handed her both. She accepted both. With a lingering look, he returned to the chicken in the pan as coils of steam rose from the boiling potatoes.

"We need to keep up appearances so we should have date nights out—so people can see us as a couple," she suggested after swallowing her water and pills.

"Add it."

Rule #4. Once a week date nights.

"*Rule #5. Three sleepovers a week*," Graham said, not looking up.

"Sleepovers?" Mina yelped. "And why three a week? Isn't that a bit excessive?"

"Most people in relationships spend the night at their partner's house. Has it been that long since you've dated anyone?"

Mina's nostrils flared. Graham didn't need to know that it had been eight months since David had dumped her via FaceTime and had been unabashedly cheating on her while he did so. It stung—not because she'd loved David, but because of the principle of it. It made her self-worth diminish, and to be frank, it was fucking embarrassing.

"Will we take turns?" she asked, not rising to the bait.

"That depends."

"On?"

"Isn't your apartment a one bedroom?"

"Yes?" She was unnerved that he knew that.

"Unless you want to share the bed or one of us take the couch we should stay at my place. I have a guest room you can use."

Why was she simultaneously relieved and disappointed to find out they wouldn't be sharing a bed?

This is not like one of your romance books, Mina, she chastised herself. *Just because the one bed trope is a thing in books does not mean it's going to be a thing here.*

"Is anyone really going to notice if we're having sleepovers or not?" Mina asked—clearly searching for an excuse.

Graham turned around and carefully assessed her in that way he always did. He was always hyperaware of everything and everyone. She didn't know where that perceptiveness came from, but she'd never encountered anything like it before in all of her twenty-seven years of life.

"Kieran lives just down the road and goes to the gym from seven to eight, five nights a week. He's going to notice your car here or my truck not here."

She couldn't argue with that. Her apartment was central to town and anyone could notice. Plus, Mina shared her location with Illiana and Madeline.

"Fine," she agreed begrudgingly.

She made it clear the conversation was over as she flipped through the notebook that Graham had made about her personal details. He allowed her this privacy as he snapped the ends off the asparagus and tossed the stalks and buds into the pan, sizzling against the garlic butter. Shockingly—though not actually—he'd gotten everything right—with some fine tuning of details and additional comments.

He knew her birthday—September 7th—and that she worked at Ocean Motions as a physiotherapist, with a specialization in pelvic floor physiotherapy. Her parent's names, Laura and Dean were scribbled with the rest of her family tree, including Lacey—Laura's twin—and her husband Walt—Mina's uncle—and their son Nate—who was Mina's cousin and one of Graham's best friends. He had her address, phone number, work number, a question mark where email would be, and her listed social medias—Instagram, TikTok, SnapChat, and Facebook.

She blinked rapidly at the list of known favorites. Chocolate chip mint ice-cream. Peanut butter cups. Deluxe pizza. Chai lattes. Gummy bears. The color sage green. Genre of books: fantasy romance. Music: 80s rock.

He knew it all.

Mina had to practically lift her jaw off the floor.

She downed her water to try to hide her shock.

"Should we call this sleepover number one?" Graham asked while straining the potatoes.

Mina choked on her water and fought to clear her airway. It burned in her throat and she sputtered against the invasive feeling.

"What about clothes and all my toiletries and such?"

Graham was mashing the potatoes and mixing in a generous amount of butter and sprinkling it liberally with a salted garlic herb mixture.

"I have spare stuff here or we can stop at your place." There was a distinct pause. "I have three sisters—which is why you'll find a lot of feminine products here. They visit here out of the blue sometimes and I like to be prepared."

Mina flipped through his notebook and sure enough his three sisters were listed there as well as their ages, jobs, and partners—none of them had children.

"I prefer my own stuff."

"Completely understandable. After we eat, we'll go to your apartment and then maybe get some snacks or dessert?"

Graham slid their dinner onto the island, and Mina salivated at the heavenly scent—she'd give him that; the boy could cook. With that, the plan was set and they dove into dinner.

Flavor exploded across her tongue. Salt and garlic, rosemary and thyme, pepper and something else. The chicken was moist and savory, the potatoes creamy, the asparagus perfectly seasoned. This, perhaps, was the biggest perk of the fake dating arrangement.

Definitely not the fact that he was disturbingly attractive and he was going to pretend to be all over her.

Mina flushed profusely.

There was also the fact that he couldn't stand her, so she hated him in turn.

This was going to be a long three months.

When they finished with dinner they got into Graham's truck and headed over to Mina's apartment. The interior was warm, and Phil Collins was softly crooning from the speakers. Within seven minutes they were at her place, but it was possibly the longest seven minutes of her life as they sat in silence—sans Phil Collins.

There was a lingering air of excitement, though Mina couldn't discern why. It's not like anything was going to happen between them. It was all fake. So, why was her stomach in knots? And why was she trying to remember the last time she shaved her legs?

Graham pulled into her designated parking spot—number 3—and put the truck into park.

"Do you want me to come up with you?" he asked.

Mina hesitated. "Um, sure."

"Maybe I shouldn't. You hesitated. Take a moment alone, I'll be here."

She was internally grateful for his observance, but at the same time she felt a flash of guilt for potentially hurting his feelings or making him feel unwanted.

But that didn't make sense.

She'd never worried about hurting his feelings before, and he'd never acted like anything she'd said to him had any negative effect.

"I'll be right back." And then she hopped out and fished her keys from her bag.

Mina made quick work of the lock and was in her apartment in minutes. She flicked on the hall light, illuminating her second-hand furniture that she had intentions of flipping, and casting long shadows from the various throw pillows on her rust-colored couch.

She dug out her PINK duffel bag from her small closet, the black canvas worn from traveling to the gym and work with her. She began stuffing various clothing items, deodorant, perfume, hair care products, her toothbrush and toothpaste, a couple of books protected in special fabric sleeves, her silk pillowcase and hair wrap, skin care, plus a few cozy items, all into the bag.

For whatever reason, when she was done packing, she was all too eager to rejoin Graham. Maybe it was the mental stimulation. Or maybe it was a reprieve from the loneliness.

Locking everything up, she padded down the stairs, duffel slung over her shoulder, and slid into the warm leather seat of Graham's white Silverado. Butterflies tumbled through her stomach, spilling all around her as she became a puddle of nerves.

"You all right?" Graham questioned.

"Are we doing the right thing?"

"I don't think it's as black and white as that. But a better question is—are we well-intentioned and will this harm anyone?"

Mina sighed. "Okay. I just…I'm not used to lying."

"Neither am I."

"Are you sure about that?"

Graham's brows narrowed. "What do you mean by that?"

"You're so mysterious and secretive. People don't seem to know you, but you seem to know everything about them."

"And that's a bad thing?" he queried.

"It can be a bit unnerving," she admitted.

He was quiet for a breath. "I see."

"I didn't mean to insult you."

"You don't need to lie to me, Jasmina. I know how you feel."

For some reason those words opened a sickly pit in her stomach. Was that genuine hurt in his voice?

And without further word he pulled out of the lot and merged with traffic.

Mina didn't understand. This was how they'd always talked to each other. Slightly insulting, barely tolerating, scathing.

The seven minutes back to his house were even longer this time. She must've struck a nerve because it seemed he'd forgotten to stop for the snacks—that was very out of character.

Graham broached the silence first. "Do you want to be alone or maybe watch a show?"

He was helping her by carrying her bag in—she allowed him the chivalrous offer as an olive branch—and was taking her up the stairs.

"Do you mind if I shower and then we can watch a show and go over our study guides?"

"That works for me. Bathroom is directly across the hall," Graham said, pushing open the second door on the right. "This is where you'll be staying when you sleep here. I'll leave you to it."

Setting her bag on the floor, Graham departed and left Mina alone, staring at a fluffy white bed. She sighed and then turned to the shower.

CHAPTER FOUR
Graham

Jasmina was in his house.

Naked.

He tried really hard not to think about that last part, but it was difficult considering he could hear the shower running. His brain was busy imagining the hot water sluicing down her luscious brown curves, over her ass, between her breasts, down to her—

He forcibly yanked himself out of the reverie and awkwardly adjusted himself, the growing erection conspicuous against the sweatpants he'd just changed into.

The Good Vibes Fake Dating Contract notepad sat on his lap, recently added rules waiting for Jasmina's approval.

Rule #6. Visit at work twice a week—once each.

Rule #7. Nightly Facetime or phone call to update on days and life just in case and for plausible deniability.

Rule #8. Sporadic texts throughout the day to sell the ruse— minimum three each.

Rule #9. If anyone finds out about the arrangement, tell the other party <u>immediately</u>.

The squeak of the shower shutting off indicated Jasmina was finished and Graham quickly exchanged the contract for the study guide—making sure he didn't knock over the crackling balsam candle—and tossed a blanket over his lap. Jasmina didn't need to see his boner straining in gray sweatpants.

Some time passed, he wasn't sure how long, but his eyes were bleary from reading his handwriting over and over again, before Mina entered the living room.

She was in a distressed Def Leppard t-shirt and cut-off sweats that showed the smooth expanse of her thick thighs, with her curls tied up in an emerald silk wrap. The vision was so…domestic. So, at ease. Graham could perfectly imagine their nights like this, of her dressed down in sleepwear, her nighttime routine completed before she curled up on his couch.

Jesus, fuck, this blanket wasn't going to be enough.

Three months wasn't going to be enough.

Jasmina settled on the couch in the opposite corner, but even that was close enough for him to smell her floral peach lotion and some kind of coconut scented hair products. She smelled delicious.

He had the sudden desire to add subtle peach décor to his house. Maybe Willow had some suggestions for a repeating wallpaper of peach bundles? With those little white flowers? Or maybe he could find a canvas of some still life ones? Surely discreet peach décor existed? Willow was all about cottage core aesthetics and botanical prints. She could figure it out.

"I added a few more rules to the list," Graham announced, reaching to the coffee table for the notepad. "Take a look and tell me what you think."

Jasmina delicately took it and perused it.

"These are all fine. I just have one to add."

"Go for it." He handed her a pen.

Graham watched her smooth handwriting flow from the pen and as each word appeared, a weight sank in his belly.

Rule #10. Do not fall in love with each other.

Jasmina then sketched two lines at the bottom of the paper and on top of one she scratched her signature with a flourish.

"Your turn," she said.

Was that a challenge in her voice?

He took the pen and signed, even as an anvil of dread dropped through him. Agreeing to Rule #10 felt wrong, disingenuous, limiting. But for her, he did it.

He didn't know if it was a coincidence or not, but they ended up putting on the movie *A Walk to Remember* and suddenly Rule #10 felt very concerning. It was also taking a lot of will power to remind himself that his life wasn't a movie and Rule #10 wasn't going to be broken.

Jasmina put it there for a reason, so it seemed she was very clear that she wasn't attracted to him. It hurt, but it wasn't a new pain.

The thing was, they weren't paying attention to the movie—they were focusing on their study guides.

"The names of my three sisters and their ages. Go," Graham commanded.

The closed study guide on Jasmina's lap contained the answers she was clearly wracking her brain for.

"Willow, twenty-four. And the twins, Piper and Sabrina, twenty-two."

"And their partners and jobs?"

"Willow is the Interior Designer and with Evan, Sabrina is a Marketing Analyst and dating Drew, and Piper's the university student—studying to be an anesthesiologist. Single."

"Sabrina is the student and Piper is the analyst, but you got everything else right."

"Dammit," Jasmina said, covering her face and hanging her head. "So close."

"It's all right, you'll get it."

"You say that because you have it easy," she griped, head still in her hands. "I'm an only child."

"True," he conceded. "But you're more than a handful enough to make up for your three missing siblings."

"Fuck off," she said laughingly, and something about the playful tone of her voice had an ember of warmth glowing beneath his sternum. "How'd you grow up to be so insufferable with three sisters?"

"*Because* I had three sisters. What's your excuse?"

"I'm ready to toss this contract into the fire."

"And disappoint Illiana and Em?"

Graham was pretty sure she growled at that point.

"What is my boss's name and my coworkers?" she challenged.

And so, it went like that, back and forth.

"Favorite movie?"

"Knives Out." Hers was Stardust.

"Favorite song?"

"*I'll Be* by Edwin McCain." Jasmina loving *Under Pressure* was no surprise.

"Color?"

"Green." Only because he couldn't say green-gold.

"Same as me," she said. "Specific shade?"

This was when he had to lie to her. Or did he?

"Olive green."

Close enough.

"Sage green," she countered.

On and on it went, and with each passing question the more Graham felt himself sliding down a slippery slope—but he didn't care that he was falling, he was enjoying the sensation of it.

At some point his eyes fluttered and when he jolted awake, he noticed Mina slumped onto the couch, her head mere inches from his lap. He had the near irresistible urge to caress her sleeping face. In sleep she looked so peaceful, all the vitriol and harsh words bled out of her, her features soft, her lips lightly parted.

Reaching out, he gently shook her shoulder.

"Jasmina," he whispered. "Let's get you to bed."

She shuffled blearily into a sitting position, rubbing her eyes, and stretched. He had to avert his eyes from the way her breasts strained at her shirt and most notably her peaked nipples—she definitely wasn't wearing a bra. And her tits looked perfect.

He blushed profusely as he sat up with her, guiding her down the hall and up the stairs. He wasn't even certain if she was fully awake—her gentle lip smacking seemed on par with that course of thought.

Jasmina slowly, and near clumsily—like a baby fawn—crawled into bed and flopped facedown onto the mattress. Graham chuckled, but gently tucked the white down duvet around her. He had the oddest urge to kiss her forehead goodnight, but settled for a gentle whisper.

"Goodnight Jasmina."

Carefully, he crept out, Jasmina already snoring softly. Closing the door with a delicate click, Graham went to the bathroom and flopped into his own bed. The only problem was that sleep would no longer claim him. Not when he was hyper-aware of Jasmina just down the hall, sleeping soundly, when all he wanted was her in his bed, wrapped in his arms. It's like he could smell her floral peach scent, the warmth of her skin, the coconut wafting from her hair.

Fuck she was a dream girl and he knew he'd be having no dreams tonight.

Graham stared at the ceiling and he was haunted by the fact that he couldn't touch her. He didn't know what he was going to do. He couldn't survive doing this constantly. Could he? Okay, he was being stupid. He wasn't some feral animal with uncontrollable impulses. He was a man—a breathing, red blooded man—but he prided himself—and his friends—for not falling into toxic masculinity, nor stupidity when he came to thinking with the wrong head. Especially when alcohol was involved—even though it wasn't here tonight.

He was spiralling.

Utterly fucking spiralling.

His brain was rambling.

Thoughts coursing like an endless tide, crashing on the shore of his mind. His brain was overwhelmed with Jasmina.

Jasmina. Jasmina. Jasmina.

He covered his face with a pillow and groaned as he felt his groin become uncomfortably tight. The thoughts of her had his mind in a snare, thoughts that had his hand coasting downward, slipping beneath his waistband.

He stopped himself.

That seemed disrespectful. To masturbate while Mina was in his house? Utterly fucking rude—regardless of she was dead to the world.

He pressed the heels of his hands into his eyes, expecting a long-suffering night.

He was right.

Blearily, he started at the computer screen, trying to make sense of the emails before him as he sipped his coffee—the second cup already. He'd finally drifted off sometime around four and woken several times after that fact.

Words wavered on the screen as if underwater, his comprehension of them as clear as hieroglyphics—and he was no Egyptologist.

A shave-and-a-haircut knock sounded at his door and Graham looked up to see Jeff from Occupational Therapy standing in the entry. His buzzcut made efforts to hide his male pattern baldness, and though Graham didn't know him very well, he did know that Jeff was a pretty decent guy with a sense of humor.

"Hey bud, it's Luke's last day today and we were going to celebrate with drinks tonight. You in?"

Graham scrubbed his face with his hand, trying to clear some of the fatigue from his sight.

"I'm pretty beat, man. And besides, I have plans with the girlfriend tonight."

Jeff's light brows quirked up. "Girlfriend? When did this happen?"

Shutting his eyes against the spreading lies, Graham realized just how much this ruse was going to effect. "Pretty recent. Around Valentines Day."

"Congrats! That's awesome," Jeff said, clapping him on the shoulder. "Happy for you."

Graham smiled, but he could tell it didn't reach his eyes, even if Jeff didn't notice. But that was the thing about being as observant as he was—he knew people didn't pick up on as much as he did.

"Thanks, Jeff."

With a nod, Jeff left his office, and Graham pressed his forehead to the cool surface of his desk. His hours today were 8-4, but he had to commute to Victoria for work, which added a twenty-minute drive that prevented him from a highly required nap. Six hours to go.

Those six hours passed slower than molasses in January, but he'd survived the work-day. He'd managed to shoot Jasmina a couple of texts—just a couple check-ins—and organized their plans for the night.

It was Illiana's birthday party—her actual birthday wasn't until Monday—and they were planning it to be the first social outing that they attended as a "couple" together. To say it was nerve-wracking was an understatement.

His sister, Willow, texted him, telling him that grandpa's health was deteriorating, and she and their sisters were planning a visit just in case. She was asking if he wanted to join. He texted back that he did.

Collapsing on the couch Graham didn't even shut his eyes before sleep took him.

Knocking woke him.

The arm he had flung over his eyes blocked out the dim glow of the hall lamp, but through the glass panes he could make out Jasmina's silhouette.

"I figured we should go to the party together," Jasmina said when he opened the door. She entered without invitation, but Jasmina always had an open invitation—verbal or otherwise.

"Well, don't you look good," he complimented.

Jasmina's golden-brown curls cascaded down her back, and glitter was dusted all over her rich brown skin. She wore a Rolling Stone's t-shirt that hung off her shoulder and a pair of faux leather pants with white sneakers.

"Try to say it a bit more honestly next time."

"Good call," he said, closing the door behind her. "I meant that in regard to going together. I did mean the compliment. Mind if I shower?"

"Go for it. I'm already ready." She clearly ignored his verbal amendment. "Just be prepared to have your every move watched tonight and at least pretend to like me."

"Can you manage the same?" he asked quizzically.

"For Ana, I'd do anything."

CHAPTER FIVE
Mina

Music pumped from Emmett and Ana's house, some top 100s chart stuff that was unoffensive and palatable to the masses. The sun had recently set, and the blue-dark night descended upon the semi-modern structure.

The house was sided in white with cedar accent beams and columns, charcoal railings and a gate with Indigenous art ironwork on it.

Mina and Graham entered the house with his arm around her waist, giftbag in her hand, alcohol in his. His touch was warm and surprisingly comforting in an almost familiar way. She found it oddly pleasant—though, she'd never tell him that. And she couldn't lie that he smelled heavenly—something floral like magnolia and heady notes of timber with the slightest spice of cardamom.

People were scattered about the house, drinks in hand, snacks being eaten, conversations rising in cacophony as the alcohol flowed freely. Mina found Ana standing beside a mass of pink balloons, chatting to a tall, sandy-haired guy. She was dressed in a short tulle dress, half her blonde hair up in space buns with ribbons dangling from them, the rest of her waves hanging down her back.

Together, Mina and Graham made their way toward her.

When Ana caught sight of them her jewel blue eyes sparkled with delight. "Hey!" She grabbed the guy's wrist and tugged him to meet them in the middle. "Mina, Graham, this is my cousin, Leo! Leo, this is Mina and Graham."

"Nice to meet you," Leo said, his voice a calming timbre. "Illiana's told me so much about you."

"Likewise," Graham said, shaking his outstretched hand.

Ana blushed. "All good things!" she proclaimed. "Leo just got in today, but he's staying in Rose Point. Isn't that exciting?"

"That's great!" Mina said.

Leo was tall, almost as tall as Graham's 6'2", with the same soft blue eyes as Illiana. A light shadow of stubble graced his angular jaw, and there was something about him that just shouted *friendly*.

"Do you have a place yet?" Graham asked.

"I'm staying at the inn for now, but I'm viewing a couple places this coming week. It's nice to finally put down some roots. I've been traveling so much for work that I haven't had a real home base since I was…I think seventeen? It's surprisingly thrilling in an unorthodox way."

"What do you do for work?" Mina asked. It didn't escape her notice that Graham curled his arm more firmly around her waist, saturating her in the scent of magnolia and timber. She allowed herself to ease into it and place a hand on his chest. His strong heart thundered beneath her palm.

"I'm a photographer. I've done a few stints with National Geographic and a few independent organizations, but I want to start expanding my portfolio to represent all the nuances of the world—a sort of self reflection project of the human condition related to our environment."

"That's fascinating," Mina said, awed. "I'd love to hear more."

Leo's eyes flashed to Graham and then his arm around her waist, then he cleared his throat.

"Yeah, absolutely. So, the project is going to compare flora—indigenous and exotic—to the people who live in their environments. To try to find that perfect shot where you can see the leaves line up with the shape of their nose, or the branch following the curve of their arm, and then split the image in half and have them split into a mirror image of itself." Mina could see the passion glowing in his eyes about this project. "I'm playing around with either shooting in black and white, or to lean into the vibrancy of the plants. If I do that, then I want to find some iridescent fractals against the verdant growth.

"But I'm rambling, I'm so sorry."

"No, it sounded wonderful," Madeline said, coming up on Mina's left. "The way you talk about your photography is magical."

Leo blinked several times at Madeline as if dazed.

"Hi," she pronounced, a wide, white grin present on her pretty, tanned face. "I'm Madeline Fitz."

"Pleasure to meet you," Leo said, all charm.

Mina giggled and lightly hip bumped her. A flash of caramel eyes told her everything she needed to know.

"Want to get a drink?" Mina asked Graham.

"Lead the way."

Arm still around her waist, the two of them weaved their way to the kitchen and opened a bottle of wine. When they clinked their glasses, Mina felt a flash of *something* strike her chest and settle in her stomach. She fought to dismiss it.

This was not one of her romance books.

It was *not*.

She forced herself to remember the words she wasn't supposed to overhear all those years ago.

I can't be around her.

A snarl curled her lip and she hid it behind her wineglass. It was ten years ago.

Graham's fingertips dug into her waist.

"What's wrong? What happened?"

"Nothing," she bit out.

Graham leaned down, his hand finding the small of her back, his lips brushing the shell of her ear. "Don't hide things from me, Jasmina."

She shivered.

Was it the way his tongue curled over her full name? Or the way his low voice brushed her ear like a sinful caress full of filthy promises?

"We can't have our first couple fight already," he continued.

Mina leaned toward him—her turn to whisper in his ear. Her hand found his abdomen, feeling the hard lines of him beneath his t-shirt as she smiled a small, wicked thing. "For us, fighting is as natural as breathing."

"Things have changed."

She leaned closer, her lips touching his neck—he trembled in response.

"Not that much."

Then she patted his chest in finality and walked away.

A while later Mina found herself standing beside Madeline as Chappell Roan's *Pink Pony Club* pounded from the speakers.

"You two were getting cozy," Madeline quipped with a glitter in her eye, smirk hidden behind her mango margarita.

"Who?"

Madeline raised a brow. "You and Graham? Your boyfriend?"

"Oh!" Mina gasped. "Right. Yeah. Sorry it's kind of surreal. Do you really think so?"

"I always thought you two would, but…" Madeline shrugged. "I managed to convince myself I was just seeing things that weren't there."

"You did?" Mina asked in shock.

"Oh, yeah. Totally. And not that I've talked to anyone about it, but I'm pretty sure I'm not the only one."

Mina could only stare.

It was common knowledge that her and Graham didn't get along, but now she was learning that people—*plural*—saw something else between them that wasn't loathing.

"I had no idea."

"Most people are blinded by what's in front of them. Such is the folly of the human brain," Mads reassured. She tilted her head to rest on Mina's shoulder. "It's all right, you have a great brain."

"…thank you?"

"You're welcome."

"Speaking of brains—how is that official psychologist brain treating you? Are you settling into your office well?"

Madeline was finally a graduated and practicing psychologist after years of hard work and sacrifice. There were many nights she had to cancel plans and events in lieu of studying, but it had all paid off and culminated in this pinnacle of success. Mina was so proud of her and hoped her career flourished.

"Yes and no. I'm trying to set a good balance of comfort and professionalism. Especially in my decorating and furniture choices. But I'm really enjoying it, even if it's a bit surreal."

"Graham's sister, Willow is an interior designer. She could probably help you."

"Ooh, I'll have to take you up on that. Do you have her info?"

Luckily, Mina did, and she sent her social media profile over.

"And your client list is still growing?"

"Every day. I'm going to have to get my own therapist soon, some of this shit is so heavy. But Chase has been helping a lot."

Chase, one of Graham's best friends from university, was a psychologist as well, and last year when they were introduced, they hit it off incredibly well based on that alone. Purely platonic, of course, considering Chase was a happily married gay man, and he and his husband, Patrick, were in the midst of the adoption process.

"I think I've had three of these mango margaritas already and now I have to pee so bad," Mads said, setting her large glass down. "I'll be back in a bit."

Madeline departed and left Mina alone, realizing she was still holding Illiana's giftbag by its handles. She hunted Ana down and found her sipping on a glass of white wine, a perfect little pink bow hanging from the stem. Someone had put a birthday tiara in her hair.

"I know it's not your birthday until Monday, but here is your present," Mina told her, raising her voice above Benson Boone's unparalleled voice screaming about wanting and needing. She handed the pink floral bag to her best friend. "Happy birthday!"

Mina had the distinct feeling of eyes on her and when she turned in the direction of the sense, she found Graham's crystalline gaze locked on her and Emmett's amber one on his beautiful fiancée. And while she noticed Emmett's looking in a peripheral sort of way, she couldn't tear her eyes from Graham. She was captured. Entranced. Enchanted.

Ana opened the gift and pulled out a mug that said TALL, DARK, & FICTIONAL, powdered matcha, two coloring books, a book sleeve, and a pack of seasonal bookish bookmarks.

"There's a gift card in the book sleeve," Mina commented, still not managing to pull her eyes away from her fake boyfriend. It was to Sugar & Spice Books—the little shop Emmett had taken Illiana to on their first date. She and Mina had also gone to a few book signings there.

"Thank you, so much," Illiana said, voice full of emotion. It was then that she could look away from Graham. Ana threw her arms around Mina and she returned the hug, her friend smelling of strawberries and wine.

When they broke apart, their men descended.

Emmett wrapped his arms around Ana's waist and kissed her cheek, then tilted her jaw up so he could kiss her lips. Mina ducked her head as her cheeks grew warm and Graham coiled his arms around her from behind, pressing her ass against his groin. She grew very aware of that fact, and so did her body.

Mina stiffened against the strong lines of him. Graham's hand splayed against her lower stomach—her heart pounded. His mouth dipped to her ear, just like it had earlier in the night, and just like earlier, she became electrified by it—her body turned to a livewire.

"Relax, baby," he murmured.

She became lightning. Heat poured through her like she was struck with a bolt, frozen by the power of it all. She was aware of every fiber touching her skin. Everything became too much and not enough.

Baby.

Baby.

He'd called her baby, and it had her short-circuiting.

Mina became acutely aware of Emmett's and Illiana's eyes on her. Forcing herself to relax, she managed to soften against Graham, tilting her head back against his chest. He dipped his mouth to her throat.

"Good girl."

Lightning struck again.

This was going to be an unbearable three months.

CHAPTER SIX
Graham

Jasmina cut the tension from their charade with wine. She coasted through the party on liquid courage, chatting with girlfriends, conversing with his friends, laughing with them all. Her voice was filled with the ease that came from lowered inhibitions, and although she wasn't wasted, she was certainly tipsy.

Earlier, Graham had made his rounds saying goodbye to all his friends and wishing Illiana happy birthday as he sensed the restlessness and fatigue of the party goers.

As the night drew to its natural close, Jasmina gave Madeline and Illiana quick and sweet pecks on the cheeks, told them she loved them, then looped her arm through his as they stepped out in the late night.

"Holy fuck, it's colder than a witch's tit out here," Jasmina crowed.

Graham laughed boisterously as he helped his fake girlfriend into the warm interior of his truck—thank the inventor of auto start for that one. He saw her lack of coordination and predicted where her head was going, so as discreetly as he could, he put his hand in the way as a buffer to prevent her from hitting the edge of the door.

She grunted softly as she knocked against his hand and huffed heavily as she slumped into the seat.

With a small smile curving his lips, he buckled her in and made sure all her limbs were inside before shutting the door. When he got inside, he told her there was water in the center console for her and some of the crackers he knew she liked—solely based on the night she propositioned him for fake dating.

"Damn, all this but no Tylenol?" she joked, taking a swig from the bottle.

"Glove compartment," he said, as he turned off of Fisher Street.

Jasmina found the Tylenol and whistled. "You sure know how to treat a lady."

Graham flushed. He didn't know how to cope with a Jasmina who was flirty—drunk, but flirty.

The rest of the drive passed as Graham put on some Creed, silent, aside from the music. When he pulled in the driveway, Jasmina was already hopping out.

"Hurry up, I really need to pee."

He chuckled, but acquiesced.

She ran inside the moment he unlocked the door and bolted for the bathroom—albeit a bit clumsily. Graham took to the kitchen and pulled out his toaster, popping in two slices of sourdough. Jasmina joined him once she finished attending to her personal business.

"We need to get more comfortable with touching each other, I feel like people were noticing," he said casually.

"I agree," she replied.

He hesitated before he let his tongue curl over the letters that stuck over the gate of his teeth.

"I also think we should practice kissing."

There, he said it. He dropped that bomb.

Mina froze, her full lips parting in a delicate O. She blinked a few times, her green-gold eyes glassy with intoxication.

Then, she leaned forward.

Terror intermingled with terrible desire gripped Graham and he leaped backward, hitting the counter. His blood roared and his hip smarted from the impact on the marble. He'd only had two drinks but it suddenly felt like he'd had ten. His brain was muddy with want, all the booze-imbued blood in his system heading straight south.

"I didn't mean right now," he said in a panicked rush.

"Oh." Hurt crested over her features, a light within her dimming—like an ember suffocated.

Guilt struck him directly in the chest, his heart panging with the pain he'd inflicted. The last thing he wanted to do was hurt Jasmina. Sure, they'd traded barbs, but it was all surface level—a shallow nick—this was a deeper wound, like a hook stuck beneath the skin.

Graham stepped toward her. She curled inward.

"I just meant—we've been drinking…we should wait. Until tomorrow."

"Scheduling kissing? Way to take the romance out of it."

"I think the fake part has already taken care of that."

"Right," she bit out, her mouth thinning into hard line.

There was an awkward breath of silence and then the toaster popped.

"I, uh…I made you toast," Graham said softly. "To help prevent a hangover."

Mina glanced over at it blandly then at him. "I'm not hungry. Goodnight."

"Goodnight, Jasmina."

It was said to her retreating back because she didn't wait for him to return the farewell.

He leaned backward against the counter, hands over his eyes.

"Graham Starling, you're a fucking idiot."

Breakfast the next morning was a much-needed affair. While Graham's ritual of water, Tylenol, and toast the night before to prevent a hangover was successful, nothing assuaged the malaise of post alcohol regret like a greasy breakfast and a chocolate shake.

Graham and Jasmina sat in a long pleather booth with Emmett, Illiana, Madeline, Nate, Sloane, Delilah, Kieran, Chase, Patrick, and Leo. The diner was a staple in Rose Point, Daisy's having been around since the 50s, serving the best milkshakes on the island.

Everyone was in varying degrees of hangover-ness—Sloane not at all, as she doesn't drink—with Nate being the absolute worst, cringing at every source of light and staring into his coffee cup like it had all the answers in the world.

"You okay?" Illiana asked Jasmina from her left.

Jasmina jolted and glanced at her best friend in a surprised sort of way. "I'm fine," she continued that affected air. "Why?"

"You just seem on edge. Guarded."

Graham tuned into their conversation as discreetly as he dared, his eyes trained on his menu, but his ears locked onto them. Jasmina was steeling herself—he'd learned her cues there—and he could tell she was realizing he was right about touching. They needed to get more comfortable with it.

"No, I'm good. Just lots on my plate right now. I'll be all right."

"Well, I hate to add more to your plate, and I know this isn't the best timing—and I definitely don't have the Pinterest worthy announcement for it—but I was wondering if you'd be my Maid of Honor?"

Jasmina utterly squealed. "Of course! I'd love to!"

"Oh yay, I'm so glad!" Illiana cooed. "And I know the whole wedding is a short notice thing—I know its crazy to get married before we've been together a year, but it just feels…right."

Graham could understand that. He'd never seen his best friend so happy until he'd gotten with Illiana. In his own opinion, Emmett and Illiana were soulmates.

"Well, since Illiana has let the cat out of the bag," Emmett said from beside him. "Want to be my Best Man?"

Here it was. The confirmation of the whole reason requiring the fake dating ruse. It was a little startling how much it did still come as a surprise. He knew it was coming, but somehow having the actual words out was something else.

"I'd be honored, babe," Graham said, clapping him on the shoulder.

In their friend group, calling each other babe was as commonplace as saying, man or bro, or even asshole. It was purely platonic in every sense of the word.

"Great!"

"Who are the rest of the groomsmen?"

"Nate, Kieran, Chase, and Riley."

Riley was Emmett's older half-brother that he hadn't known existed until he was in his late teens. Riley had a whole family already, a wife, kids, all of it. Despite the King children having the same dad, not one of them followed in his footsteps—thanks to their three mothers.

"And the bridesmaids? Do you know?"

"Sloane, Madeline, Delilah, and someone else hopefully."

Their server came by then and orders were placed, everyone easing into various conversations. Illiana and Delilah were talking about Delilah's next book—Delilah was a successful contemporary romance author, which was how her and Illiana (a romance reader), originally hit it off, being Emmett's ex not-withstanding. Nate and Patrick were barely alive after last night, Chase, Leo, and Madeline were all discussing a thriller movie—everything to do with the psychology of the protagonist, to the artful descriptors of shots, camera angles, and color choices—and Emmett and Sloane kept up a steady stream of sibling bickering. It was all perfectly mundane and normal.

What wasn't normal was the fact that he was lying to every single one of them.

"What do you want to do from here?" Graham asked Jasmina after they'd all finished breakfast.

They were on their way out the door and he pulled her aside.

Jasmina looked down and scuffed her feet on the worn linoleum floor, the checker pattern done in strawberry pink and mint teal. "I think we should go back to your place and start practicing."

A riot of emotions flooded through him—shock, fear, hope, longing, and so much more. It all swallowed him up beneath the tide of feeling that he didn't know how to draw breath. How to organize his thoughts. How to get his head on straight.

Jasmina was the only one who affected him like this.

The only one who ever had.

The only one who ever would.

CHAPTER SEVEN

Mina

The study guide—as she'd affectionately started calling it—was incredibly detailed and resourceful. Together, Mina and Graham were curled up on his couch, feet delicately touching.

Their touches were starting small, unoffensive, and unpresumptuous. They were trying to quell the startle from the initial contact until the strangeness became familiar. Slowly, occasionally, a foot would slide up a calf, and her skin would catch fire. Mina's breaths would come short, and Graham would whisper that phrase that turned her into a puddle of honey.

Relax, baby.

Fucking relax baby, my ass, she internally griped.

It had been meant as condescending, she was sure, but it did not have a condescending effect on her, which made her mad that she had a lustful acknowledgement of it. Which just snowballed that frustration into a bigger thing than it was.

"We should set some ground rules," she announced, sticking her pen in the spine of the notebook.

"In addition to our fake dating contract?"

"Yeah. I meant in regards to this—" she gestured between them. "The touching. What's off limits, what's not, etcetera."

"Okay." He sat up straighter. "What's off limits?"

"Um…" Her face flushed. "Between the legs is a no-go."

"Understood and agreed."

"My hair—I prefer it not to be overly touched. A little bit is fine, though."

"I can respect that. Is what I've been doing too much?"

Her cheeks flared hotter. "No, that's been fine. Just don't…pet it."

"I would never."

She didn't know how to respond to the sincerity in his voice so she just nodded. "Okay, good. And for you?"

Graham looked taken off guard. "Oh, uh, same as yours. But you can touch my hair."

"Like this?" she asked, boldly running her hand through his dark chestnut waves.

His eyes fluttered shut as her gold nails slowly raked over his scalp, his hair feeling like silk beneath her touch. It was actually unfair how soft his hair was.

"That's perfect," he breathed.

Her heart stuttered as she kept brushing through his locks.

"So, just the groin?"

"And the backs of my thighs—it's ticklish there."

"Odd, but okay."

Mina found herself content to keep touching him, so she did as she flipped through the notebook. Graham did the same next to her, practically melting under her touch.

"I have your favorites and such here," she said. "But I don't have anything you're afraid of."

"What, besides capitalist greed, the elite's agenda, and a developing oligarchy?"

"Yeah, aside from that."

"Centipedes."

"But millipedes are fine?"

"Fuck, no. They're what nightmares are made of."

"Noted." Mina scribbled that into the book, her handwriting so different than his. His was more sharp and concise, while hers was more flowing and soft, bubbly.

"Let's figure out a schedule," he proposed.

"Anything pre-promised?"

"I go to Blue's every Tuesday with the boys, sometimes Fridays too."

Mina did know this—from Ana, of course.

"Then Tuesday should be a workday visit day, considering it's not as feasible for a sleepover."

"That makes sense."

"I work Monday, Tuesday, have Wednesdays off, then work Thursday, Friday, with the weekend off," she listed, "I do Monday and Friday in Rose Point, and Tuesday and Thursday in Victoria. So, Tuesdays you come visit me, and Thursdays I visit you."

"Done," he said, scribbling in the notebook.

"Date nights should be either Wednesday, Friday, or Saturday."

"Not Sunday?"

"I need a day to rest and do nothing—but also, Ana will probably need help wedding planning and I'd like to keep Sundays free just in case."

"Ah, very considerate of you."

She shrugged. "She'd do the same for me."

Mina knew she would. Mina didn't leave Ana alone in Toronto when everyone else abandoned her, even though she hated it there and was horribly homesick. Mina had been raised in Rose Point, as close to Nate as siblings—especially considering their mothers were twins—but had felt she had to spread her wings a while on her own. So, she'd gone to university across the country, to a city she didn't know, and forged one of her closest bonds. But aside from Illiana, the draw of Ontario waned.

It wasn't until Ana had said she wanted to stay in Rose Point after their vacation that Mina had finally let it out that she also wanted to be on the island. It was like finally breathing clearly after inhaling smoke. Within months they'd both completely packed up their Toronto lives and threw down roots here.

"What are *you* afraid of?" Graham asked, knocking her out of her inner thoughts.

She glanced over at him and was struck by the naked curiosity in his face.

"Besides being stuck with you forever?"

"Haha," he said flatly.

"Flying. Heights."

"I sense a pattern."

"Yup. My feet like to remain firmly planted on the ground."

"When did you figure out you were afraid of flying?"

"On the way to Toronto for the first time." She blushed at the memory. "I had such a bad panic attack that one of the stewardesses had to pull me aside and help me breathe through it. She was really nice. Now I have to take meds anytime I get on a plane." She sighed. "Heights have been for as long as I can remember. I went on a Ferris Wheel for the first time when I was nine and I passed out from fear. I've never seen my dad panic so bad."

She remembered her father's face. All the color draining from his pale features, his brown eyes wide with terror, him yelling, *"Laura, something's wrong! She's not responding!"*

Dean Coulter was not one known to overreaction, but that day, he did. He'd always been a protective father, especially since him and her mother had only managed to have one child, despite efforts of fertility treatments. Even IVF failed. They'd called Mina their miracle baby. But after her there were no more.

"Do you have any trauma with bugs?"

"Nope," he said, reaching out and tracing the line of her knee. She shivered—it felt good. He kept doing it. "I just can't stand them."

There it was again.

Can't stand.

Can't stand them.

Can't stand her.

She stiffened and pulled away from him, removing her hand from the stroking of his hair. Rejection shooting through her like a poison.

"What is it?" he queried, worriedly.

"Nothing," she shut down.

"Well, no, it's clearly something. Did I say something? Did I do something?"

"Not everything is about you, Graham!" she hissed.

Graham was taken aback, but she couldn't find it in herself to feel guilty for it. She wanted to steamroll on, to hide that feeling of not being enough—not enough, never enough.

"Not everything is an attack, Jasmina," he fired back.

"You calling me that, even though you know I don't go by it is a psychological attack."

"That's a bit far."

"Is it?" she challenged. "We've never gotten along. Let's just try to get through these next few months as argument free as possible and we can go right back to how things used to be—comfortable animosity. 'Work for you?"

Graham's face was unreadable. "Perfectly."

"Great. Well, on that note, I think we should call it quits for today and we can readdress everything tomorrow. All right? I'll keep you posted on whatever you need to know—for the ruse."

"Right. For the ruse."

"I'll see you later."

"See you later."

She didn't know why, but his defeated tone dug itself into her heart and made its grave there. She felt every shovel full of dirt thrown on the casket as she made her way to the front door. She just kept burying it deeper as she left.

Mina got into her RAV4 and returned to her apartment. When she collapsed on the couch, she wanted to think of nothing at all.

Gloss was full of people. Unsurprising for a Saturday night. Mina was meeting Madeline for a couple of drinks and a small celebration of her graduation.

The pink, girly-themed nightclub was a favorite of theirs, and security was really on top of everything. The bouncers also were not ones to be bribed, so if a fuck boy came lurking around with a wad of cash, looking for an easy pick, he found himself black listed instead.

It was refreshing.

Mina was in a pair of tight jeans and a see-through lace top with a cute black bra. The sleeves and trim were all sewn with a lettuce edge and it was all paired with gold jewelry. Madeline wore an ice blue cardigan with only the middle button done up and no shirt beneath and a pair of loose-fitting light jeans with white sneakers.

"So, things with you and Graham, hey?" Mads asked, sipping on her tequila sunrise. "It's good?" Her brows waggled. "Like is it *good*?"

"Mads!" Mina said aghast.

"Jas!" Madeline chastised in return. "It was a valid question. You don't need to act like a shy little virgin."

Madeline was the only one who still called her Jas—a hang on from high school. In college she'd opted to go by Mina and everyone else adopted it.

Well, nearly everyone else.

"Things are great," Mina told her. "And no one is acting like a virgin—we're just private."

"Mmhmm," Mads teased, sipping her drink.

"You're one to talk," Mina began deflecting, hoping this wasn't a total shot in the dark. "I saw you getting all googly-eyed at Ana's cousin, Leo. Have anything to share with the class?"

This time Madeline blushed furiously. "We're just friends. Besides, he has a girlfriend. Probably some gorgeous swimsuit model or Tomb Raider looking explorer chick he met on one of his National Geographic gigs."

"You're worried about a Lara Croft?"

"Uh, yeah. Have you seen Angelina Jolie?"

She had—she supposed Madeline's complaints were founded.

"Don't sell yourself short—you're gorgeous."

"Awe, thanks, love," Mads said cupping her cheek. "But have you seen him? He's so far out of my league."

"He's blond," Mina argued.

Being blond was the cardinal sin of fictional men—let alone real-life ones.

"He's barely blond, it's almost brown," she argued.

"Not my type."

"Right. You like them tall, dark, and Graham."

"Oh, hush," Mina scolded teasingly.

Mina hated to admit it, but Graham *was* her type. And once upon a time, so long ago, she had considered it. With him. But then she'd heard what he said and she squashed all those budding feelings, erecting a brick wall between them so high there was no way to see past it. She'd met his every word with condescension, every look with derision, every touch with disgust.

If he thought she was so abhorrent, then she'd *be* that abhorrent.

Graham brought out an intensity in her that no one else did—or could. There was something about them that charged the air—what was the opposite of chemistry? Whatever it was, that's what they were. Oil and water.

A text vibrated in her pocket. Mina took it out and read the message from Graham.

My ears were ringing, were you talking trash about me again?

Mina chuckled to herself.

Always, she responded.

Typical girlfriend behavior.

Fake girlfriend.

I'm deleting that last text. Too much evidence. Especially since I have Kieran over.

Okay fair. She did the same. *I made sure it's gone as well. I'm with Mads.*

Girl's night?

"Who're you texting with that massive grin on your face?" Madeline asked. "Definitely couldn't be your boyfriend who you used to hate."

"Definitely not," Mina said sarcastically. Though, she wasn't sure which part she was being sarcastic about.

Graham double texted.

I hope you're giving Madeline all the sordid details of our sex life. Make sure it's saucy.

Saucy? Ick. Try spicy.

Oh, I can make it spicy, baby.

Heat flushed through her like a volcanic eruption. She tried to cool herself with her mojito. It didn't help; it just made her blood warmer.

Fuck, fuck, fuck, fuck, fuck.

"Are you dirty texting over there?" Madeline inquired.

"No," she said, a bit too quickly.

"Liar," she said, chortling.

"Believe what you want," Mina said on a sigh.

"Oh, I'm an expert at reading body language and non-verbal cues."

"Okay, Dr. Psychic Mads Fitz."

"Hey, drop the doctor—I'm not there yet."

"You going to go for your doctorate?" Mina asked, swiftly changing the subject.

"Still thinking about it. I want to take a break for a while. But I know the longer I put it off, the less likely I am to pursue it. Especially if I have less time to dedicate to clients. It's a tricky situation."

"That's super hard to navigate, but definitely not something you need to think about right now," Mina said. "Right now, is for drinks."

"Amen to that."

Graham texted her again.

Did I scare you off?

Mina's heart lurched at the challenge. She wouldn't back down from Graham, she would not let him have a win over her. He would have nothing over her.

Never, she texted, *Besides, I think your definition of spicy will be vanilla to me.*

Let him sit on that. She smirked to herself.

Her phone vibrated.

I know all those delightfully filthy books you read, trust me. I know what I'm talking about, baby.

She was wet.

Embarrassingly fucking wet.

Was this even pretending right now? Or were they testing the waters of a sexual tryst while maintaining a continued animosity?

Smells an awful lot like enemies-to—

Mina shut that little voice up in her head.

This was *not* one of her books.

They were not going to be enemies-to-lovers.

They were not going to fall in love.

This was pure convenience. For the greater good of their friends' marriage.

Her mind was so mired in her books. So mixed up in her feelings of hatred and whatever else she felt for Graham Starling. She didn't know where her head was and he had her completely unsettled. She didn't know how to respond.

So, she left it.

For now.

Until she was home.

Her home felt empty without Graham's presence. She laid in bed, thinking of him, soft-limbed from booze, heart aching with a pang of loneliness.

She tried to convince herself to put him out of her mind and just go to sleep. But she tossed and turned. Kicked off the blankets. Laid at the foot of her bed.

Heaving a sigh, she stared at the ceiling.

She pulled her phone out.

CHAPTER EIGHT
Graham

Kieran had his feet up on Graham's coffee table, beer bottle to his lips, when he asked the question that had been nagging him for months. Years, even.

"How do you deal with having secret feelings for someone and not tell them?"

Kieran shifted uncomfortably. "Are you asking a rhetorical question?"

Graham met his gaze pointedly. "You know I'm not."

Kieran visibly squirmed, looking over his shoulder as if someone else were in the house but the two of them. As if all the boys were waiting with a camera to record him with a "Gotcha!" moment.

Although, that was completely out of character for any of them to even contemplate doing. Still, anxiety was one hell of a poison.

"No one's listening," Graham assured him. "It's just the two of us, babe."

"Does anyone else know how I—?"

"No one else knows," Graham told him softly. "And I'm not planning on telling anyone."

Kieran deflated with relief.

"How'd you figure it out?"

"I have eyes. Mine just happen to work better than most."

Kieran playfully punched him in the bicep, his brown eyes shining with mirth. "You're such a shit."

Graham chuckled, happy to be letting loose—just a bit—with his friend. "I am, but you love it."

"What brought on the question?" Kieran asked, returning to the original matter, that, for some reason he suddenly didn't want to talk about it. To have those words out in the world and confirmed.

He couldn't help but notice how effortless it was to speak to Jasmina over text. How easily the flirting and banter flowed. How much he enjoyed toeing the line of what was appropriate and what wasn't. To see how it was received and respond in kind—reading between the lines they'd laid. Even still, he was aware of his body—how it felt, how it *needed*. Even now, he was thinking of her.

He took a drink and forced himself back to the conversation.

"The question you still haven't answered?"

"Yes."

Graham waited.

Kieran huffed out a long breath and took a pull from his beer. "It fucking sucks," he finally said. "Seeing her, but I can't—because it would be wrong."

"How do you think she feels?"

"Oh, I'm sure she doesn't feel the same way—or have any fucking clue how I feel. And at the same time, I want nothing to change, but simultaneously everything to. I want her, but I'm afraid of ruining the status quo. Regardless of that, the entire concept is a mess. So, I've accepted my fate and choose to suffer in silence."

"That's really dark, man," Graham said carefully. "Are you all right?"

Kieran cracked a sad smile, his slightly pointed incisor indenting his lower lip. "Yes and no. It's a lot. And it's even more knowing that you know."

Graham clapped him on the shoulder. "I'm here for you, you know that?"

"Yeah," he mumbled.

"And no one would be mad if you pursed—"

"I'm just not ready to risk it."

Graham knew when a topic was shut down so he closed his mouth and accepted it. "Okay."

"Want to tell me what prompted you to ask me this? I'm guessing you're feeling a similar way about someone?"

Pinching the bridge of his nose, the knot of stress coiling up in him, Graham sighed.

"It's about Jasmina."

"You mean your girlfriend? How is this relevant?"

This is where he had to fudge some of the details and twist the truth into something palatable that didn't breach the contract. He didn't want to betray Jasmina's tentative trust. But also, he didn't want to share this small little truth with the world yet. For now, it was them and he liked it that way.

"There are still some unresolved things from the past that we're working on, and until then, I don't think she can fully be in this. But the thing is, I don't know how to fix it. I don't know where I fucked up."

"I'm going to give you the simplest advice," Kieran said, shifting on the couch to set his bottle down on the coffee table. He took Graham's face in his hands. "Talk. To. Her." Kieran released him. "That's it."

"Damn, how much do I charge for this therapy session?" Graham teased.

"That's a question for Chase. I'm the teacher."

"Speaking of teaching—have you heard anything more about that transfer yet?"

And just that easily, the conversation switched, drifting to easier patterns, lighter comments, less loaded phrases. It turned to work and working out, hobbies and health, comments on thinking about cutting down on drinking and offers of moral support. It was far less complicated than crushes and love.

Love?

Oh, fuck no.

He didn't love Jas—

No, he couldn't.

Could he?

No, he'd been drinking. It was the two beers he had that were talking. Not how he actually felt. A crush was one thing. *Love* was another beast altogether.

Eventually, words drifted into yawns and Kieran declared he needed to get home. They said goodnight and Kieran made the walk home with promises of a text to confirm he hadn't died in a ditch on the short trek home.

As he settled back on the couch, flipping through Netflix, a text came through.

So, if we're going to talk spicy, tell me the wildest thing you've ever done, Jasmina texted.

Sexually, she added.

Graham's cock jumped, hardening in his pants. He shifted uncomfortably, trying to staunch his arousal but failing miserably when the third text came through.

You tell me yours; I'll tell you mine.

He was highly motivated.

I had a threesome, he told her.

I knew about that actually. From Never-Have-I-Ever last summer.

He did recall this. It was around a fire and it didn't end well.

Tell me the details of it, she commanded with a winky face. *Were the girls fun?*

Who said there were multiple girls? he challenged.

The three dots flickered on screen. Paused. Resumed.

How do I say this without sounding like I'm fetishizing you? Because I'm not, she said. But I do think that's hot. (Disclaimer: I'm a little drunk.) Tell me more.

There was something about it that he didn't want to tell her. Not because he was ashamed of it—it was an experience, he had it, he didn't regret it, but he felt no need to repeat it, nor have another—but because he didn't want to think about sex with anyone but her. And those were dangerous thoughts.

He forced himself to recall the details for Jasmina. She wanted to know so he'd acquiesce.

Well to start, you know I'm bi, right?

I do.

Okay, so, it was in the summer a few years ago, he began, *I was in Greece and a couple approached me. We had some drinks, one thing led to another, then we were in their hotel. It was fun, but I wouldn't do it again.*

It was a wild romp, he remembered how it felt to give and then to take, to have so many hands on him, lips on his skin. It was hot, but it didn't have a wild allure. It didn't have him hardening.

Did you use protection?

He laughed. *Yes, we all did, and I got tested after.*

Good, she said. *That's good.*

Worried about contracting an STI from me? he sent with a winky face emoji.

A girl can never be too careful.

His heart and cock throbbed with the response. That wasn't a no. That wasn't a clear shut down.

Your turn. He paused. *You scared, baby?*

Ha. You Wish. I once played strip poker with a bunch of people and then slept with one of the guys in the bathroom.

His interest was piqued.

And is that something you like? Games like that? His hand drifted to his waistband.

A bit. Yeah. A lot. Games are my favorite.

Mine too, he sent back.

His hand slid beneath his boxers. He palmed his boner and groaned. What he wouldn't give to have Jasmina being the one to wrap her soft little hands around his length, pumping him.

"Fuck," he growled to the empty house.

He bit his lip as he wrapped his hand around himself, picturing her doing it, her gold-green eyes devilish as she worked him.

What else do you like? she queried.

You.

You, just you.

But instead, he told her, *Voyeurism. I like to be watched. But I don't like to share my partner.*

Oh, fuck, that's hot. I've never tried that.

Do you want to? he asked boldly.

Are you propositioning me?

And if I was?
The three dots danced in the message thread.

CHAPTER NINE
Mina

Mina was completely hot and bothered. She was rubbing her thighs together, searching for friction that wasn't quite there. Wasn't enough. She sought the pleasure her body was aching for, but it needed more. It needed a touch.

It wanted him.

But that was foolish.

But her body sang a different song and it was crying out for Graham's hands, lips, and cock.

Which was utterly absurd.

She hated him.

But why was talking sex with him getting her so riled up? The idea of him fucking two other people was simultaneously hot and jealousy-inducing. Which made no fucking sense. She never wanted to a have a threesome, and she didn't actually want to fuck him, so why the aggression? Was she ovulating?

What if I was?

What if I was?

She kept rereading that last message, trying to compose her own response while she started spiraling with sexual craving. Her vision was lust-hazed, her thoughts clouded with yearning. She was wanton desire made incarnate.

It had been so long since she'd had sex with anyone.

She reached for her bedside table drawer.

Not letting herself think further on it, or dwell on the consequences, she grabbed the trusty purple toy she preferred.

With thoughts of Graham in her head, she shimmied down her shorts and underwear, baring herself to the night. Her limbs were all warm and languid, smooth and soft. Carefully, she took a finger and circled a nipple through her shirt. She gasped as it peaked beneath her touch and continued the motion, working herself up.

Slowly, she attended to herself the way she liked to be touched. Caresses and gentle pinches, a little flicking that had her biting her lip. All the while, she imagined it was Graham. She grew wetter with every fingertip against her electrified skin through the thin cotton of her t-shirt.

Everything was over sensitized. Her bedsheets, her blankets, her pillows. Even the spill of light from her bedside lamp felt like it was heating her up.

When she felt like she couldn't take the edging anymore, she reached down, feeling the shorn hair down at her pussy, and set the vibrating toy to her clit. The sensation was immediate and divine. Mina arched off the bed with a half moan, half gasp as it zinged through her. She kept rubbing her nipple and massaging her clit as something built within her, coiling low in her belly, making her core clench.

Relax, baby.

She heard Graham's voice in her mind and her brain short-circuited, her orgasm flashing to the surface. Imagining Graham talking her through it, whispering filthy, sweet nothings, had her on the edge within moments.

As the climax crawled through her, on the edge of breaking, her toes curled, and she gasped a wordless plea.

And then she said something very much not wordless.

"*Graham,*" she moaned as she came.

The orgasm crashed through her, tearing her from the cliff and casting her out to sea as she shattered through the vibrations, her hands still working in a frenzy, carrying herself through the waves.

She collapsed, boneless, against her mattress, chest heaving, sweat made glitter on her skin. Breaths sawed out of her. And with them came the post-orgasmic bliss and abruptly interrupting that came the post-orgasmic regret.

"Oh my god," she gasped to the empty room.

Holy fuck, I just made myself finish thinking of Graham. I am so fucked.

Mina blinked, staring at the ceiling, pondering all of her life's regrets and wondering if the universe would take pity on her and open up a hole beneath her bed, swallowing her whole.

It was Sunday and Mina was at Illiana's house, thinking very hard about not thinking about last night. About touching herself and imagining her fake boyfriend. It took much of her self-preservation to not scream into the void about it.

In front of the two of them were pages and pictures spread across the dining table; a notebook dedicated to wedding planning in front of Ana.

"So, I've narrowed down the colors to these three—" Ana said, indicating three swatches of green. "Which do you like best?"

"I love the green, but I have to admit, I'm surprised," Mina said, fingers drifting to the sage swatch. "I figured you would've chosen pink."

"I love pink," Ana admitted, twisting a blonde coil around her finger. "But while I know you'd look stunning in pink, green is your color, and I want this to be about you, too." Ana giggled. "Besides, there's going to be enough pink accents, I figured I'd give Emmett a reprieve from it."

Mina felt a swell of warmth from her best friend's consideration.

"Will you come get the dresses with me? I want you there when I pick out my wedding dress and all the bridesmaid dresses. I want all the bridesmaids there, and Ashley and Danika."

Ashley and Danika were Emmett's moms, both having gotten pregnant by the same man, and who banded together to raise their kids together while also falling in love. It was one of the sweetest love stories Mina had ever heard.

"I'd love to," Mina told her. "Just let me know when, and I'll be sure to get the day off."

"Will do! Also," Ana said, flattening her palms down on the notes, pink nails pointing at hearts in the margins, reining in her excitement. "I've cleared it with Lacey and Walt, and all the necessary insurances, so the wedding is confirmed to be at the lake house."

Ana had confided last month about her desire to marry in front of the lake at the Ellis family lake house and Mina and Nate had dropped hints to her aunt and uncle so they ended up suggesting it to Emmett and Illiana anyway. It had been perfect and her best friend was beyond thrilled.

Walt was already building them an arbor.

The conversations continued as such, Illiana gushing about her future—the marriage and her trip tomorrow to Tofino for her birthday—Mina nodding and gushing appropriately before Ana slowed down, assessing.

"Are you all right?"

"Fine," Mina replied.

"Did you and Graham have a fight, or something? You seem really tense. Do you want to talk about it?"

"No, it's nothing, but I appreciate the thought."

Ana didn't look like she believed her, but that was the thing with their friendship—they never pushed. When Ana was working through her eating disorder, Mina never pried or made her talk about it. Luckily, that seemed to be something she'd largely overcome. It was the same for Mina. When Mina shut down about her relationships when they started going south, Ana just sat by her and was there whenever she needed her. It was what they needed.

"Don't worry," Mina said. "It's all good."

It would be, because she and Graham would be working on getting more comfortable with each other in earnest. Tonight. They'd have to if they had a hope of surviving this.

CHAPTER TEN
Graham

Jasmina was on his doorstep. Her golden-brown hair was haloed in the golden aura of his automatic porch light, the haze like a corona about her head. It casted her in an awed, angelic glow. She took his breath away.

"We should kiss," she said without hesitation.

His lungs completely stopped working.

"No, '*hello*?'"

"You were right. People noticed. We need to get more comfortable with each other."

"How hard was that for you to say?"

"Like pulling teeth," she confessed.

And then she was kissing him.

Jasmina's hands were cupping his face, her smooth brown fingers caressing his jaw as her lips molded against his.

Her mouth parted against his and his thoughts raced in disbelief. As his hands went to her waist, one of hers roamed to his hair, fusing with the waves as he felt the gentle prod of her tongue.

This was what he'd wanted.

For so long this was what he'd craved.

What he never let himself have.

Never let himself even imagining it could be true.

All he tasted was her—the slight sweetness of tea and the bite of spearmint gum. All he could smell was her—peaches and floral. He wanted to devour her.

Graham's heart hammered in his chest, thundering an unbelievable rhythm. This…this was better than he could have ever possibly imagined.

Graham tugged her closer and pulled her over the threshold, firmly into his house. He shut the door and wildly pushed her against it, every curve of her pressed to every line of him.

Jasmina let out a soft, startled mewl and he chased it, his tongue slipping into her mouth. Hers met his in a wild gasp and then the kiss turned feral. His hands went to her ass, cupping those voluptuous cheeks in his palms, hoisting her up. Her core was against his abdomen, the heat of her searing him—he felt desperate for her.

All he wanted was more, more, more. He never wanted this to stop. Jasmina in his arms was pure heaven. He was damned sure he was going to leave a lasting impression on her because she'd branded herself into him.

Her hands went to the edge of his shirt between them, her fingers splaying over his abs and he shivered at her delicate touch. He kissed her deeper, her fingers tracing up from the fine trail of hair below his navel, climbing higher.

He froze when her fingertips brushed a scar.

Suddenly, that touch was a douse of ice water to his arousal. With an abruptness that startled him, the spell was broken and he broke the kiss and set Jasmina down on her feet.

Even if she had fully felt that scar, and even if she'd lifted his shirt to see it, she wouldn't find it. Each of the five surgical scars were covered with tattoos. So expertly hidden that it took touch to unveil them.

"Well," Graham started breathlessly, lips swollen from Jasmina's kiss. He could still taste her on them. "If that's the way you kiss someone you don't like, I can't imagine it when you *do* like someone." Or love them.

Graham really took her in after that. She was clearly flustered, fidgeting with her hands, not meeting his eyes. Her breaths weren't even, her chest heaving, and he forced himself to tear his gaze from her full breasts.

"Well," he started again. Didn't he start his last sentence that way? "Since you're here, are you hungry?"

"I am," she finally said.

"Good. Stay in or eat out?"

Jasmina's breath caught and Graham felt of shiver of lust chase through him at the latter option. She hesitated before choosing to stay in and cook.

Graham motioned for her to follow him to the kitchen and she kicked off her shoes before doing so. He reached the fridge and pulled out peppers, cucumber, red onion, feta, and Greek dressing, setting them all by the glass cutting board. As Jasmina wordlessly went to the vegetables and began washing and chopping, Graham prepped the chicken souvlaki and preheated the oven. He sidled up next to her and began scooping the chopped vegetables into a waiting glass bowl.

"You know," Jasmina said nonchalantly, slicing the cucumber. "I think we need to practice a basic kiss. Just a peck. Because while that last one was great, it's a bit intense for the friends."

Graham couldn't help the smirk that curled his lips. "It was great, huh?"

"Oh, shut up. You know what I mean."

She rolled her eyes and Graham swept in for the opportunity—belatedly worrying about the very large knife in her hands. Gently and eagerly, he kissed her, just an easy meeting of lips, catching her full mouth with his. She didn't flinch. She kissed him, too.

When he pulled back, he could see that it affected her—deeply.

Positively.

Jasmina cleared her throat. "See, that was perfect. Very acceptable for our friends to witness." She brandished the knife. "And don't make a comment about me calling it perfect."

Graham held his hands up in surrender, quelling a playfulness that rose to the surface. Amusedly, he watched her. "I would never dream of it."

"Liar," she said, waving him off with the blade.

She wasn't wrong.

He laughed to himself.

Jasmina eyed him with a slight disturbance.

Perhaps it wasn't to himself.

They made the rest of dinner in companionable silence, cooking, eating, and cleaning it all up in the same manner. When all of that was done, they settled onto the couch with their respective hobbies.

Graham was reading a domestic thriller and Jasmina was coloring, sitting on the floor in front of the coffee table like a child. The faint scent of alcohol markers tinged the air as she colored a picture of cute animals. Nearby, she had a book on standby, just in case her interest changed. It was some sort of fantasy, and judging by what he knew of current trends, the genre, and what she and Illiana liked to read, it was probably smutty, too.

He wondered if she ever wanted to act out any of those scenes.

He banished the thought immediately.

But he couldn't stop himself from thinking about something distantly attached to that thought. The idea that this exact situation—this exact moment—could be their life. Having had dinner, engaging in their hobbies, and then perhaps the reenactment. It felt like a flimsy dream, but goddammit, he wanted to catch it and keep it.

Eventually, they retired to bed—separately—with a lingering goodnight that felt filled with double meaning and questions. But he couldn't act on it or even ask about it. What if he was wrong? He knew how he felt; he wasn't certain about her.

The thoughts plagued him while he tried to fall asleep.

CHAPTER ELEVEN

Knocking woke her.

It wasn't knocking on the door of Graham's guest room. It was knocking on the front door.

Mina leapt out of bed, straightening her t-shirt and shorts as she dashed into the hall. She met Graham there, her fake boyfriend tugging on a white shirt that gave her a glimpse of those abs she felt yesterday—and was that ink underneath?

Did Graham have tattoos hiding?

Mina suddenly wanted very much to have him naked and discover what else he had going on under those clothes.

As Graham padded down the stairs, Mina followed and found him at the front door. When he opened it, he was surprised to find Emmett and Illiana standing there.

"I am so sorry," Emmett said in a rush. Mina had never seen him so frazzled before. "I know it's early, but we were on our way to drop Leia and Gimli off at the dog sitter, but she cancelled at the last minute and our vacation rental doesn't allow animals. Is there any way you can take them for the week?"

Graham seemed to blink to process this information before leaping to acceptance. "Yeah, of course! Bring them on in."

"Thank you so much, babe," Emmett said before him and Illiana went back to their SUV.

Graham turned to her quickly and bent low to speak lowly. It was the morning. How did he not have morning breath? "Run to the guest room and make it look like you haven't been staying there. That's where the dogs will be sleeping."

Mina's eyes widened but she nodded before racing up the stairs.

Fuck, fuck, fuck, she was chanting internally.

She rushed into the guest room and grabbed her bag, running across the hall and tossing it in Graham's room, not even bothering to consider any of the furniture or décor. Back in the guest room, she threw the blankets together, removing every trace of her once sleeping presence. The pillows were haphazardly fluffed, coverlet hastily smoothed, and her previous day's clothes tossed onto Graham's rumpled bed.

For good measure, she tore the blankets off the slightly more made side of Graham's bed to give the illusion that she'd been sleeping there. She didn't know if they'd even bother to look in his room but she was not taking the chance. Making a quick chopping motion to a pillow, she hoped it looked like her head had been resting there.

Distantly, she noticed his bedspread was a really pretty shade of olive green with gold thread and his bedsheets were a soft beige-brown shade.

She slapped the mattress once in finality.

It would have to do.

Just as she returned downstairs to Graham, Emmett and Ana led the two dogs into Graham's house. Ana had Leia, the princess of all chocolate labs, on a pink leash printed with lighter pink roses, and Gimli, the laziest English Bulldog in town was led in on a red leash decorated with sparkly hearts.

Clearly, Illiana's touch on Emmett's life had translated to the dogs, too.

"Thank you again, so much," Ana said as she corralled the dogs into sitting calmly.

"Of course. The dogs are always welcome," Graham told them warmly—surprisingly bright for just having woken up.

"Why haven't you gotten one yet?" Emmett asked as he hauled in a bag of expensive looking dog food and some chew toys.

"I don't know. I just haven't yet." Graham shrugged. "Just waiting for the right one to pick me, I guess."

Emmett and Illiana shared conspiratorial look. "The one, huh?"

Graham grumbled something under his breath.

"I'm going to start on breakfast," Mina announced. "Do either of you want anything before you go?"

"No, no, we're good, thanks," Emmett said.

Mina and Ana hugged goodbye and Mina whispered in her ear.

"I hope you're still practicing safe sex."

Ana laughed. "Fuck off. But I hope you are too. And I hope it's good sex." Ana pulled back and wiggled her brows.

Mina laughed and she hoped Ana didn't hear the slightly forced sound running as an undercurrent to it.

Emmett and Illiana left, and the dogs settled on Graham's couch as Mina made for the kitchen.

She worked in Rose Point today, considering it was a Monday, so she had a bit more time to get ready. At the stove she cooked scrambled eggs and bacon, slices of sourdough bread ready to be toasted, and half an orange sliced on a marble cutting board. The scents of grease and butter filled the kitchen with a scent like home, the salt and pepper adding to the aroma. The bacon sizzled and popped as she danced away from the grease splatter, just as Graham entered the large kitchen.

He was dressed in loose pants—not quite sweatpants, but comfortable pants, to be sure—and a pale blue button down, the top two buttons undone, exposing the delicious line of his collarbone where a drop of water traced the shape from his damp, shower tousled brown hair.

"Business on the top, party on the bottom?" Mina quipped, scrambling the eggs with a wooden spatula.

"It's a work from home day today. Gotta be ready in case they want a Zoom meeting."

Right, she mentally scolded herself.

The schedule. She knew this. She knew Mondays he worked from home.

She wished, distantly, that she was as perceptive as Graham. What would it be like to be that aware? That ease of just knowing? He made it seem so effortless, whereas with her, it wasn't unusual for her to click "*I forgot my password*" more than once a month.

The thoughts bothered her all throughout the rest of the day, even after she'd eaten her breakfast, made enough for Graham, and gotten ready for work. She wondered if there was something wrong with her. Was she just careless? Forgetful? Or was Graham really just that special?

Special?

Special?

She was thinking of her enemy as special, now?

Mina scrubbed at her cheeks from her desk as she wrote down some client notes about diaphragmatic breathing to help with some pelvic floor issues. Typically, helping patients with their concerns helped take her mind off the issues in her personal life, but today it wasn't working.

Her phone vibrated with a new text. She opened it to find a picture from Graham.

I have a portable heater, he texted. The picture was of Leia sleeping on his feet while he sat at his desk, her nose pressed into her paws.

Where is Gimli? she sent back.

He thought you'd never ask, he returned.

A pictured joined it and Mina couldn't bite back the laugh that burbled out.

Gimli was on Graham's lap, tied to him in a makeshift sling, almost like a baby. He seemed content, dozing without a care in the world, his white and tawny wrinkles on full display.

Before she could compose a reply, an incoming phone call interrupted her, a picture of her mother's smiling face peering up at her. Mina hit answer immediately.

"Hey mama," she said, twiddling a pen between her fingers.

"Hi honey. What's this I hear about you having a boyfriend?"

She had to give it to her mother. Laura Coulter didn't beat around the bush; she liked to get directly to the point. It was something she did not share with her twin sister, Lacey.

Mina pinched the bridge of her nose between her thumb and forefinger, breathing in slowly.

"It's new. We've just recently put a label on it."

"When did it start?"

"Valentines Day."

"Oh, honey! That's romantic. What did you do? Wait—is it appropriate for your mother's ears?"

"Oh my god, mama," Mina groaned. "It was, but even if it wasn't, do you think I'd tell you that?"

"Some children are closer with their parents. You never know. Elaine's daughter tells her everything. She knows all about her sex life."

Mina screamed internally. "Mama, I love you, but we will not be discussing sex. At all. Ever. We just got dinner and sat at the beach and looked at the stars."

"Well, that sounds romantic."

It was. And it twisted in her gut that it was a lie. She wanted it to be true, and it made her sick that she felt that way. But she couldn't admit that. Graham was doing this whole ruse out of the goodness of his heart for his best friend, and to make sure his wedding went off smoothly. Not because he secretly wanted to be with her. She had to remind herself of that.

This was *not* one of her books.

It wasn't.

"Yeah, it was really nice."

"So, when do we get to meet this young man? He is a young man, right? He isn't some old man giving you money for your dates, right? A sugar escort?"

Jesus fucking Christ.

"It's a sugar baby and sugar daddy, or an escort. But no, it's neither. He's my age, mom. Perfectly acceptable."

She was careful not to say it was real. Because it wasn't.

"Well, I'm glad to hear all that is good and well. So, would you two like to come to dinner so you can introduce us? I'd like to meet him."

Should she just say she already knew him and rip the bandage off now? Should she tell her mom that she already adored Graham, much to Mina's chagrin? No, that would extend this phone call far past the non-spoken allowable time to.

"Sure."

"Okay, we'll see you both Thursday at six!"

Her mom left no room for argument.

"All right. Love you, mom."

"Love you, too. Bye!"

They hung up and Mina sighed. She was left looking at the text thread with Graham. It was odd to see it, how it had once been so sporadic, only there for emergencies and bare necessity pleasantries. Now, they had hours of banter, logistics, pictures, quips, emojis, and so much more.

The dots on the lower left side indicated Graham was writing.

Mina quickly told him about the dinner plans with her parents on Thursday, then tucked the phone away as she closed out the client notes and prepared for her next patient, Hannah.

She quickly skimmed the previous intake form from her initial appointment and mentally checked what kind of exercises and exams she'd be doing with Hannah. When she felt ready, she got up off her little black rolling stool, and went to the front to grab Hannah for her appointment.

She'd known Hannah in school, so while there was a touch of awkwardness, Mina was a professional. But it was when Hannah spoke that the awkwardness began for an all-new reason.

"Forgive me if this is too personal, but I heard through the grapevine that you and Graham Starling are together. I thought you two hated each other?"

Three. More. Months.

CHAPTER TWELVE
Graham

Tuesdays were for Blues. Sometimes Fridays, but Tuesdays were the go-to day. Every week the boys got together for dinner and a beer and talked about their week, or even just to catch up.

Blues was their preferred kitschy-styled bar with mismatched seating—the red pleather booth was their unofficial official spot—multicolored Christmas lights strung around exposed wood beams, and records dangling from the ceiling. Movie posters hung on the walls, several of them signed. The floor was a perpetually sticky linoleum, but the food was good, and the service was immaculate.

Graham, Emmett, Nate, Kieran, and Chase were regulars, but Emmett wasn't in attendance tonight due to his vacation with Illiana. Sometimes, like tonight, Chase's younger brother tagged along. Typically, it was a drag when this happened as none of the guys had liked Jace, but something was different with him lately. It was subtle, but Graham had noticed it.

"I can't believe you didn't tell me you were seeing my cousin," Nate razzed, punching Graham playfully. "You better treat her well, otherwise, she'll make you regret it."

"You're not going to threaten to beat me up?" Graham teased, taking a pull from his beer.

Nate scoffed a laugh, his green-gold eyes, so like Jasmina's glittered. "Have you met Mina? She can take care of herself. Besides, you know we're not into that toxic macho shit. We talk about our issues like regular emotionally regulated humans." Nate flashed a look at Jace, and to Graham's surprise, Jace noticed and ducked his head into his own drink.

Peculiar.

That was another thing about their friend group—they were very much against toxic masculinity and felt comfortable sharing emotions with each other and talking out problems, rather than punching them out. Which came in handy last summer with the whole clusterfuck of Illiana's identity.

"I'm with Nate on this one, too," Chase interjected. "I really didn't see this coming."

Kieran flashed Graham a look that said, 'I *did*.'

"Yeah, yeah, I know, it's unexpected, all that jazz. What can I say? A moment changes everything."

"A moment?" Nate asked, quirking a dark brow. "You two had a moment? One where you weren't scheduling pistols at dawn?"

Graham gave him an unimpressed look while the rest of the guys laughed.

"I'll have you know, we're more than capable of talking civilly."

"That's a new development," Chase quipped.

Graham's brows drew together. He wasn't enjoying being ragged on like this. To his chagrin, he was feeling sensitive about Jasmina and all his tangled feelings with her. He was about to say something, asking them to knock it off, when Jace piped up.

"Can I ask you all a question?"

The entire table fell silent, every hand froze, each expression stone.

Graham was the first to gain his composure. He cleared his throat. "Yeah, sure. Shoot."

"So, there's this girl, and—"

"Jace? That you man?" a belligerent voice crowed from across the bar.

A frat bro type stumbled over, a few pints deep, his squeaky-clean sneakers, light blue washed jeans, and white polo shirt gave every negative signal he could imagine. His hair was gelled within an inch of its life, his slimy smile just as falsely shining.

Jace looked mortified at the guy's approach and his cheeks reddened even more when a second guy joined frat bro. This guy was slightly less pompous-looking, but more unpredictable.

The second guy was in a navy hoodie and black jeans, his sneakers showing signs of wear, a silver chain flashing around his neck. His brown eyes were hazy, movements jittery, jaw jutting and clenched—Graham recognized the tell and mentally prepared himself.

"Hey, Chad," Jace said resignedly to frat bro.

Because of course his fucking name was Chad.

"Have you had any luck with that chick from the bookstore or wherever she works?"

"Yeah, man. Heard you had the hots for her bad," the second guy interjected.

"Trevor," Jace greeted, looking like he wanted to do nothing less. He continued to Trevor—AKA: the guy coked out of his skull beside Chad. "You doing well?"

"Feeling great," Trevor said, sniffling. Snorting every last speck of blow into his nasal passages. "But hey, when you're done fucking her, maybe let me know if she's game for more."

Palpable tension thickened in the room, as touchable as an electric current. Every guy at the table was a fine-tuned bow string, ready to leap into action—save for Chase, who was trying very hard to disappear. He was not going to risk his career for two losers.

Trevor's gaze flittered over all of them, assessing them in a predatory manner. Sizing them all up.

Graham's hackles rose, and he was ready to throw fists—despite his earlier thoughts of abhorring toxic masculinity, sometimes needs warranted a little rule breaking.

Jace flinched at the crass language. "Okay, cut it out, Trev. You're being gross. She's a person. A person I'm interested in and I'd appreciate it if you were a bit more respectful when referring to her."

"What the fuck, man?" Chad gaped. "Since when do you talk like a lil' pussy? Can't take a joke?"

"A joke usually means someone laughs," Jace deadpanned.

The table went silent.

Kieran's dark brown eyes were hard as he stared threateningly and unblinkingly at Chad and Trevor. It was his disciplinary teacher's stare. The one that made you feel like you were in trouble, even if you hadn't done anything, and made you feel supremely fucked when you knew you had.

"Man, fuck you," Chad spit. "We're just messing around. Being a little bitch about it isn't going to get you into Olivia's pants any faster."

"Okay, back off," Jace hissed. "I'm not talking about this anymore."

Was Jace turning over a new leaf? Never did Graham expect Jace, of all people, to stand up for women like that, especially to his own friends. Or at least, Graham thought they were Jace's friends.

Sort of.

"You've changed," Chad accused. "You think you're better than us now? Is that why we haven't seen you around Mitch's lately?"

"I've just been busy. Focusing on other things."

"Like sucking these guys dicks?" Trevor snarled.

Graham fisted his hand in his lap and had the distinct thought that if looks could kill, his blue gaze would've had Chad and Trevor in caskets.

"No, I'm not sucking any. This is my brother and his friends."

Trevor scoffed something that sounded suspiciously like *bag*, but Graham was pretty sure he used an F, and not a B.

Chair legs screeched across the floor as Nate stood. Rage outlined every part of him, his frame and features were a mask of wrath that sent chills through Graham's blood.

"All right, it's time you left. Now," Nate gritted out firmly.

They were drawing attention now. Servers were watching with bated breath, large-framed kitchen staff stood in the doorway, ready to defend if need be. This wasn't the kind of establishment that had security.

"You going to let him talk to me like this?" Trevor sneered. "This—"

Graham stood before Trevor could manage another slur.

"Get the fuck out. Now." His voice was timorous. Dark and gravel and every ounce of intimidation his 6'2" presence allowed.

"Seriously," Jace said quietly. "You should go."

Chad and Trevor stared, agape with shock and disgust. Then finally, they turned on their heel and left, spitting expletive laden insults the entire way,

Jace deflated in his seat, his head falling forward, his light blonde hair flopping to cover his eyes.

"I'm so sorry," Jace whispered into his hands. Frustration laced his words, angry tears silvering his eyes. Graham pretended not to notice.

"Friends of yours?" Kieran asked.

"Sort of," Jace admitted with shame. "Used to be. We hung out in the same friend group, but lately I've been really not okay with a lot of the stuff they've been saying."

"Like?" Graham prompted.

"Stuff like what they were saying just now. Talking shitty about Olivia like that. Like she wasn't a person, just a thing. It made me feel sick."

It wasn't too long ago that Jace had been referring to girls as bitches and what they could give him, but it seemed those days were over. It seemed he was growing up.

"Was that the girl you were going to ask us about?" Graham inquired softly. "Olivia?"

Jace's cheeks reddened. "Yeah. I met her at Cupid Café and we got talking a bit, then she mentioned she also worked at the bookstore in Vic that Emmett and Illiana like, so I—" Jace blushed furiously. "I started going into it to see her, not knowing it was romance only."

Oh, Emmett would love to hear about this.

"Have you been forcing yourself to read Orc Smut?" Graham teased.

"Okay, not Orc Smut—does that exist? Just regular smut."

"Oh, yeah. It definitely exists."

Jace looked a little green.

"You know," Graham said contemplatively. "Delilah might know her if she works at Sugar & Spice. Maybe she can talk to her."

Kieran's head snapped up at the name and Graham had to force himself not to roll his eyes.

Not subtle, babe. Not at all.

Graham shot Kieran a cautious look. Kieran turned to his magically delivered chicken wings—courtesy of Gina. Graham turned back to Jace.

"Does she know you're interested?"

"I don't know," Jace muttered despairingly. "I don't know how to talk to girls when it's something serious. Hook ups are one thing, the real thing is another."

The real thing?

Who was this and what had he done with Jace Laurier?

"Want some advice?" Nate asked.

Jace was fumbling with the label on his beer. "If I'm getting advice from the four of you, I have a confession to make." All the guys held their breath, waiting for something horrible. "I fucking hate beer—it tastes like piss. Can I get a watermelon margarita?"

Jace got his margarita and the boys divulged their advice. After that was done, the conversation evolved into bachelor party plans. Activities were discussed, locations suggested, and ideas vetoed.

It was during this time that Graham got a text from Jasmina, and he realized how much he missed her. It was just a basic check in, but it was enough to set his heart galloping.

He couldn't imagine ever getting sick of it and he wondered if she was even beginning to feel the same way. If she was falling into the habits and lifestyle they were faking just as effortlessly.

Could they renegotiate the contract?

Graham let his mind wander as he finished his beer.

Just maybe they could talk about it tomorrow at their next sleepover.

CHAPTER THIRTEEN
Mina

When Mina arrived at Graham's Wednesday evening, she realized three things.

One: Leia and Gimli were there, meaning they were taking up the guest room, and with that bed being a twin, there was not a chance of sharing it with them. Not if she wanted a decent night's rest.

Two: Either her or Graham would have to sleep on the couch—and again, if she wanted a decent night's rest, her back would not thank her for that.

And three: She didn't want to contemplate why she wanted to sleep in his bed instead.

Mina and Graham were lounging on the couch after dinner, playing two truths and a lie, drinking non-alcoholic beverages and snacking on whatever they rummaged from the pantry.

"I once fell asleep while driving, my sisters waxed my eyebrows off as a joke, and I used to have night terrors as a kid."

"There's no way you fell asleep at the wheel," Mina declared. "You're too observant for that—you wouldn't risk it, but if you were really overtired..."

"So, if that's your theory—which is the lie?"

Mina stared at him, taking in his face.

"You never had your brows waxed off."

"Correct," Graham confirmed. "But it was a regular threat in the house."

"I can see that. Especially from Sabrina."

"Oh, yeah. She was the worst."

They went back and forth

"I went to the Bahamas after my third year of college, I hate Smirnoff Ice, and I lost my virginity in the back of a car," Mina said, counting off her fingers.

Graham's brows drew together in contemplation. He and Mina had gone to school together but had never been close due to separate social circles. Not to mention she completely cut any contact with him after graduation.

"I've never heard you talk about the Bahamas before," he said, eyes faraway and thinking. "And you hate flying."

"I've never told you about my first time having sex either."

"True. But I do know how you got blackout drunk off Smirnoff Ice that one time, and I had to carry you to bed."

"That was one time!" she defended.

"One time is all it takes."

"Regardless, continue."

Graham tapped a finger to his lip in thought. She had the wild urge to bite that lip. To pull it between hers and—no.

"It must be the Smirnoff Ice."

"Nope," she said, popping the P.

"Bahamas?"

"Incorrect."

Graham's brows rose. "So, how *did* you lose your virginity?"

"You first," she said coyly, sipping on her sparkling water.

"Your cousin Sasha's friend, Carmen. I had a crush on her for a while, but I just think that's because she was older and therefore, I thought cooler. We never would've worked out though. It was awkward and definitely not good."

"How old were you?" she asked, ignoring the flame of jealousy that ignited beneath her skin.

"Seventeen."

"I was fifteen," she told him before his obligatory ask. "It was my high school boyfriend. We dated for four years, but I think it happened around our second-year anniversary." Mina shrugged. "It was okay, nothing amazing, nothing traumatic. We got the hang of it eventually."

"Why'd you two break up?" Graham asked, a thin edge to his voice. Was that jealousy, too, she sensed?

"I wanted to go to Toronto for school, he wanted to go to Alberta to work in the oil fields. It was hard at the time, but I'm over it now."

"Do you think you'd still be together if he followed you or if you went with him?"

Mina considered this. "No, I don't think so. He seems happy now. Married with three kids and another on the way."

"Oh, shit. Wow." Graham's face turned pondering. "Is it weird for you to think about that?"

"In an odd way, yeah. Not that I want that with him, but what if that's the life I could have had—you know?"

"Is that something you'd want one day?" he asked.

Mina didn't get a chance to respond before Graham's phone went off on the table. Nate's name and picture popped up, a grinning shot of him with two pitchers of beer, and probably half of one spilled down his shirt.

"Mind if I get this? He doesn't usually call unless it's something serious."

"Go for it."

It saved her from having to answer his question about a life she could have had. She didn't know why, but Graham asking her that had her questioning so many things. Not to mention, wondering why he would even ask, and if he even cared.

"Yeah, man. Hang on a sec, let me talk to Jasmina."

Mina tuned into the conversation Graham had been having just as he turned to her, covering the speaker of his phone.

"Everything all right?" she asked. She was ready to grab her things and run for the door, to race for the hospital if that's what her cousin needed.

"Kind of. Something happened at work and Nate wanted to know if he could come by. He doesn't want to be alone. You okay with that?"

"Oh, yeah. Of course. I can go," she said beginning to get up.

"No," he said quickly, latching onto her wrist. His grip was hot on her skin, and she swore electricity crackled between them. "Stay. I want you to."

I want you to.

I want you to.

It repeated over and over.

He wanted her to stay.

"But you asked—"

"I just wanted to make sure you were okay with him also coming by."

"It's your house, though."

"For the time being, it's also yours."

That had butterflies ascending in her stomach. A whole storm of them fluttering and rapidly flapping their wings in a too cramped space.

Ten minutes later, Nate arrived, a six pack beneath his arm. He was in joggers and a gray hoodie, his face drawn, his mouth etched with hard lines of stress. Her cousin stuffed the beers in the fridge and returned with one in hand, cracking it open, and flopping on the armchair across from them. Gimli scrambled onto his lap.

"What's going on, babe?" Graham asked one of his best friends.

"I think I'm getting fired," he said, defeated.

"What?" Mina gasped, nearly launching off the cushion. "Why?"

"The business is apparently restructuring and they told me to take tomorrow off."

"Is there a chance that they're just giving you the day off while they manage some paperwork bullshit?" Graham inquired, searching for options logically.

"Doubtful. But, yeah, technically, I suppose so." Nate took a swig of his beer, his other hand on Gimli's wrinkled coat. "I just...I didn't want to be alone with those thoughts. You know? Like, what about my mortgage? How will I pay my bills? How soon can I find a new job?"

"Okay, those are all valid points," Graham placated. "But, let's table that for now. There's nothing you can do about it right now. Tomorrow, we can figure it all out."

Nate nodded, emotion a roiling storm across his face.

Laura and Lacey had been encouraging in supporting their children's emotional needs, as well as emotional expression. With that said, Mina had seen her cousin cry on more than one occasion—less now that they were adults, but it had happened.

Surprisingly enough, he didn't seem all that close to breaking right now. He just looked drained. Like the fight had gone out of him. She worried something deeper was at play here and she mentally vowed to get to the bottom of it and make sure Nate was truly okay.

"Do you have any cards?" Mina asked Graham.

"Uh, yeah. Junk drawer in the kitchen."

"Perfect," Mina got up and headed to said drawer, finding two decks there. Leia followed her curiously. She grabbed them both, as well as the Good Vibes notepad they'd originally written their fake dating contract on, and returned with glee, shuffling all the cards together. "We're going to play a game."

"What's it called?" Graham asked, his eye nearly twitching as she mixed the two decks together. She could separate them later—she wasn't all that worried.

"To be honest, I don't know, but it's fun."

Mina explained the rules while she put the fat stack of cards on the table before them. She prompted them to cut the deck to pick up twenty-three cards, if they managed to pick up exactly twenty-three, it was minus ten points from their total score.

"It's like golf, that way," she told them as she placed four cards facedown in front of her and four faceup on top of them. "You want the lowest score possible."

Graham and Nate copied her as she began organizing her hand. Highest on the right, lowest on the left.

"Aces are low," Mina said, stuffing two aces into her left hand. "Kings are highest, with queens and jacks following. Tens are wildcards and can be put in the place of anything to clear the pile. The goal—" she explained, moving her four tens together, "is to get rid of all your cards. Whatever is left in your hand goes against you points wise. Each card is worth their face value except jacks, queens, and kings are all ten points, and tens are worth twenty. Remember—you do not want these points."

"I think I remember playing this a long time ago," Nate said wonderingly, his brows knit together. "Our moms liked to play it out camping, right?"

"I think that's the only time they would. If we were home, it was board games, so this got pushed to the wayside."

"So, if I have this right," Graham started. "You can clear a pile by being the person to put down the fourth card of a like card, or with a ten?"

"Correct." Mina grinned.

"And how often do you lose this game?"

Mina's grin widened. "Not often."

Graham's eyes turned challenging. "We'll just have to see about that."

"You're on."

Those words, Mina grew to regret. The entire game—more than ten rounds—her and Graham seemed to win back and forth with Nate scraping by with a mere two wins. Unfortunately, points were in varying degrees of getting racked up and they were in the 200s by the time Mina called it quits. By that time though, Nate was more than his six beers deep and asked to crash on the couch.

That left only one option.

Mina and Graham locked eyes and held a wordless conversation between them. They didn't want to be rude—and kicking Nate out when he was drunk and down would certainly convey that—so that left them with one problem to solve between them.

How were they going to handle sleeping in the same bed together?

There was no time to figure it out logistically. They just had to wing it.

"I'm pretty tired, so I'm heading to bed now," Mina announced, standing up and stretching.

"Graham?" Nate asked. "You heading to bed, too?"

Graham's eyes flickered to Mina and back to Nate, clearly sensing something in Nate that Mina hadn't noticed.

"I'll come to bed in a bit. You get comfy, baby."

And then Graham stood up, placed a warm, firm hand on the small of her back, and dipped down. The kiss was soft, pleasant. Like a honey-sweet hum, she closed her eyes and melted into it, letting her lips part and linger on his. Mina's blood rushed beneath her skin, and her hand found his chest, centering over his thundering heart.

When they broke, their eyes met and there was a thinly veiled glitter between them. She didn't know what it meant, but it had her veins singing like angels, euphoria bubbling through her limbs.

She was careful to pace herself as she headed to the bedroom, not to go too fast and catch suspicion. Quietly, she sneaked into the bathroom and freshened up everything that needed freshening up, washed her face, brushed her teeth, applied her very meager skincare routine—hyaluronic acid and lotion—and wrapped her hair in a protective style.

In Graham's bedroom, she undressed and slipped on an old gray t-shirt—it was so soft and worn that it was see-through in places—and a pair of cheeky shorts. It was her preferred sleeping clothes, although, last time she was over she'd packed longer shorts—she didn't want to begin contemplating why she didn't this time.

It meant nothing.

Mina stared at the bed, daunted by its intimidating presence. Not that it was an overly large bed, but it was what it symbolized.

It might be the 'only one bed' trope, but they were still not falling in love.

Psyching herself up, she paced the room.

"Get a hold of yourself, Mina," she muttered to herself. "It's just a bed. It doesn't mean anything."

She jittered and stared at the inviting blankets and groaned.

How hard was it to get into a bed?

"You're being stupid," she chastised herself.

Without thinking it through further, she dove into the side of the bed she noticed he left unoccupied last time. Climbing in, she settled in, feeling the soft sheets on her bare legs and—

She froze.

Did he have…a *silk* pillowcase?

She looked.

He did.

But only one.

And on her side.

Well, not *her* side, but the side designated for her because he—she assumed—preferred the other.

She stroked over the olive fabric. It felt new.

Did he…buy this for *her*? Had he researched the kind of care her hair would require? Had he bought any other things for her she hadn't noticed?

Or was she reading far too much into this?

She put the silk pillow in the middle.

Flopping down onto the not silk, but still soft pillows, Mina waited anxiously for Graham to join her in the bed. Her limbs were electric, like a thin live wire current coursing beneath her skin. Anxiety ratcheted up in her chest, churning in her stomach, spoiling her insides with nervous nausea.

Time began to do that odd thing where she couldn't tell if it had been twenty minutes or an hour, just that she was viscerally aware of time passing. Like a broken section of consciousness that demarcated when she was aware of the waiting, and when she wasn't.

Whether it was twenty or sixty, though, did not matter as she heard the click of the dogs' nails on the wood and Graham's whispered voice prompting them to go to bed. As soon as the door creaked open and Graham's tall frame filled the gap in the doorway, she felt immobilized. A golden glow from the hallway backlit him, haloing him like Prince Charming. Mina held her breath as the door clicked shut behind him.

He approached the bed, and through the watery light of his phone flashlight clutched between his fingers, she saw him pause. She had the sensation of eyes on her—of being watched.

"You're still awake," he whispered into the gloom.

Perceptive as ever.

"Yeah, I couldn't get to sleep." Her heart was hammering in her ears. Taunting her with the one bed trope.

"I was kind of hoping you would be."

"Why?"

"So, you wouldn't feel awkward about sharing a bed."

"Oh."

She watched Graham's gaze flick to the floor, reluctance on his face. "I can sleep on the floor."

"Don't be ridiculous," she said, opening his side of the blankets. "We're approaching thirty. Our backs will not thank us for the abuse of hardwood floors. Just get in the bed."

Her voice was cool and reasonable, but she felt anything but.

"All right."

Graham disappeared into the ensuite bathroom and she felt the tension pull taut between them, the anxiety a thread so tight you could strum it. The sound of water running and a toilet flush came from the room, light spilling from beneath the doorway.

When the bathroom door opened, Graham was wore a worn gray t-shirt and a pair of flannel pajama pants.

Wordlessly, he climbed into bed next to her and pulled the covers up underneath his arms. He was flat on his back. Mina turned on her side, sitting up on her elbow. Graham turned his face towards her, and she caught the scent of spearmint toothpaste.

She wasn't sure what she was doing, why she was trying to initiate conversation, so she just blurted out the first thing that came to mind.

"Why do you have a silk pillow?"

She watched him freeze, the light from the street cutting through the gap in the curtains. Mina saw the way his eyes glittered in the dark as they widened, his mouth parting ever so before he bit it closed.

"I bought it for you," he admitted in the darkness. "I heard that it's good for certain hair textures."

"It is," she confirmed. "It would also be fine for yours. It really helps to reduce frizz."

"Ah," he said.

"I'm assuming you've never dealt with it before."

"No, I haven't."

"Typical lucky man. Non-frizzy hair and long eyelashes that you don't even notice."

"Are mine that long?"

Mina sighed. "My point exactly."

"Anything else this ignorant man is yet to discover about himself?"

"Don't turn this into a self-deprecating thing."

"I'm not."

"Then don't try to make it an argument."

"Jasmina, I'm not," he said patiently. "I was just playing around."

"Oh." She felt her cheeks warm, realizing she had her defenses up before she'd even registered if Graham tapped on the walls. "Sorry, I'm just…I'm so used to us bickering."

"It's what we always did best. But maybe we can learn to do something better."

"And what's that?" Her heart caught in her throat.

"I don't know yet, but we can figure it out together."

"Is this the start of a truce?"

"Is our fake dating not already the start of that?"

Mina's hand flew to cover Graham's mouth, as she shushed him. "Don't say that too loudly. Nate might hear."

Graham gently wrapped his fingers around her wrist, and though the touch was soft, she felt as if his fingerprints were seared into her—his touch like a flash of lightning. He pulled her hand from his mouth. "Jasmina, he's practically passed out on the couch. Unless I yelled it, he's not hearing it. Even then, he might sleep through it."

"Oh. Right," she said, feeling silly.

Graham was still holding her wrist. For some reason, she didn't want him to let go. She was content to let him hold it, suddenly craving the physical contact.

Fuck, how long had it been since a man had touched her?

She wasn't counting the fake kisses with Graham, no matter how pleasant they were.

They stayed like that a moment. In stasis. In silence, in the dark. For a moment they were just two people—Mina and Graham. Not two fake dating frenemies. They were just them.

It hit Mina with a wave of calmness that she discovered that she liked his presence. She liked the way she felt with him. How he made her feel.

Alive.

Charged.

He challenged her. Thrilled her.

Every touch was a live wire.

What did it all mean?

Certainly not what her books had always said—no matter how much the heroine was blind to it, because she certainly wasn't. There just had to be another explanation.

Wordlessly, they parted and went to their opposite sides of the bed. Apparently, so in sync they'd felt that slight shift of inner conflict and confusion.

In the dark, Graham whispered.

"Goodnight, Jasmina."

She whispered back.

"Goodnight Graham."

In the morning Mina woke, limbs languid, tepid sunlight peeking through the drapes, and an arm wrapped around her waist. She came to more clearly and realized her face was pressed into Graham's chest, his shirt smelling of spice and timber and that elusive floral note. His fingers were grasping her shirt, her own tucked between them.

Alarm filled her as she realized she and Graham were cuddling.

"Fuck."

CHAPTER FOURTEEN
Graham

He couldn't shake the lingering effects off the morning from his skin.

He'd woken wrapped up with Jasmina, her smooth skin pressed against him, her bare legs tucked into his pajama-clad ones, her peach scent seared into him.

Luckily, his raging hard-on hadn't been touching her—small mercies. He would have been mortified had she noticed it, morning wood or not.

Their disconnect and departure was a blur. He couldn't remember anything but her touch and her smell and her. Just her. It replayed, haunting him.

Even now, hours later, when they were sitting in the truck on the way to her parents' house for dinner, he couldn't push the memory from his mind.

"Are you nervous?" Jasmina asked him from the passenger's side.

He looked over at her, her profile catching the fading evening light.

"Kind of?" Graham felt his brows knit together. "I've met your parents plenty of times, but never under these circumstances."

"The fake dating ones?"

His mouth twisted into a wry line. "Yeah, fake dating ones."

"Are you worried that they're going to see through this?"

"Are you?"

She shrugged. "My parents know me well, but they also know not to pry. They've always been good at giving me space as long as we keep healthy communication."

"That's good."

He felt her side-eyeing him from his peripheral vision. "Do you have a good relationship with your parents?" She cleared her throat. "I know we went over the basics with our contract, but I feel like there's more nuance than I know."

Graham scrubbed a hand over his jaw as he turned onto the Coulter's road. "Yeah, I'm good with them. Closer with my sisters though. With so many mouths to feed mom and dad had to work a lot, but we were never without love. When we were all together it was…special. Like postcard perfection—only it wasn't fake. Did we have regular family squabbles? Of course. Piper was really bad for hiding the remote, and Willow would scream at Sabrina to get out of her room, and Sabrina would stand in the doorway taunting her, because technically, she wasn't in her room. I kind of became one of the girls, too. Dad and I became well-versed in all things female." He held up a finger in caution. "I realize I may have overstepped with my last sentence—but you understand what I mean."

Jasmina's lips twisted into a smirk. "I do."

Something about those two words spilled something in him. Warmth and something like nostalgia or déjà vu. Something he couldn't pinpoint. Something good.

Graham pulled into the Coulter's driveway and applied the brake. What had once been a generic 70s BC box house had been renovated over the years and turned into a modern traditional dream. Big glass windows, proud wooden beams, stonework, and white siding shingles. The front door was painted red and upon it hung a white floral wreath, heralding the coming spring.

The porch light flicked on as they approached and Jasmina didn't bother knocking, just opened the door and called out a welcoming, "hello!"

Laura Coulter came around the corner from the polished white kitchen. Graham couldn't help the shock of seeing her because, one, she looked so much like Jasmina, and two, she was identical to her identical twin sister, Lacey—the mother of one of his best friends.

Like Jasmina, Laura had golden brown curly hair, except hers was tighter and her skin was a few shades darker. They had the same face shape, the same doe eyes, high cheekbones, and full lips, but age had marked Laura in gentle lines. They traced the corners of her mouth and teased the edges of her eyes, but if one didn't look too closely, they could be mistaken for sisters.

It made him think briefly of his own sisters and how they scarcely resembled their mother. How they'd all taken after their dad. It was Graham who looked like their mom.

"Hi honey," Laura greeted, throwing her arms around Jasmina. She looked right past Graham. Dressed in white, she brought with her the scent of Dior perfume and the feeling of joy. "How're you? How's the boyfriend?"

"The boyfriend is right here," Graham stated with a slight wave.

Laura pulled back from the embrace with her daughter and did a double-take. She blinked her hazel eyes—a color Jasmina had inherited—and her mouth parted as she glanced between the two of them.

"Graham?" she stage-whispered, though Graham thought it was supposed to be a regular whisper. "Graham Starling?"

"Hi, Mrs. Coulter."

"Yes, mama," Jasmina confirmed on a sigh.

"But…you two hate each other."

This was it. Laura was going to see right through them. The ruse was over, and they were going to be outed. Laura and Dean would tell everyone, and Emmett and Illiana would find out, and it would be a complete catastrophe.

"Feelings change," Jasmina said evasively, discreetly extending her hand by her side.

Graham took her hand and pressed a kiss to her knuckles—fuck, her skin was so soft. He let his lips linger a moment, catching that floral peach scent, and allowed himself a breath to close his eyes and savor it. When he brought their hands down, he noticed a brightness to her brown skin.

"Evidently," Laura said dryly, eyes suspicious. "You seem awfully…smitten."

"*Mama…*" Jasmina said warningly.

Laura gave her a playfully rebuffed look that involved scrunching up her nose and huffing. It was the same reaction he'd seen many times on his fake girlfriend.

"What's for dinner?" Jasmina asked, changing the subject, and craning her neck as if she could see into the kitchen.

"Roast beef dinner," Laura responded, waving them to follow her to the kitchen. "Oh, and Graham—you know better than to call me Mrs. Coulter, it's always been Laura to you."

"Of course," he said, nodding with a small smile. "Do you need any help making dinner?"

"Graham is an excellent cook," Jasmina inserted, boasting about him.

It thrilled him. Hearing pride shine in her voice like that—even if fake—had his stomach fluttering.

"Oh, I'll have to take you up on that offer next time. It's already all prepped, just a few more minutes to cook."

Next time.

Next time.

The words rang over in Graham's head.

The prospect of next time seemed so distant. Like a far-off galaxy. There was no way they'd be cooking dinner together once this ruse was done. And for some reason, his heart panged at the concept.

Some reason? A niggling voice in his head taunted.

Okay, he knew the exact reason.

He wanted Jasmina.

He'd wanted her for years.

And he couldn't stand that she couldn't stand him.

Still, despite it all, he still knew she was it.

He wasn't creepy or stalkerish, he just…knew. Knew like some people knew when they're in danger. Like how detectives get that gut feeling. Something primal and instinctual in him just knew.

It was what had started his entire view on The One.

Just then, Jasmina's father appeared from the walk-in pantry. Dean's blue eyes lit up at the sight of Graham. On the odd occasions they'd met, Graham and Dean had bonded over their mutual love of fishing. They'd shared some techniques over beers and the rest was history.

"Hey there, Fisherman! What're you doing here? You joining us for dinner with Mina's new boyfriend?"

"Dean," Laura said with caution. Her hand rested on her husband's broad shoulder. "Mina and Graham are together. This *is* her boyfriend."

There was a pause of breath holding before the light that entered Dean Coulter's eyes turned into luminance.

"Well, how about that!" he boomed joyously, throwing his arm around Graham's shoulders. "Glad to see she found herself a good one. You know, she never brings her boyfriends around here."

"Dad!" Jasmina chastised, aghast.

"Sorry, pumpkin. But it's true."

Jasmina sighed and scrunched up her nose. As she scrubbed a hand over her forehead, she sat herself on one of the island bar stools. Graham, as if compelled by a magnet, followed her and wrapped his arms around her upper body from behind, resting his chin on her head.

"You're doing great, baby," he murmured.

If he had to confess, then he'd say he liked calling her that a bit too much. If by using the fake dating scheme to call her by a term of endearment was a crime, then he was guilty on all charges. But the secret thing he didn't want to admit was that he was hoping this arrangement would convince her to give them an actual shot.

He still didn't know what had caused this animosity. How they'd been okay one day and then overnight it was outright hostility.

Right when he'd confided in Kieran about his feelings for her.

He didn't know how it had gone so wrong.

For now, though, he pushed that out of his head and enjoyed the moment. Relishing the touch of Jasmina, how it felt to hold her in such an intimately casual way. How she leaned into him and heaved a sigh of relief, how her breath ghosted across his skin, her fingertips digging into his forearm.

Graham felt as if the wind was knocked from him.

She was luxuriating in his touch, too.

He couldn't kick the smile from his face so he tucked it into Jasmina's hair, floating on a heavenly cloud of peach.

The dinner passed without much affair. The food was excellent, the conversation playful with enough serious interrogation to balance out. Throughout the meal and following card games, he and Jasmina kept up the carefully orchestrated touches and glances—even if his were involuntary because he was compelled by her completely. What he was learning, however, was that games were an integral activity to the Ellis-Coulter clan—which he made a mental note of curiosity to discover Laura and Lacey's maiden name.

That night, they—like the studious souls they were— discussed the events of the dinner and completed an overview of the touches and methods of affection to see which were most effective in selling the charade.

They were curled on opposite ends of Graham's caramel colored sectional; a queen-sized blanket stretched between them. Graham had his trusty Good Vibes notepad and Jasmina had a spiralbound notebook decorated in peaches.

"The chin grab was a nice touch," Jasmina commended, scribbling in her book.

"I wasn't too rough?" he asked.

"I would have told you if you were."

"Right," he chuckled. "I forgot who I was talking to. Nothing but blunt honesty from you."

"And that's why you love me," she said, completely blasé.

But Graham was paralyzed.

Did he love her?

His heart was racing, his eyes—though he obviously couldn't see them—were round orbs in his face. Was his jaw on the floor? It must be.

Love.

Love.

Did he love Jasmina Coulter?

What was her middle name?

Did he love her?

He looked at her and somehow composed his face into something new. But when she met his eyes, her gold-green ones shimmering with mischief and warmth, a true smile blooming on her lips, only one word echoed in his skull.

It was Tuesday at Blue's, Emmett had since picked up his dogs—who'd been very eager to see their dad—and thanked Graham for helping him out. Graham didn't comment on how he should be thanking him, because without those dogs—and Nate crashing on the couch—he and Jasmina may not have shared a bed.

Something he was very eager to repeat. Even though he knew he shouldn't get his hopes up.

Graham had been the first to arrive, so he'd ordered his beer and reclined in the old, red, pleather booth, warm in his gray hoodie, jeans, and once white sneakers. The booth was cracked, but familiar, this particular booth having hosted the boys every week.

Earlier, Emmett had texted the group chat and asked if they'd be all right with Leo joining them. None of them had objected, so Graham made sure there was enough space at their table.

Graham took a swig, beer in one hand, phone in the other and searched for his friends. None had arrived yet, but there was a mid-twenties brunette eyeing him at the bar. He noticed, in a completely objective way, that she was pretty, but that fact only made him miss Jasmina more. Graham looked away and returned his attention to the recent picture his fake girlfriend had uploaded to her profile.

They'd amended that in their contract; posting about each other. Graham wasn't a big poster, but Mina typically published something to socials once a week, so it was agreed that every so often—dictated by their regular posting status—they'd say something about each other or use an actual photo of them.

This was her first post of them.

They were cozied up in her parents' kitchen after dinner, smiling at each other. Neither of them had taken it, and neither had been aware of it being taken. They were completely in the moment. It was a true candid moment. The thing that really got him though; was the way they were looking at each other. Like they'd actually liked each other.

The two of them were in stark contrast against the polished and elegant white of the Coulter's kitchen. Graham couldn't tear his eyes away from the golden brightness of Jasmina. How everything about her seemed illuminated by some intangible warmth.

He realized it was just her.

Her being.

Just *her.*

Graham's heart gave an uneven thump as he liked the photo and commented with a heart. As an afterthought he screenshotted it, too, and pocketed his phone before anyone could ask about it.

Nate slid into the booth beside him, and shrugged off his corduroy coat. He noticed he was growing his hair out. Last summer he'd shaved it to a buzzcut, but now he sported dark coils tapered to a fade. The two of them knocked knuckles as their regular server—Gina—brought over Nate's preferred beer. Nate thanked her and leaned back.

"Hey man, how're things? Did that restructuring shit get sorted?" Graham asked just as Chase walked through the doors.

Chase was adjusting his glasses on the bridge on his nose, frustration lining his shoulders. He stopped at the bar and was conversing with the bartender.

Nate scrubbed the back of his neck. "Yeah, actually," he responded, shamefaced. "They promoted me with a salary increase, so I kinda overreacted for no reason. Sorry, man."

"Don't worry about it, babe," Graham reassured. "It was a logical train of thought. So, are there any new responsibilities with this promotion?"

From there, Kieran joined, and conversation continued to safe and banal topics, including Chase's gripes about child services and adoption. As he sat, he downed a tequila shot and swallowed half his cocktail.

"Fuck me, the adoption process is endless. I feel like a TSA strip search would be less invasive," Chase growled into his glass.

"Still going through safety checks?" Graham asked.

"Yeah," Chase sighed. "Apparently we need a portable fire escape ladder because our house has two floors."

"That's a thing?" Nate asked, brows arched high.

"Apparently."

They empathized and commiserated with Chase and Patrick's struggle for a child when Emmett and Leo found their way over to their table.

Once they found seats, their table was full, and Gina came by for Leo's drink order. She also asked if they were ordering food this time. They all did, and Gina, as usual, took off with her perfunctory serving services.

"Thank you, guys, for having me," Leo said, a slight shyness to his tone. He hid most of it behind his cola and whiskey, but Graham was observant, and he made it his mission to put Illiana's cousin at ease.

He was the cousin of his fake girlfriend's best friend. Graham had to ensure all was well—as to avoid the dog-house, and just generally be a nice person; which he always strived to be.

"Of course," Graham said cheerfully. "And I mean, what better bonding time, than an upcoming wedding—am I right?"

"Speaking of!" Nate added, clearing his throat of beer. "Are we planning your bachelor party?"

"Yes, but—" Emmett said, holding up a halting finger. "No strip clubs, no dancers, and I kinda just want it to be low key. Just my guys, you know? Not a bunch of randoms."

"It's like you don't even know us," Nate said with mock offense, clasping a dramatic hand over his heart. "As if we would ever dare."

Emmett flicked a stray bottle cap at Nate who tossed it back. Emmett dodged it and Graham simply reached out a hand and caught it. He started fiddling with its sharp edges between his fingertips, forearms resting on the table.

"Do you want to do just one night or a weekend?" Graham asked.

Emmett shrugged. "Depends what it is. If we're bar hopping, probably just a night. But if we do something else, like camping, then a weekend would be ideal."

"I like the sound of camping," Kieran inserted. "I know a few free sites if we want to go that route."

"I think we should go with that," Emmett confirmed. "And onto another wedding adjacent topic—we need to pick out suits soon."

"Does Illiana have a color preference or anything so that we match the bridesmaids? What is their color anyway?" Nate asked.

"Sage green," Graham responded easily. "Jasmina told me the other day."

"Yeah, what Graham said," Emmett answered. "I think we were leaning towards lighter suits. Gray pants and jacket, white shirt, and brown suspenders and shoes."

"Tie?" Leo inquired.

To Graham, it seemed like Leo was compiling a mental list in his head. No, Graham realized, no a list, a picture. Leo was a photographer. He was setting the scene in his mind.

"Either gray or green."

Leo nodded. "I don't want to seem like I'm imposing, but I'd love to offer my photography services as a wedding present if you two were interested."

Appreciation shone in Emmett's amber-brown eyes. "Leo, that's so kind of you. But we were going to have you attend as a guest."

"I honestly appreciate that, but I want to thank you for taking care of my cousin when I couldn't—when I should have—and this is me starting to make reparations for that."

Emmett seemed to contemplate the offer. "Only if you're really okay with it and feel like you can still be part of the party for Illiana—and me."

Leo pursed his lips with a playful curl to the corners. "I think we'll have a deal."

They shook on it and both men grinned.

Then Leo turned to Graham.

"All right, Best Man, with that in mind, want to help me scope out some locations with the Maid of Honor? The two of you can help me navigate the town and do some trial portraits. I'd love to see how the light and shadows play on the height dynamic with the season." Leo glanced between Emmett and

Graham. "I think you're a few inches taller than Em, but Mina is a little taller than Ana, so it should work out all right."

Graham tried not to lunge at the opportunity. Another chance to spend time with Jasmina, especially publicly as a couple? He was hoping that these moments they faked, her feelings would shift and it would all be genuine, natural, *real*.

"Yeah, absolutely. Name the time and place and I'll clear my schedule," he said as casually as he could manage.

"It'll probably be in the spring, since the daylight will be better."

"I'll keep that in mind." Graham wanted Leo to feel more comfortable with the group, so he switched topics up. "Will your parents be attending the wedding?"

"Mine are invited, yeah. Illiana's aren't though," Leo told him.

"Yeah, she's still no contact with them. Though I imagine it's probably hard."

"It is. I'm trying to make up for it anyway I can. Her parents are real pieces of work, totally lied about so much. It did a lot of damage. My parents tried for years to have a relationship with my aunt and uncle, but now knowing the truth, they want nothing to do with them. Last I heard though, divorce was in talks."

"Does Illiana know?"

"I told her," Leo said, taking a drink. "She didn't have much of a reaction. Either she doesn't care, or she hides it well." He tipped his head towards Emmett. "I'm sure Em knows, though."

"Probably," Graham said, sipping his beer. "There's not really any secrets between them."

"Excuse me," a delicate voice asked from Graham's shoulder.

Graham turned in surprise to find the brunette from earlier standing behind him. She was wearing a small white tee shirt and jeans with several butterflies tattooed on her arm. It immediately reminded him of his sister, Sabrina, and her sleeve of flowers and butterflies.

"I noticed you earlier and thought you were pretty cute. And I was pretty nervous, especially when all your friends showed up, but I decided to throw caution to the wind. If you're not seeing anyone, maybe you'd like to get together sometime?"

Graham felt a softness at the girl's confidence but was firm in his resolve and answer. "I'm flattered, but I'm happily taken."

She shrugged with a smile. "It was worth a shot. Have a nice night."

And then she turned, taking the rejection gracefully, and returned to her seat. When he turned his attention back to the table, Nate held his gaze.

"Smart boy," Jasmina's cousin commended with his beer extended in salute.

"Fuck off," Graham said on a chuckle. "You know I'm loyal."

"I know, but that's my cousin you're with. I'm a little protective."

"Don't go all macho man on me now, babe," Graham teased.

Nate flipped him off and laughed.

Just then, Graham's phone went off with a text. He grinned when he saw the name.

Saw a s'more, thought of you.

Graham blinked at the text in confusion.

What? he answered back. *Why?*

The dots danced on the screen as his brows knit together.

The messaged arrived.

Graham cracker.

He couldn't contain the bark of a laugh that escaped him.

It was official.

He was in love with her.

CHAPTER FIFTEEN
Mina

Girl, I forgot to tell you. The bridesmaids and groomsmen will all be doing a dance with us after our first dance. You and your new boyfriend need to start practicing your slow dance skills. Keep it PG though hon.

Mina stared at the text from Ana.

Her phone felt like a lump of lead in her hand. Heavy and toxic. Dangerous.

Her and Graham had to slow dance in front of everyone to a—presumably—romantic song.

Mina flopped on her couch; the rust fabric soft beneath her cheek. She covered her face.

"Ana, honey. Why are you torturing me?" Mina whispered into her empty apartment.

In an unusual flair of dramatics, she rolled off the couch onto her wavy, checkered rug and wallowed in self-pity, facedown on the floor.

You dumb, bitch, she chastised herself. *You could just come clean now. Sure, it would be awkward, but this whole thing is fucking awkward.*

But she knew she couldn't.

What she was doing was wrong, she knew—and immature—but it helped save face and stress during a time of extreme stress. Mina knew her best friend well, and even though Ana was handling it well, she was under an immense amount of pressure planning a wedding that was rapidly approaching. She didn't need the implosion of Mina's lies adding to it. Not to mention, the overthinking that would accompany it and distract her from what really mattered at this time.

No, as much as the guilt was eating at her, she knew the right course of action was to continue on the predetermined course of action.

Enacting the fake dating contract in full.

Groaning, Mina took out her phone and skimmed the rules again.

It was Saturday, which meant it was a sleepover at Graham's night, and because of that—for reasons unknown that she would not analyze—she'd had an everything shower and done extra treatments to her hair so that it was extra shiny and springy.

Graham's name flashed on her screen.

Ready for our sleepover, baby?

Mina battled the wave of excitement and irritation that rose up within her.

It was fake.

Fake. Fake. Fake.

She didn't know which one got a rise out of her more, Jasmina or baby.

She knew she was delusional if she thought it meant more than antagonism. It was not flirting. It couldn't be.

Still on the floor, she threw her legs onto the couch and texted back.

You're not scared I'll suffocate you with a pillow?

I couldn't think of a better way to go.

Seriously? Suffocation? I've heard that's painful.

I've heard there's worse ways. Plus, that new silk pillow is very soft. And breathable.

You're being morbid.

You started it, he retorted.

And I'm ending it.

Fine, fine. No, murder via pillows. Deal?

Deal, she accepted.

Great. I don't know about the kitchen knives, though.

You have villainous ideas of me.

Ah, but what better way to romance thy enemy?

"Did you hear about the dance?" Mina asked Graham the second she walked into his stupidly gorgeous Victorian house, dropping her overnight bag in the foyer. She was dressed in gray leggings and a pink off the shoulder sweater. Around her neck was a golden heart necklace.

"I heard," Graham responded, stooping to pick up her discarded luggage. "We've also been nominated to scout locations with Leo for photos and act as models."

"For Emmett and Ana?"

"For Emmett and Illiana," he answered in an echo.

"Oh, the joys of being heads of the bridal and groom's party."

"I second that," Graham said, leading her to the living room.

Big glass windows spanned floor to ceiling on the entire western wall, letting in all the afternoon sunlight. On the northern wall were bookcases painted in a dark, moody, navy blue housing a variety of books, but more knickknacks.

Mina briefly pictured her fantasy book collection on those shelves, rather than the sad, sagging one she'd purchased from JYSK in desperation. She could imagine curling up in a chair—that north-western corner was the perfect space for a papasan chair—reading by the fading sunlight, bundled up in blankets with a chai latte nearby.

It would be so easy.

As natural as breathing to fall into patterns like that with Graham.

But of course, it was *Graham*.

The man that challenged her, antagonized her, ruthlessly taunted and teased her. The man that drove her utterly fucking wild. The man she couldn't stop thinking about and it boiled her blood until she didn't know if she wanted to fight him or fuck him.

Oh.

That thought jarred her so sharply she flinched.

And of course, Graham noticed. More perceptive than any one person had any right to be.

"Are you okay?"

"I'm fine," she squeaked. "Just got a shiver down my spine."

"Ah, someone walked over your grave."

Mina cocked a brow. "Death talk, again?"

"What can I say? You bring out sides in me, never before seen."

Mina's heart gave an uneven thump.

"Sadist," she tossed at him.

"It's the best way to get you in the mood, Jasmina."

"For what?" she asked, eyes narrowing, nose scrunching.

With a flourish, Graham tapped on his phone screen, pocketed said phone, and said, "For this." Just as Ed Sheeran's *Thinking Out Loud* came on over the wall speakers and he took her in his arms.

Graham's touch was perfect. Firm, yet undemanding. Soft, yet unyielding. He gracefully wrapped her in his embrace and spun them around the room as Ed Sheeran continued to croon and cry out about love.

Graham could dance, Mina realized distantly.

Her hands went to his shoulders as if on instinct and followed him through the song. Their socks glided across the hardwood floor, buttery sunlight bathing them in its warmth.

Graham spun her out from a hand and pulled her back in. She returned with a dip so deep her hair brushed the floor. A pure, and joyful laugh spilled out of her, and the grin that overcame her face became near permanent. Graham also had a matching smile.

The lyrics flowed through the room, words about falling in love by a voice filled with emotion. Graham expertly guided them through the rhythm; slowing and picking up when it warranted, tugging close and twirling out, swaying to the music. Hands on waists, and shoulders, and hands.

His scent of spice and timber suffused her, filling every cell of her being until she became utterly enthralled by it. Her mouth parted in surprise; his blue eyes locked onto her mouth.

And suddenly, after a breath, his lips were on hers.

She met his kiss with a rush of breath, her mouth pliant on his, molding to his desire. Her hands fisted in his shirt, his pressing into the small of her back. He was dipping down because of their significant height difference, but he was devouring her like a man starved.

Their tongues met, dancing, battling, fighting, fucking. Their tongues lashed each other just like their words, hard and soft, and sharp and tender. The kiss was unequivocally theirs. Quintessentially them. It filled her with bliss as his teeth scraped her lip, earning him a slight whimper from her.

Graham's breath caught at the sound. His fingertips tightened.

And suddenly, her back was against the window. Golden light limning them as they kept kissing. And kissing. And kissing.

"*Jasmina*," he practically moaned.

Wetness bloomed between her thighs, an ache developing there that alarmed her. She'd never had such a visceral reaction to Graham.

But his kiss…

His touch…

His smell…

Fuck, he knew what he was doing. And that unintentionally celibate part of her wanted him to ruin her.

For him to take her here, right now. Right against these pretty floor to ceiling windows.

Mina's hands went to the hem of Graham's shirt, exploring beneath, finding the ridges of his abdomen.

Holy shit, Graham Starling most certainly had a six-pack.

Graham shivered beneath her touch, and his hand went to her jaw, tipping her up for deeper entry, his other hand roamed to her hip, cupping the swell there, fingertips dancing over the round globe of her ass.

Fuck, how she wanted him to squeeze it.

Just then, the screech of the oven timer broke them apart.

They came apart with a gasp, the music having disappeared, the only sounds their labored breathing. Mina's hand went to her lips, feeling how swollen they were, noticing how bee-stung Graham's looked. There was a rich flush to his face, a glitter in his eyes that sent butterflies dancing through her stomach in a routine that would've rivaled Cirque du Soleil.

"Sorry, I was baking," Graham announced into the post kiss—bliss?

Gloom?

Haze?

Despair?

"You were…baking?" she said to the empty room, completely befuddled. So much so that she hadn't noticed Graham scurrying out of the room.

As if in a fog, Mina made her way to the kitchen and found Graham pulling a banana bread out of the oven with checkered mitts. The steam was coiling from the pan and Mina could smell the chocolate chips sprinkled in.

Was this real life?

Mina blinked as Graham set the bread on a kitchen towel lined trivet and shucked off the mitts before turning off the oven. She watched all of this with a detached sort of assessment.

"You bake," she said baldly.

"I bake," he confirmed with the same sort of non-clarity as her.

That kiss was different.

It had altered them both. Both were tilted off their axis. Both were lost. Floating in confusion.

The silence in the room was ringing.

"My bananas were going bad."

"And you didn't put them in the freezer with promises to make banana bread soon and then immediately forget them for eternity like a normal person?" she somehow managed.

It was if she were operating on autopilot, running over the routines she knew were familiar to her and Graham.

"If I didn't do it right away that's exactly what would have happened."

Words failed her.

"I, um…" she cleared her throat. "Sorry, I'm just going to go to the bathroom."

Without waiting for a reply, she darted away and locked herself in the half-bath down the hall. Splashing cold water on her face, Mina tried to restart her brain—and body's systems—into something somewhat functioning into what it was before. Distantly and eternally grateful she'd gone for a clean-faced look earlier, she knew she wasn't washing off too much time and effort in her makeup.

What the hell had she done?

She'd kissed Graham outside of their contractual stipulations.

Or had he kissed her?

She couldn't remember.

What she could remember was that she'd wanted it and that didn't make any sense.

They hated each other. Didn't they?

She'd been so caught up in the moment, that had to be the reason. There was no other logical explanation.

Who else wouldn't be charmed when dancing with someone—objectively handsome—while Ed Sheeran crooned about love?

But *hypothetically*, if her feelings were shifting towards him, that didn't mean that his toward her had changed.

You could just talk to him about it, a logical part of her brain offered.

She could. *Technically*. But it would ruin all their plans for fake dating before the wedding, which was the whole reason they were in this mess. She could, however, tell him *after* the contract was over. If she destroyed whatever was between them, well big deal, the friend group had already survived this far with them disliking each other—what was a little more?

The more she thought about it, the more she settled on it. She couldn't risk it now, but she could later. Sure, it could be embarrassing and the most mortifying moment of her life, but she was not going to chicken out about it, no matter if it worked out or not.

It was decided.

She stayed in there a long time. She wasn't sure how long, but when she'd finally composed herself and returned to the kitchen, the banana bread had cooled enough to cut, and Graham had plated her a slice with a pad of butter ready to go.

"You want to talk about…that?" Graham asked as she sat down and spread the warm butter on her slice of loaf.

She took a dainty bite. It was warm and moist and perfect. The perfect balance of banana and chocolate-chips with the salted butter adding that extra rounded flavor.

Mina swallowed then looked up at Graham.

"Mm, no. But I do think after that, we're going to be quite convincing."

CHAPTER SIXTEEN
Graham

"When the fuck were you going to tell me that you had a girlfriend?"

Sabrina's furious face took up the screen of Graham's phone as she berated him over FaceTime. Her green eyes were blazing beneath the wild glitter of her eyeshadow.

Graham rubbed the heel of his hand against his temple. "I hadn't gotten around to it."

"*You hadn't gotten around to it?*" she screeched, the microphone cutting out. "You've been with her since last month! Valentines Day! It's almost Saint Patrick's!"

"I feel like Willow or Piper would have been more chill about this."

"Piper thinks she did something wrong and you're icing her out, so now she's upset. And you know how she is—she's non-confrontational—which is why I'm here now, defending my big sister and ripping you a new one."

"She's three minutes older than you."

"Graham!" she hissed, showing off her milky teeth that he knew bit. Sabrina was ruthless as a toddler. "Why are you keeping secrets from us? Are you ashamed? Did you think we wouldn't approve, or some bullshit like that?"

"No! Never that!" Graham sighed. "It's complicated."

"Well, uncomplicate it," she demanded, stabbing a pencil through the messy pile of pastel pink hair on her head. "Because I had to find out you're with Mina Coulter from Kelsey Kowalski!"

"How does Kelsey know?"

He remembered her vaguely. She'd been at some of the twin's birthday parties in elementary school before she fell in with a preppy clique and thought she was too cool for people who didn't have individual identities—as if twins were completely synonymous. It was a gross underestimation of Piper and Sabrina's persons.

"I don't know! She heard it from someone who told someone. You know how small towns are! I'm shocked people didn't find out about Emmett and Illiana before they announced they were a couple last year. I mean, for fuck's sakes, they went on dates and walks, and—no. This is not about them; this is about you being a shitty brother."

"I resent that."

"Well, what the fuck, Graham?" she asked, voice softening, trying a different tactic. "What's going on? We don't keep secrets."

Graham shuttered his eyes.

She was right. They didn't keep secrets—except one. None of them—except him.

He'd never told anyone about his true feelings about Jasmina. Everyone just assumed they'd never gotten along and never read into it more—or at least, he thought they didn't.

The four of them were surprisingly close, even despite his six-year age gap between the twins. They were usually adept at sussing out each other's bullshit, and with that, imagined that they weren't withholding anything.

That's one of the only reason's he'd survived the Starling Perception—something the four of them all possessed; the ability to be keenly observant.

"I've always liked her," he confessed.

Sabrina's head cocked to the side. "Even when you two fought all the time?"

"Even then."

"So, what's the problem?"

"It's not..." he trailed off.

"It's not what?"

"Never mind."

Sabrina growled. "Okay, fine. Is your girlfriend sleeping over tonight?"

"No."

She'd slept over last night. After their impromptu kiss. Where he'd virtually slammed her against his glass windows and thought about fucking her raw right there. It had killed him to wash the window later and erase their fingerprints.

"Good, we're coming over tonight. Piper and Willow are free as well so we're bombarding you. Do you have any more banana bread?"

"Why? And yes." He didn't question why she knew about his baking yesterday; he'd posted it on his story and she'd immediately harassed him for some via DMs.

"Because we need to figure out what's going on and I want banana bread. And you need to reassure Piper that you don't hate her.'

"I don't hate her!"

"Good, tell her that. We'll be there at seven. *Byeee*."

And without ceremony she'd ended the FaceTime call like that.

Graham groaned and tossed his phone across the kitchen island, lying flat on the cold marble, and pressing his cheek against its surface.

He hadn't been able to stop thinking about the kiss with Jasmina yesterday. Hadn't stopped thinking about the way she felt. The way she smelled. The way she tasted. He'd wanted to drop to his knees and taste her where she'd be the wettest. He'd wanted it all.

He could've been imagining it, but he thought something might've shifted within her. She'd been just as off balance as him—just as affected. But she'd given no indication later.

She'd sat at the island after the kiss, eating the fresh banana bread, and told him—in not so many words—that she didn't want to talk about the kiss. Following that, they'd continued their evening as normal—cooking dinner, eating dinner, studying their notebooks, planning next dates and sleepovers, watching a movie—and acted as if nothing happened. When the night drew to a close and he was struggling to keep his eyes open, they'd decided to retire to bed and he'd be lying if he said he hadn't been holding his breath, hoping that she might choose to sleep in his bed again. But of course, she didn't. She said a simple goodnight and disappeared into the guest room.

He'd lain there, disappointed and feeling foolish.

This morning, Jasmina had left early, claiming she was going for a run to enjoy the rare day of sunshine. From her later social media post of the ocean and a sticker of running shoes, he'd accepted that she truly had gone for a run, but didn't believe it was for the sun.

It was to get space away from him.

So, with Sunday dread pulling him down, he'd puttered around his house, tidying up and making a grocery list. It's what he'd been doing when Sabrina had so rudely interrupted with her FaceTime.

Graham finished his list, placed an online grocery order, and went about his day. When his sisters arrived that evening a half hour late, he was in the middle of making two sheets of nachos—one vegetarian for Willow, the other topped with ground beef for the rest of them.

They were a whirlwind of sound and energy, the three of them so very different, and so dearly loved.

"I brought red wine!" Sabrina announced, flouncing into the kitchen, holding aloft cheap, boxed wine.

"Wine and nachos aren't the best combination," Willow commented as she shrugged off her quilted coat.

Willow was tall, just like their dad, with a perpetual tan, and long, wavy ash blonde hair that she kept in a feathered style around her oval face. Curtain bangs framed her jaw in a wispy way, her makeup applied to appear natural and dewy. Her eyes, like all the Starling girls, were green, but hers were soft with a dream-like quality, whereas Sabrina's were unyielding gems, and Piper's were as changing as the sea.

"You're totally right," Sabrina said, depositing the wine on the counter. "Graham, where's your tequila? We're having margaritas."

"It's Sunday," Piper inserted, carefully folding her camel coat on the back of a chair. Beneath, she was wearing a dark green, long sleeved, lounge set with hard soled slippers.

Unlike Willow, who kept her natural hair color, Piper dyed hers a deep, chocolate brown in a smooth, straight fall down her back. She was the curviest of all his sisters with big doe eyes, and a gentle demeanor that translated to everything she did—except when she was in the presence of her siblings.

Of all the Starling girls, she was the shortest at 5'5", somehow an inch shorter than her identical twin.

The twins had identical facial structures, but that's where the similarities ended. They both dyed their hair and wore makeup in opposing styles, their fashions diverged from office chic to alternative, meeting only in the middle for casual wear. Piper kept her nails in a professional French tip, whereas Sabrina went for patterns and bold colors.

In a nutshell, they were—to Kelsey Kowalski's ignorance—completely different.

"And tomorrow is Monday. We'll be fine as long as we follow my foolproof anti-hangover routine." Her eyes darted to Graham. "And maybe the booze will loosen up some tongues and we'll find out why someone's been a little secretive bitch."

Graham was fiercely protective about his three younger sisters, and while Willow and Piper called him for help more often, Sabrina didn't need him. She fought the battles he couldn't. She leveled the playing field when there was girl drama in school. She was the spitfire of their family and everyone knew she couldn't be contained. It was why now; it was so hard to tell her about Jasmina. If he was even going to.

"Are we watching movies or playing games?" Piper asked, plucking a bit of shredded cheese off the grater plate.

"I'm down for whatever," Graham responded.

"Where are your margarita glasses?" Sabrina asked, rummaging through his cupboards.

"What makes you think I own margarita glasses?"

"Ooh, can we watch a rom-com?" Willow asked, slicing limes—when had she gone to the fridge?

"Every person should own margarita glasses," Sabrina continued, slamming cupboards.

"I have wine glasses. And sure, we can watch a rom-com," Graham said, attention pulled in all directions.

Did he put the trays in the oven? He checked—yes.

"I'll pick!" Piper exclaimed, running to the living room, her dark hair swinging behind her.

"That'll do." Sabrina shrugged and grabbed four wine glasses.

"You're going to pick something from the 90s!" Willow argued, following Piper.

"The 90s are great!" Sabrina shouted, filling his blender with ice.

"Not when they're rampant with blatant sexism!" Willow called back.

"We'll find one as sexism free as possible," Piper reassured.

"I don't think that exists."

"We'll see!" Piper sing-songed.

Graham heard drawers opening behind him, Sabrina searching and metal clinking.

"What are you looking for?" he queried.

"A corkscrew."

"What do you need a corkscrew for?" he asked, brows knitted together just as she opened the junk drawer and panic launched through him. "Brina, no!"

But it was too late.

There, in his baby sister's hand, was a green and white checkered notepad with his and Jasmina's fake dating contract boldly detailed.

It was all over now. The jig was up. Sabrina would find out the truth and tell the world. It would be humiliation and he would have failed Jasmina.

No. No, he couldn't let her down. Not when she'd gone to all these lengths for their friends. Not when she'd done one of the hardest things in asking him for help.

Sabrina was quick—her reading skills and her reflexes— and was out of reach just as Graham lunged toward her.

His heart dropped.

"What is this?" she hissed under her breath. Her green eyes were like Maleficent's flame, glittering like jewels, the fury just barely contained.

"What does it look like, Brina?" he asked, defeated. There was no sense in trying to deny it. He was caught.

"It looks like you're fake dating a girl you have real feelings for." Both her voice and tone were even.

Graham sighed as he sat at the island, completely deflated. He shuttered his eyes as he admitted, "I am."

"Why don't you tell her?" Sabrina asked, uncharacteristically soft.

He chuckled mirthlessly. "Aside from the fact she hates me?" His heart panged. "It would ruin everything with the wedding."

Her lips screwed up in thought. "What about after the wedding?"

"After the wedding I'll tell her."

"Good."

"Why aren't you telling Piper and Willow right now?" he asked, hearing their two sisters arguing in the living room. "Or anyone and everyone?"

"I'm not a complete asshole. Clearly this is a sensitive subject for you. I'll give you the time to tell them yourself."

"I'll come clean eventually, but not yet."

Sabrina held his gaze, gemstone eyes hard. "Why did it take this to even decide?"

"I thought maybe this could be my opportunity to show her what it could be like. Before, I had no idea where to start. She always had her walls up, always ready to antagonize. We challenged each other every step of the way."

"And now?"

"Now...I don't know if it's wishful thinking, but I feel like something's shifted."

"Well, if it's any consolation," she said, pushing the notepad at his chest. "I think you'll win her over. But I also think you need a better hiding spot."

He chuckled. "Thanks, Brina."

"Don't mention it," she said as the oven timer went off. "I'll take care of this. You go hide your dirty little secret."

"You're the best."

"That's why I'm your favorite sister."

"I will neither confirm, nor deny that."

"I know the truth. It's fine."

Graham left Sabrina to take the nachos out and as he left down the hall to his office, he heard the blender going—he definitely needed that margarita now.

As he was reading over the contract, he saw rule number nine.

If anyone finds out, tell the other party immediately.

Graham sighed and pulled out his phone. He found the text thread labeled *Jasmina* with a red heart.

Sabrina knows. She found the contract, he texted.

The phone immediately vibrated in his hand.

What is she going to do?

His fingers flew over the screen. *She promises she won't say anything to anyone.*

Good, Jasmina responded. *Maybe lock that contract up now.*

In progress, he said, then stuck his phone back in his pocket.

Tucking the notepad into his desk drawer, he shut the room up behind him just in time for Piper and Willow to return from their movie choice debate, seemingly satisfied with the decision.

"What's the verdict?" he asked as he accepted a margarita in a wine glass from Sabrina.

"We're watching two," Piper said cheerily, sipping her own margarita. "*Chasing Liberty* and *Anyone But You.*"

"No 90s?"

Graham sipped his slush, it was good—alarmingly good; the kind of good that made you think five of these was a good decision.

"I made a compromise," Willow responded proudly, flipping her long ash blonde hair over her shoulder.

The coffee table was laden with nachos, guacamole, salsa, sour cream, and margaritas. And of course, banana bread. Beside the pile of napkins was a bowl of assorted candies—Skittles, gummy worms, fuzzy peaches, and peanut butter cups. Graham popped a fuzzy peach in his mouth, thinking of Jasmina.

He felt bad that Sabrina had discovered their secret, but he was half grateful that he wasn't alone in it anymore. That he did have someone he could confide in. And someone, who somehow didn't condemn his plan, had validated his actions.

They put the first movie on and they all settled on his couch. Piper and Sabrina were curled under a mint blanket, and Willow in the corner, a knitted throw over her lap.

By the second movie they were all asleep on his couch. Sabrina was curled up against Piper and snoring before the first one ended. Willow delicately nodded off halfway through the second film, while Piper and Graham were last to lose the battle with slumber. When Graham awoke to the credits rolling, he simply turned off the TV, got more comfortable, and fell back asleep to the sounds of his sisters' snores.

CHAPTER SEVENTEEN

"So, you really didn't do anything for Saint Patrick's Day?"

Mina shook her head as she sipped her chai latte from a bubble gum pink mug. "I'm too old for that."

Ana narrowed her brows—which were a few shades darker than her naturally blonde hair; hair she did get highlights in—and her blue eyes became watchful. "And who is the one who just turned twenty-eight?"

Mina cringed behind her mug. "My bad. I will say though, you are aging gracefully," Mina paused teasingly. "For an ancient crone."

Ana gasped in mock offense. "You heinous bitch."

"I think your eyesight is going with your age, sweetie. I am an ethereal forest nymph."

"You've been reading too many fantasy books," Ana chastised, sipping her green tea.

"Now you've gone too far. You speak such sacrilege?"

"I know," Ana submitted, "It was too far. It hurt me, too."

The two of them fell into a fit of giggles, forgoing their fake argument as chatter continued around them, the scent of sugar thick in the air.

They were sitting in Cupid Café & Bakery, the day after Saint Patrick's, taking in the most unique, locally owned establishment. It was all creamy whites, rose hues, and dreamy peaches, decorated in celestial clouds, vintage renderings of cherubs, and golden bows and arrows. Swooping stylized calligraphy that spelled out the name and items were on a chalkboard, with a serif type in juxtaposition describing ingredients and details. Seating consisted of bistro tables in white with chairs cushioned with patterns of cherubs. The bay window held pillows in a ray of sunrise—tepid blue, soft pink, baby orange—with a thick white blanket that emulated a cloud. On the far wall, where a mural of the heavens was painted, hung a pair of angel—or rather, cupid—wings, all snow white and golden tipped. In the center was an anatomical heart, struck with a golden arrow. There was no gore to the image, just a tiny trickle of gilded blood. It was absolutely stunning, the whole aesthetic of the café stuck to a theme so simultaneously dreamy and refined. It was a feat to be acknowledged.

"Which one do you like more?" Ana asked.

Mina's attention returned to her best friend, then immediately flittered to their table. In front of them were two cupcakes; samples they were trying for Ana's upcoming wedding. Cupid Café & Bakery was catering the desserts and wedding cake. They were here to select six flavors for cupcakes, while Emmett and Illiana had a second appointment for the wedding cake itself. The tiny, handwritten tags in front of each sample spelled out Cherry Chocolate and Chocolate Cookie.

"Hmm," Mina considered. "The chocolate cherry was good, but I do find cherry flavors are often associated with cough syrup. Chocolate cookie though, sounds like homemade goodness."

Ana's full, pink lips curved up in a smile. "I feel the same. Cherry out, cookie in." She frowned. "Why did that sound dirty?"

"Because you have a filthy mind. It's all that porn you read."

"Shut up," Ana laughed. "You introduced me to it."

"Guilty as charged," Mina accepted, putting her hands up. "You're welcome."

Just then, the girl from behind the counter, Olivia, came and dropped off the next two flavors; Lemon Lavender and Red Velvet.

"Do you want boxes for the leftovers?" Olivia asked, her voice sweet and honeyed, with a slight click that indicated a tongue piercing.

"Yes, please!" Ana beamed. "These are all so good, I can't wait to show my fiancé—he's going to love them."

"I'll make sure I bring some out," Olivia said.

Olivia left them with the new flavors and returned behind the counter, wiping up invisible crumbs and coffee spills. Her dyed black hair fell around her shoulders as she scrubbed a particularly sticky spot and her short, emerald nails clicked against the glass case housing the freshly baked treats.

As Mina and Ana dug into the new flavors, a surprising individual appeared from the doorway. Mina tilted her head, mouth full of red velvet, fork poised in the air as Jace crossed the café and sauntered up to the counter.

Mina blinked in confusion.

Jace was tall with casually messy light blond hair and dressed in a basic hoodie and jeans. His shoes were simple sneakers and seemingly clean. He appeared…boyish. Like the boy next door and not the douche canoe she'd always known him to be.

The Jace she knew would've never been caught dead in an establishment like this. He would've said it's too feminine, or something worse. This was the guy who called Ana too skinny last year, the same that Graham, Nate, and Emmett had complained to her about more than once.

The Jace she knew wouldn't be smiling at Olivia the way he was right now.

"Are you seeing this?" Mina whispered.

Ana nodded silently, slowly chewing lavender lemon cupcake.

"Hey, Olivia," Jace started warmly.

Mina briefly considered the idea she'd choked to death on a cupcake and her spirit had blocked out the memory and now she was viscerally hallucinating from oxygen deprivation, because *who* was *that?*

"Oh, hey, J!" Olivia greeted enthusiastically. "What's up? You coming in for your usual?"

Jace scrubbed a hand over the back of his neck in nervousness. "Actually, not specifically." He cleared his throat. "I've been trying to work up my nerve for a while, but I'm finally going for it. I think you're really cute and funny, and I was wondering if you'd like to go out sometime?"

Olivia visibly deflated.

Uh oh.

Mina cringed, fork in hand.

The only thing worse than a rejection, was a public rejection.

"I'm so sorry, J. I think you're great and all, but I'm like…super gay."

Mina watched Jace's back straighten as he physically processed this information. She got ready to stand and was willing to fight him if he went all homophobic toxic masculinity incel behavior on her.

"Oh," he said, surprise in his voice. "Well, I still think you're cool. Want to hang out sometime? You mentioned paint and sip before—want to do that sometime?"

Mina and Ana were utterly silent. Eyes blinking, jaws slack.

"Um…did we slip into a parallel universe, or something?" Ana finally managed to whisper.

"We must have. Or we're having a joint delusion."

"Either is more likely than what we're witnessing right now."

"Agreed."

"Is Jace growing up?"

"I think so."

They watched as Jace and Olivia kept chatting, a genuine smile gleaming on Olivia's face as she became more and more animated with each passing second.

There was no way this was real.

"Oh my god, I have to tell Graham about this."

Mina hadn't even processed what those words really meant until she had her phone out and was typing of a message detailing the past several minutes. She was startled when the realization struck her.

She had new information—gossip, if you will—and the first person—the only person—she wanted to share it with was Graham. Was that…foreboding? Did that spell more of an attachment than they agreed on? More than she'd prepared for? But, then again, it did fall under the umbrella of terms in the contract that dictated them messaging throughout the day to keep up appearances. So, what if it wasn't just surface level?

Graham responded back with similar surprise and informed her about Jace's run in with some "friends" at Blue's recently. It seemed it was official—Jace had gotten a wake-up call. She wondered what Chase thought of his character development, or if he had even noticed with the stress of the adoption process and his job.

A short time later, Jace left with a pink paper cup in hand and a small smile on his face. It didn't seem as if he'd noticed them. As soon as the bell on the door chimed his exit, Olivia retrieved the next flavors of cakes; Strawberries and Cream and Cinnamon Chai—both were instant yesses. The following two didn't quite hit the mark and then the last two were carried out, not by Olivia, but someone new from the back.

"Oh," Ana gasped with delight. "The owner is coming over."

The owner was an early twenties,—well, the simple word to describe it was: tattooed baddie. Mina was straight, but this girl could make someone reconsider. Her long dyed gray hair was tied up in a ponytail with a pink scrunchie that matched her pink apron. Her eyes were a light hazel and above her full glossy lips were a Medusa piercing and septum piercing. Sleeves of tattoos wound up her arms and down her legs, revealed in her steel blue corduroy dress, and disappearing into her Doc Martens. She was thick in the hips and snatched in the waist, her entire physique the sort you'd see only on social media.

How did she own a bakery and look like *that*? All the power to her, Mina applauded her.

"Hi!" the owner said with a grin, revealing straight white teeth and a little diamond imbedded in her right eye tooth. "How's the tasting going?" She had a husky voice, all low and sensual.

"Amazing!" Ana cooed. "These are all so delicious."

"Thank you," she preened. "They're all my own creations."

"Seriously, Harlowe, you are making magic with these."

"Oh, stop." Harlowe glowed with pride. "You haven't even tried the last ones yet. There's only a slight difference, but it can be the divisive. We have Vanilla Bean and French Vanilla."

Harlowe deposited the tray of cupcakes before them and pulled up a chair, straddling it backwards. She rested her chin on her folded hands topping the chair back.

"Tell me what you think, I won't be offended. Unless you choose wrong." Harlowe winked.

"How do we know which one is which?" Mina asked, these cupcakes lacking the handwritten tags.

"You don't. You taste and choose with your heart, sweet one."

Mina eyed her warily, wondering if she was serious or playful. Her beaming grin indicated the latter.

Selecting the cupcake on the right with ivory frosting and tiny dark specks, Mina took a big bite and let the sugary sweetness melt on her tongue. It was divine, the best vanilla cupcake she'd ever had. After swallowing, she picked up the other and noted the more yellow-toned frosting free of dark specks. When she sank her teeth into this one, flavor exploded in her mouth, filling it with the decadent cream and moist cake.

"*Oh my god*," Mina moaned, mouth full of cupcake. "This is divine."

Harlowe smirked. "I know. I'm a cupcake wizard."

"*Harlowe*," Ana groaned. "This is so good."

"Careful there, Ana, keep that up and Emmett is gonna get jealous," Mina teased, cackling and stuffing her face.

"Hush, Emmett is confident in our relationship, and has nothing to worry about. Not even supremely talented bakery owners that can make vanilla taste like heaven."

"And that's why I never complain about vanilla," Harlowe giggled. Mina wondered if she knew how clear that innuendo was.

Ultimately, they decided on the French Vanilla over the Vanilla Bean—Harlowe remained cryptic over which one was the right choice. Among the French Vanilla, Ana also chose Lemon Lavender, Strawberries and Cream, Cinnamon Chai, Chocolate Cookie, and Red Velvet. Olivia packed up their remaining cupcakes—plus a few additional samples at Harlowe's behest—and sent them out the door with encouragement to return soon.

"Holy fuck," Mina said, snagging another cinnamon chai cupcake from the box. "I see why you chose Cupid."

"I know, right?" Ana beamed. "The shop is new but I decided to take a chance on her and I have zero regrets."

"I will be going there weekly now."

"I was thinking the same thing."

Mina was so proud of her best friend. It was an unspoken thing, but Illiana had overcome a restrictive eating disorder, courtesy of her ballet upbringing. She'd measured every calorie, mentally catalogued every morsel, and starved herself if she perceived herself to have over eaten. Even a year ago, the idea of cupcake tasting would've sent her best friend into a spiral. Today, Illiana clearly had shed some of those qualms and even gained a slightly fuller figure. She was still slender to the extreme, but not so worryingly so.

Since moving to Rose Point, they'd both come such a long way.

"So," Ana started, sipping her iced matcha she'd ordered for the road. "We have the venue, photographer, catering, DJ, tables and chairs rented, the arch custom built, officiant, bouquets, hair, makeup, nails, decorations, and invitations all secured." Ana had been listing the items off but ran out of fingers. "Now, we just need to finalize the wedding cake and bachelorette party planning."

"You leave the party to me," Mina announced, stopping her. "That is my responsibility as Maid of Honor. You have enough on your plate."

Illiana visibly softened—her graceful shoulders dropped, her full mouth curved up, her eyes brightened—and she wrapped her arm around Mina's waist.

"What would I do without you?" Ana asked, nuzzling Mina's neck as they walked.

"You're capable of anything, but I'd be sad to see you go."

"Me too."

They walked together a little while longer, the cool March air touched with the scent of sun and early blooms, the damp asphalt sticking dirt and leaves to their shoes. They chatted until they came upon Illiana's little ballet studio, all glass windows and brick with pastel pink accents and an adorable window box that would soon be filled with flowers.

Since she'd moved to Rose Point and had to pivot her career, teaching dance, particularly to little ones, had given Ana a new fulfilment in ballet. She'd never be a principal dancer again—never reach prima ballerina status—but Mina thought Illiana had healed from that blow.

"I have a class in a half hour, so I need to set up. I'll talk to you later." Illiana gave her a tight hug. "Love you."

Mina returned the hug, breathing in her best friend's strawberry scent. "Love you, too."

They broke apart and Illiana slipped inside the building while Mina pulled out her phone and texted the bachelorette party group chat that she'd created a few weeks ago.

If you're free, come to my place tonight for wine and bachelorette party planning! Mina texted. *Address is 22, Unit 3, Westbrook Way.*

Immediately her phone lit up with confirmations from each of the bridesmaids and Mina made her way home to prepare.

It was eight o'clock and four bottles of wine had been drunk between Mina, Madeline, and Delilah. Mina's oversight had been not realizing—or not remembering—that Sloane didn't drink.

They'd mapped out the plans, the dates, and activities for the party, and now the laptop that they'd used to book, search, and veto was now sitting stationary, playing a Spotify hits list. It was fortuitous they'd confirmed everything via bookings, email, and writing, before truly getting into the wine, because if Mina had to do it now, she would be virtually useless.

She knew better, one bottle was usually her limit, but she was having so much fun with the girls and both Madeline and Delilah had higher tolerances than her. And so, in her effort to keep up, she'd crossed her line.

Giggling as she sipped the Pinot Grigio, Mina nudged Madeline with her hip.

"I think I like Graham," she whispered in Mads's ear.

Madeline laughed, eyes glittery with drink. "I sure hope so, he's your boyfriend."

"No, I really—" she hiccupped. "Ah, fuck. I'm a mess."

"No, you're not, Sweet Love," Delilah reassured, her wine glass poised delicately between her fingers, her eyes lacking the drunken sheen she knew hers had. "You're just having fun. It's okay to let loose."

"I can't remember the last time I drank like this."

"Was it when you got too drunk of Smirnoff—?"

"Why does everyone bring up the Smirnoff Ice situation?" Mina despaired.

"Because it's *romantic*," Sloane teased, drawing out the word. "Your boyfriend, before he was your boyfriend, took care of you like a boyfriend would? That's very memorable."

Mina blew a raspberry. "It was not one of my finest moments."

"We've all had them," Delilah reassured.

"Yeah," Madeline agreed, slurping the dregs of her glass. "Like that one time I got way too drunk at my exes staff party, fell out of the cab, then got stuck in my dress before puking on said dress, only to slip in the shower and smash my tailbone on the faucet?" Mads sipped her empty glass. "Now *that* is glamorous behavior."

"How bad was the bruise?" Mina inquired.

"The size of a baseball."

There was a chorus of hisses in sympathetic pain.

"I think my worst was when I fell in a snowbank outside of Gloss and showed my entire ass to a group of forty-year-old dudes, then screamed at them for being perverts," Delilah revealed demurely. "I wish I could say that only happened once, but I'd be lying."

"I don't drink," Sloane started, sipping her sparkling water. "But one time I was hanging out with this guy I really liked and his friends, and we were on a walk down this trail. I climbed onto a stump, but my dumbass didn't realize how slippery and rotten it was, and I ended up faceplanting into a mud puddle." Sloane's nose scrunched up as she remembered the moment. "They all laughed, but the guy I liked did try to hide it, and he did help me up."

"What happened with him?" Mina inquired.

"We probably would've dated, but he moved to Alberta. Haven't seen him since. I hope he's doing well."

"A guy I was seeing moved to Alberta once," Mads began, emptying the rest of a bottle into her glass. "Turns out I was the side chick and he had a whole ass family there. I was furious, and of course told his wife. He called me a conniving, jealous bitch for that. I feel bad that I imploded her life, but she had a right to know. Him? He could fall off the face of the Earth and I wouldn't give two shits."

Mina cleared her throat, steadying herself. "My most recent ex dumped me over the phone by telling me that he'd been seeing someone else and he was done with me. He had zero remorse and just said it like he was reading off a dictionary definition. It was so…" she searched for the word. "Clinical."

"Ugh," Sloane groaned. "Was that the doctor?"

"Yeah. David."

"They're the fucking worst for that. They think their hot shit and so many of them don't have empathy. Don't get me wrong, there are some wonderful ones, but the ones that have egos—have *egos*."

As a public health nurse, Sloane had more experience than most with doctors.

"Wait," Delilah interrupted, holding up a hand. "Wasn't he your ex from last summer?"

"He was. Why?"

"So, Graham's the first guy you've dated since him?"

"He is," Mina confirmed, swallowing her nervousness. She dumped some extra wine into her glass. "Why? Is that bad?"

"No! Not at all. But I'm just wondering…is he the *first* since him?" she asked pointedly.

Color rose on Mina's cheeks. She felt the heat fill her and she was thankful she could blame in on the nitrates in the wine. Rather than trusting her voice, she nodded and drank deeply.

"Girl," Mads practically purred. "Give us the dirty details. How was he?"

Oh, fuck.

She had not thought their entire fake dating scheme through. She had not considered these questions. But she should have. She fucking should have. Her and Madeline—and her and Illiana for that matter—had candidly recounted their sex lives to each other, it wasn't a stretch for Mads to expect that now.

A wild and unwelcome thought struck her—they'd practiced kissing for the agreement, should they practice fucking? Just once?

That hot flush grew hotter, burning beneath her skin.

The idea of Graham's touch, of his fingers skimming over her skin, brushing over her breasts, pinching her nipples. The thought of him drifting those hands lower, swirling around her navel before finding her clit and playing her like a harp. The fantasy of him over her, driving in, giving her untold pleasure—

"He's the best I've ever had," she blurted.

Fuck. Me.

Why did she always say the wrong things about Graham while she was drinking? It was only him, and it was only because of wine. Those two should never mix, they were a combination for disaster.

"Give us more than that," Delilah pressed.

Mina drank again. "He…um. Well, he's very dominant, but also is willing to hand over control."

She was just spouting nonsense now. Babbling and hoping something stuck. Praying they didn't dig deeper.

"I'm sensing you don't want to talk about this," Sloane interjected.

"I just—I…I'm sorry, I'm just really drunk and my head is swimming."

Sloane gave a reassuring smile and stood. "Totally understandable, girl. Mad, Del, finish your drinks, I'm taking you home."

Relief soared through Mina. All she wanted was to have a shower, take some Ibuprofen, and go to sleep. She knew the hangover tomorrow would be predominantly a headache and she wanted to make sure it didn't decide to station itself into a migraine—something she was horribly prone to.

"Good call," Madeline agreed, draining her wine in one long swallow, tilting her head back and letting her long fall of auburn hair cascade behind her.

Delilah finished her last sip then went over to her tiny, sage green kitchen and rinsed her glass before setting it aside. When she made her way to Mina, she gave her a quick hug.

"Thanks for having us, Sweet Love. And I apologize if I made you uncomfortable."

Mina sighed softly. "It's okay, don't worry. I just passed my limit, and now I'm too drunk."

"Do you need any help?" Delilah inquired; her blue eyes cautious.

"No, I'm good. Thank you, though. Have a goodnight and please let us know when you get home safe."

"Will do."

The rest of the ladies bid their goodbyes, and finally with Sloane ushering the drunk redheads out the door, Mina was left alone in her little apartment. She sank onto her couch and sighed, drunk and emotional.

What was she thinking with this whole contract idea? It was a mess. Her feelings were a mess. She was a mess. It was insane and they were going to get found out. Not to mention, Graham was going to catch on that she didn't actually hate him. Not anymore.

She was drunk now and was more readily able to admit it.

She didn't hate Graham Starling.

Not by a long shot.

It was vindicative to say.

But it was also so heavy.

Mina groaned and flopped onto the floor. As the spins set in, she took out her phone.

CHAPTER EIGHTEEN
Graham

The phone call was unexpected, but not unwelcome.

Graham excused himself from the table at Blue's and stepped outside into the cool March air, leaning against the brick façade of the building.

"Jasmina?" he asked, plugging his opposite ear from the traffic noise.

"You have no idea," she mumbled.

His anxiety spiked. "Are you okay?"

"I'm *fiiiine*," she drawled sloppily. "Well, not *totally*." She sighed dramatically. "I had to lie to my friends, and that didn't feel very good."

She was drunk, he realized. Very drunk. Instantly alert, he pushed for information.

"What did you lie about, baby?"

She let out a sound half like a purr, half like a groan. "Why do you call me that?"

"To sell it."

"I like it," she admitted in a small voice.

His heart flew out of his chest. "I'll keep doing it then. What did you lie about, baby?" he repeated.

"They asked how you were in bed."

There was silence.

A pedal biker passed him, the roar of a custom engine echoed in his ears, leaves from the trees housed in tiny iron fences whispered against each other in the breeze.

"And what did you say?"

"That you were the best I've ever had."

Graham Starling did not have an ego, but after a comment like that…well, he was a man. The infinitesimal ego he did possess swelled at that.

He had to remind himself that she was drunk and not in her right mind.

"Oh. Well, thank you."

"And it made me start thinking maybe we should…"

His blood hummed and he could feel his cock hardening in his pants, pressing against his zipper. Fantasies were soaring through his mind. Fantasies where he and Jasmina were unclothed and sober.

She's drunk. She's drunk.

"We should what?" he pressed anxiously.

She made a sound on the other end. A sound that sounded like a heave. "Oh. I don't feel very well."

"Where are you?" He switched topics immediately, forgetting about his erection, only worried about her.

Before he even had the conscious thought, he was striding back in the doors and past the bustle inside Blue's. He wove between the tables as Jasmina groggily answered.

"I'm at home."

"I'll be right over."

At the booth, where the guys were carrying on conversations unaware of his inner turmoil, Graham snatched up his keys and coat, and tossed two twenties on the table.

"Everything all right, babe?" Nate asked with concern.

"Jasmina drank too much," Graham told him succinctly.

Nate straightened immediately, worry lined every inch of his frame. His green-gold eyes, so like his cousin's, were flared, showing the whites all around.

Jasmina groaned at the other end of the line. "I forgot it was Tuesday. Tell Nate to chill the big brother act; he doesn't need to worry. I'm in safe hands. Very nice, very safe hands."

Graham didn't even allow himself the moment to soak in that glowing comment.

"She's okay, babe," he told Nate, shrugging on his canvas jacket. "I'll let you know if it's anything worse than an impending hangover. I've got her—all right?"

"All right," Nate acquiesced.

They fist bumped, Graham said his quick goodbyes to the boys and then he was out the door and climbing into his truck. It may have been overkill, but the tires squealed on the pavement as he raced to his girl.

He wanted—no, needed—to make sure she was safe.

He wasn't sure how much time had passed, but soon enough he was at Jasmina's apartment. Ascending the steps two at a time, as many as his long legs would allow, he found himself at her front door and knocked. The welcome mat was patterned with peaches and curly script that read *Just Peachy*, and framed by thick, white tassels.

Graham heard the lock click and when the door swung open, he found himself face-to-face with a very inebriated Jasmina Coulter. There were a few wine drops on her shirt and her eyes were glazed as she took him in.

"Took you long enough," she sassed playfully, hiccupping. Sighing, she trailed golden nails along her hallway wall and went to the kitchen sink.

Graham entered her apartment, kicked off his shoes, and locked the door behind him. When he joined her in the kitchen, she was drinking water like she'd been traveling in the desert.

"Trying to mitigate the hangover," she managed between sips.

"And how is that going, baby?"

She smiled into the glass—or was that a cringe? "Too late, but I'm trying anyway."

Jasmina finished the cup and filled another from the tap, overfilling it as her reflexes betrayed her.

"Ah damn," she said, trying—unsuccessfully—not to spill a drop. Worse, when the entire glass toppled over onto her perfect tits, soaking her wrap-style shirt. "Mother of fuck."

Somehow, Graham had caught the glass before it hit her oak floors and shattered. Meanwhile, she stood there, dripping wet in shock.

"Well. That's my cue to never drink again," she deadpanned.

Graham carefully set the glass in the sink and Jasmina plucked at the sticking fabric. Her face was a mixture of disgust and despair. Turning on her heel, she went for the small bathroom and flicked on the light, but didn't close the door.

He stayed stalwartly in the kitchen, hearing the shush of fabric over her skin. Jasmina was drunk. And even if she begged him, he would not touch her—not like that. He would do whatever was needed to help her, but nothing further than that.

Not right now.

Not tonight.

Graham busied himself waiting for Jasmina to change by casually looking around her place. It was cute—albeit small.

Her furniture was modest, yet cozy. She had a rust orange couch with ecru, pink, and peach pillows, and a knitted throw tossed over the back. In the corner by the window framed with gossamer curtains and jeweled suncatchers, was a plush armchair with a matching footstool. It was dusty rose, threadbare on the left arm, with a blanket patterned with teacups, and a flat, circular green pillow.

The walls were off-white, but nearly every single one was taken up by some kind of wall art. She'd made gallery walls of thrifted gold frames, some photos, some prints, some paintings. There was a print of a baby highland cow with flowers between its ears, and another of an anatomical heart drawn in a vintage style made of twigs and florals. Pictures of Jasmina and Nate, Jasmina and Madeline, and Jasmina and Illiana dotted the collage. There were witty book sayings like, *Just One More Chapter* and *I Read Past My Bedtime*. There was also a suggestive piece of fingers spreading the pages of a book— Graham cocked his head at that one in curiosity. His eyes were drawn to a cross-stitched piece, circular, and bordered in daisies. It was only an assembly of letters—a long one—and he wasn't sure what it meant.

Jasmina let out a frustrated growl from the bathroom.

"Graham?" she asked hesitantly, a slight muffle to her voice.

"Yeah?"

"I'm stuck."

A pause.

"Would you like me to help you?"

"Yes, please."

"Are you decent?"

There was a heavy pause. "No."

"And you're okay with—"

"Graham, I'm drunk and stuck in my shirt. My options are extremely limited."

Graham stifled his laughter and made his way to the bathroom where he found Jasmina. Standing there, arms and shirt over her head, her abdomen on full display, the slight softness of her belly, and the generous swells of her breasts in her beige lace bra.

He blinked, eyes unable to pull from her cleavage, the way they jiggled when she shimmied.

"I swear to fuck, Graham Starling, if you're staring at my tits instead of helping me, I'll tell everyone you bleat like a goat when we fuck."

This time he couldn't suppress his guffaw and it spilled out of him.

"You have quite the imagination there, baby."

"Just get me out of this. I think the stupid strap thing that goes on the clothes hanger is snagged on my bra hook and this shirt is stupid tight."

"Okay, turn around."

She did as bidden, and he found that she was correct. The loop attached to the shirt was twisted around the hook that connected the straps together.

With gentle hands, his fingertips brushed the blade of her shoulder as he unwound the loop from the hook and freed her from the confines of her gray shirt.

"Can you help me pull it off? It's all wet and stuck to itself."

Swallowing, Graham grabbed the edge of the shirt and helped pull it off her head, careful not to snag her curls in the process. Once freed, she yanked her arms out and tossed the top to the floor.

From a neatly folded pile, Jasmina pulled on an old band t-shirt and from beneath said shirt, she unfastened her bra, slipped out of it, and flung it to the corner.

Jasmina sagged against the sink.

"I hate when I get like this," she admitted tiredly.

"Like what?"

"Too drunk and wishing I wasn't drunk anymore." She blinked heavy eyes. "I feel stupid."

"You're not stupid, baby," he reassured her, leaning against the sink beside her.

She hummed an acceptance and leaned her head on his shoulder. "I need to come up with a name or nickname for you. Graham…Graham. Teddy Graham." She sighed. "Oh, I love Teddy Grahams. I really like Teddy Graham."

"Oh, do you?" he teased her.

"They're so good. I could eat a whole bag of them right now. They're my love, Teddy Graham. Just like Teddy Grahams are my love."

She wasn't making any sense.

"I think it's time for bed," he announced.

She nodded her head against his shoulder. He could smell the peach floral scent of her beneath the wine. Without words he guided her to her bedroom and turned down her bed.

Jasmina turned to him with sudden strength and fire in her eyes. "Will you stay with me? In my bed? Just for tonight? To make sure I'm okay? I promise I won't try anything."

Graham weighed the pros and cons. Realistically, he didn't feel comfortable leaving her because, what if she puked in her sleep and asphyxiated? What if she fell out of bed and hit her head on the nightstand? It wasn't something he wanted to even debate risking.

"Sure, I'll stay," he told her.

Jasmina clambered into bed and pulled on the covers.

"No peeking!" she nearly shouted at him as she shimmied out of her pants beneath the covers and tossed them out the side.

Maybe he should've reconsidered this sleepover.

"Are you coming?" she pressed.

No. "Yes."

Shucking off his coat and jeans, he slipped into her bed in his t-shirt and boxers, lying on his back, as far as humanly possible from her.

Jasmina turned on her side and gazed at him with those beguiling green-gold eyes. A smile curved her mouth.

"Hi," she whispered.

"Hi."

"Thank you for coming tonight."

"Thank you for trusting me."

Jasmina paused, tracing shapes aimlessly on her pillow. "Something between us has changed, hasn't it?"

Graham stole a breath then blew it out slowly. "Yeah," he agreed. "It has."

"Was it before or after the kiss?"

"I thought you didn't want to talk about that?"

"Humor me."

He scrubbed a hand over his mouth, trying to wipe away the urge—the fervent desire he always possessed—to kiss her.

"Before."

"Hmm," she demurred, then began humming.

"Jasmina?"

"Yes?" she responded, eyes closed.

"What does STFUATTDLAGG mean?"

Her eyes flew open, hazel bright and glassy. "Where did you hear that?"

"It's on your wall."

Her mouth pressed into a thin line. "*Shut the fuck up and take this dick like a good girl.*"

Seconds later she was asleep and Graham was wide awake, dick hard as a fucking rock.

When Graham woke, Jasmina was curled around him, leg slung over his hips. Her smooth, bare skin was pure heaven against his, her gentle snores pressing into his throat, her soft hair clouding over her face.

Carefully, he extricated himself from her warm clutches—very unwillingly, he might add—and slid out of bed. Jasmina flopped onto her belly in his absence, sprawled, and began snoring like a freight train.

He chuckled, smiling at her affectionately, heart swelling with something he wouldn't acknowledge, and slipped from the room.

It was around six a.m., the sky outside deep blue. Quietly, he set about opening Jasmina's windows, airing out the lingering scent of booze. After dumping and rinsing the discarded wine bottles, he set them outside her front door, then wiped down the counters. Graham could still smell the sourness of wine in the air, so he found a half burnt candle, and lit it. Slowly, the scent of stone fruit filled the space.

Fifteen minutes later, Jasmina's dishes were done and drying on the rack, and Graham had begun prepping breakfast—scrambled eggs, bacon, toast, and coffee. He knew Jasmina drank coffee sparingly, but he assumed a vicious hangover would constitute one of those days.

In her bedroom, there were the sounds of Jasmina stirring from sheets, mixed with the sizzle of grease and the bubble of butter before him. Graham continued cooking as footsteps padded into the kitchen behind him.

"What are you doing here?" Jasmina croaked, confusing written across her face. "And why are you only in your boxers?" Horror filled her face. "Oh my god, did we—?"

"No, we didn't. You called me because you got too drunk and asked me to stay."

"Oh. Okay."

He knew Wednesdays were one of Jasmina's days off, but unfortunately it wasn't one of his and he had to be in the office at eight thirty. It was a painful thought—leaving her—but he had appointments and he knew people had been waiting months if not years to see him.

"What did I say?" she asked tentatively.

Gently, he filled her in and mortification drew its dire lines across her face. Her hand came up to cup her mouth and her previously tired eyes grew shiny with embarrassment-fueled tears.

"It's okay," he finished. "We've all had our moments when we're drunk."

"Yeah, but this isn't the first time you've taken care of me because of it."

"I don't mind."

"You did then."

"Who said that?"

"You did."

He shook his head as he plated their breakfast. "I've never had an issue with it, Jasmina."

"But..." Her brows knitted together.

Graham didn't know what it was, but he could clearly see a thought begging to be spoken on the tip of her tongue. His talent of perception had always aided him in being able to help fix problems or say the right thing, but in this moment, he didn't know what to say. Jasmina Coulter was the only person who knocked him so off-kilter.

"But, what?" he asked, sitting down.

She shook her head. "I'm sorry, my head is killing me."

Graham pointed to the tiny green dish he'd put two Tylenol in. It looked handmade, the shape was that of a flower with horribly uneven petals. Beside it was a glass of water.

"Do you enjoy taking care of people?" she asked, taking the proffered pills and water.

He chewed some of his breakfast. "I like taking care of *you*."

"Graham, you don't need to perform for anyone here—it's just the two of us."

"I know," he replied, giving her a heated gaze.

He was hoping—no, praying—that she read into it as much as he'd meant her to. He was hoping this, despite her hangover, despite last night's drunkenness, would begin to tip things into the *real* category.

Jasmina swallowed. "Why are you being so nice to me? Acting like you might even like me."

"I do like you, Jasmina."

"You never did."

"I never said that. It was you who didn't like me."

"What are you talking about?"

"You couldn't—forget about it. This is too much right now."

"Jasmina—"

"Another time," she begged. "Please. I just want to eat and go back to bed."

He held a breath. The tension had built and he thought it was all going to transform, but instead it fell through a sieve and dispersed.

"All right." Graham finished his breakfast and rinsed the plate. "I also took the liberty of ordering you some post-hangover cures, they'll be here this afternoon."

Softness entered her face. "Thank you."

"Don't mention it."

After gathering his things, he blew out the candle, said a reluctant goodbye to Jasmina and headed for the door.

"Lock it behind me," he told her.

"I will," she promised.

The door clicked shut and with that solid wood between them Graham felt the wind go out of his sails. He thought there were on a new track, but no, they were still walking the parapet of fake dating status quo.

Everything after that passed in a sun-faded blur. It was all half vibrant and all the brightness and energy had been sapped from his worldview. Jasmina had texted him letting him know she wouldn't be making it for their sleepover that night and that sun-fade turned to sun-bleached.

The next day was much the same, made worse by their sparse conversation. It was as if Jasmina were avoiding him—but why? Embarrassment? Stress? Dislike? Confusion?

He didn't know, and that unknowing unnerved him.

With a heart beating a lumpy rhythm, he focused what little determination he had into planning their weekly date. And like a lightbulb, his genius ignited, and by Friday afternoon he'd shopped for everything he'd needed, his truck packed with supplies. As a last detail he messaged Emmett for a favor.

Seven o'clock Friday evening, Graham was in front of Jasmina's apartment, plans of true romanticism searing his heart.

CHAPTER NINETEEN
Mina

Mina had dressed up a little for their date. She'd be lying if she said she wasn't a bit nervous—butterflies tumbling through her stomach—but in the same breath, she was excited.

Her makeup was minimal—some lotion, concealer, gloss, brow gel and powder, mascara, and a bit of highlight. Her hair was unbound and shiny, the curls cooperating tonight and falling over her brow in a sexy/cute sort of way. For clothes she'd gone with high waisted jeans, a semi-sheer beige blouse over a matching full lace camisole/bustier combo, and fun leopard patterned heel boots. Jewelry was even more minimal, with just a gold chain bracelet and tiny leaf earrings.

Graham stood outside his truck, passenger side door open as he gestured toward it chivalrously.

"Your chariot awaits, my lady," he said in a grand voice, almost mocking a British accent.

Mina laughed as she climbed in. "Why thank you, good sir."

Graham shut the door behind her, and after she buckled, she looked in the backseat and noticed blankets, tons of them, and reusable grocery bags filled with snacks. She also smelled the telltale aroma of pizza.

"What is this?" she asked as he got into the driver's seat.

Graham followed her gaze and pointed finger, then smirked. "It's our date." He then turned the engine over and pulled out of her lot, heading out down Seaview Road.

"How was your day?" Mina queried.

A smile crooked the corner of Graham's mouth. A mouth that she hadn't forgotten kissing. "It was fine, a regular work-day. It's better now, though." And then he tossed her a look that had her heart slamming against the cage of her ribs. "And yours?" he added.

"It was good. It was all regular clients today. My last hour was a lot of emails, so it was nice to unwind with that."

"That's good," he replied, but it had a distracted air to it.

"Where are we going?" she queried, looking out the window.

The quaint streets of Rose Point passed beneath their tires, most of the roads unmarked by paint lines, and drawn with dirt sidewalks. Trees peppered the sides, green shoots fighting the lingering fingers of winter. Spring had officially sprung and Rose Point was now a butterfly breaking from its chrysalis.

Mina recognized every aspect of the town, from the large sequoia on the Morris property, to the row of shops on Clover Street that were painted in pastels with matching lacy gingerbread trim, and the town square which backed onto a field and playground where outdoor movies were shown in the summer and seasonal festivals were held.

She'd missed the town for the almost ten years she'd lived in Toronto, but she didn't regret the move. She thought it gave her an all-new appreciation for her hometown. Not to mention, it was where she'd met her best friend.

Darkness was descending, but in the lull between, as twilight was breaking, the sky was painted in strokes of orange and lavender. Mina rolled the window down and let the budding flower season air in, the floral notes ruffling her hair and filling her lungs with endorphins.

Dreamily, she sighed as Graham turned down a dirt road pressed between some trees. The shaded canopy overhead caused the headlights to carve stark lines in their path, illuminating a red painted government gate. A gate that was closed.

"Um, where are we going?" she asked.

"It's a surprise."

Graham put the truck in park and climbed out. When he approached the gate, he took a keycard out of his pocket and swiped it in the hidden box below the gate. It unlocked and he pushed it open.

When he returned to the truck, she pressed him for answers.

"You have a keycard?" her voice was pitched high.

"Emmett does. I'm borrowing it."

Keycards for these sorts of gates were scarce. Most people wanted them for access to backroads for hunting or UTV riding, and in certain circles, they were passed around like a joint. She didn't get the vibe that Emmett would be so laissez-faire about it, though.

The process of driving through, closing the gate and locking it behind, and then continuing the drive took less than two minutes, but it was double that driving down the secluded road before Mina spoke again.

"What are we doing in the middle of nowhere?"

"I told you, our date, baby."

"It had better not be a date with death."

"I promise you it's not."

"I don't know if I would've believed you a few weeks ago."

"And now?" he asked, a hint of hope in his voice—or was she imagining it?

"I trust you now."

The smile that spread over Graham's face was slow, but bright. It reached his eyes and made them sparkle. She couldn't help the pattering rhythm of her heart in answer.

Why was he so cute? And so fucking hot at the same time? It was criminal.

Soon, the canopy of trees broke apart like open arms and exposed the violet twilight. The moon shivered over the gentle tide, the stretch of the ocean indigo in the drawing night. Starshine dappled the current and sparkled like diamonds in the sky as Graham pulled the truck onto a shallow outcropping and reversed against the waves. When he parked, the truck was only a few feet higher than the rocky shore, and the sandy grass they were on the last bastion against the water.

"I've never been here before," Mina said, awed.

"It's a bit of a secret. Kieran and I found it when we were in middle school and only shared it with the other guys."

"You mean this isn't your secret make out spot?" she asked, mockingly scandalized. "I'm offended."

"I've never brought anyone here."

"Wow. What a line."

"I know, right?" Graham chuckled. "But it's the truth. I've never told anyone outside of our group about this spot."

"And what about the others? Has Emmett told Ana?"

"I don't think so."

"And he knows you're bringing me here?"

"He does."

Mina's heart swelled, and it felt as if her chest were squeezing itself. The overwhelming emotion was not unpleasant, nor unwanted, but it was unexpected.

"Oh, wow."

She didn't know what else to say.

"Wait here," Graham told her, climbing out of the truck and grabbing everything from the backseat. He popped his head back in. "And don't look!"

Quickly, the blankets, bags, and pizza disappeared from the cab. While Mina waited, Graham had climbed into the box of his truck and was laying all the pillows and blankets down. She heard the sound of rustling fabric, crinkling paper, him hitting the metal of the box, jostling the truck, and Graham's ministrations.

A short while later, Graham returned. He opened her door and swooped his arm gallantly. "Milady."

Mina giggled and slipped out of her seat. Taking Graham's elbow, they rounded the truck, and when she saw the truck bed, her jaw dropped.

"Graham! Oh my god!"

The box had been transformed. Piles and piles of blankets—comforters, quilts, and throws—were laid out like a nest. Pillows framed the walls of the bed and two laptop tables were set with pizza, peanut butter cups, mint chocolate chip ice cream, and all the essential utensils. Water and other drinks— non-alcoholic—were set aside. A small speaker played quietly, and strung across the top of the cab were battery operated butterfly string lights.

"Do you like it?" he asked anxiously.

She gripped his arm tightly and peered at all the effort he'd put into this.

"Like it? I love it. It's so magical."

"I'm glad you like it. Hop on in."

Mina's heart soared. She kicked off her animal print boots and climbed into the bed on her hands and knees, cozying herself in the cocoon of warmth. As she settled, she noticed how plush it felt. Not at all like the hard metal of his truck.

"Is there a mattress topper under this?" she asked, bouncing up and down.

Peeling back a corner of the blanket mountain she peered down, and sure enough, there was in fact a memory foam mattress topper covered by a fitted sheet.

"Oh my god, there is. How did it not fly out on the way here?"

Graham blushed. "I glued a mattress topper to some plywood and made it fit into the box."

Mina's eyes grew wide and she felt her lips pop open.

"Can I take a picture?" he asked. "You know, for social media—to sell this."

"Go for it."

Mina carefully posed herself, attempting to look candid, not looking at the camera and then gave him another where she was grinning fully at him. When he finished the mini photoshoot, he pocketed his phone and stood there a little awkwardly.

"May I join you?" he asked, hopefully.

"Well, all this pizza isn't going to eat itself," she proclaimed, opening the box and being greeted by the mouthwatering aroma of cheese and oregano.

It was pepperoni topped with green peppers and mushrooms. Her favorite. Just like their fake first date.

She froze.

Fake first date.

She scanned the entire space and completed a mental checklist.

He'd recreated—or just created?—their supposed first date.

"How long did this take you to put together?"

"A few days," he admitted, settling beside her and pulling the blankets onto his lap. "But it wasn't too hard. The hardest part was figuring out how to make the box comfy—I had to ask Willow for her opinion."

"So, I have Willow to thank for the mattress topper?"

"You do."

"Well, Willow is my new favorite of your sisters."

"Don't let Sabrina hear you say that, she'd take it as a challenge for herself and an insult against Piper."

"She's protective?"

"Very."

"Sounds like her big brother."

"We're definitely alike in that."

Mina dug into her pizza, shutting her eyes against the flavor—it was insanely good. Beside her, she heard Graham eating, too.

"What motivated you to do this tonight?" she asked.

Graham stopped chewing, and she looked over at him. He looked contemplative. Wiping his mouth and hands on a napkin, he swallowed, cleared his throat, and began speaking.

"It seemed fun. I've never done something like this before. And, this was what we told people our first date was, so I figured we should have it for real."

"Always so considerate."

"I try."

They ate for a while, continuing with small talk and joking. With two spoons, they shared the mint chocolate chip ice cream straight from the tub. The air was chilled, but between their body heat and the copious blankets, she was perfectly content. Besides, the view more than made up for any discomfort.

The sky and the ocean were stunning. Something out of a painting. And in this moment, under this moon, and these stars, over this water, was her and Graham.

Sharing a moment.

It felt poetic.

Beautiful.

And she gravitated toward it.

Toward him.

Awareness fluttered between her legs and she found herself shifting her thighs, trying to ease the ache. In her effort to sate her need, she moved closer to Graham mid-conversation, and he beamed in response. Her response was to shiver.

"Cold?" he asked.

She took the out he offered. "A little."

Graham shuffled closer, even going as far as to wrap his arm around her shoulders and tug her in. She didn't fight it, which surprised her. She, Jasmina Coulter was willingly being pulled into the embrace of her enemy, her nemesis, Graham Starling—and she *liked* it.

Famous last words floated through her mind—

Fuck it.

Mina nuzzled Graham's throat, right where the scent of him was most potent—that damned timber spice got her so worked up—and she pressed a kiss to his pulse. He stiffened, and she watched his hands flex on his thighs, opening and closing like he was trying to regain control.

She let her tongue dart out, and he groaned.

"Jasmina, what are you doing?" he asked, and his voice was anguished. Like that of a man in pain.

"I was thinking…" she whispered, kisses trailing to his collarbone, her hand coasting up his chest. "For the sake of authenticity with this fake dating contract—we should have sex. Just one time—so we know what it's like."

"Jasmina…" She felt him clench his teeth. "I don't want you to say things like that because you feel obligated to sell this."

"I'm not. I want this."

"You…you do?" he asked, as if he couldn't believe the words, as if by questioning them, they'd evaporate like a mirage.

"I do. Very much so."

Her fingers slid beneath his green flannel, beneath his t-shirt and quested across his abdomen. There, she scraped her gold-painted nails across the ridges.

"I don't have any condoms," he blurted. "I wasn't expecting this."

Mina straddled him, resting her arms on his shoulders. She gazed at him, taking in his breathtakingly blue eyes. There was so much hope swimming in them, so much care. Fuck, he was good looking, and fuck, did she like him. How did she ever find herself hating him? How did she ever imagine hatred between them? When had it shifted? Where had it gone? When did bygones become bygones?

"I'm on the birth control ring," she told him, fingers toying with the silky brown hair at the nape of his neck. "And I'm clean. After my ex cheated on me, I got tested, and I haven't been with anyone since."

Graham's breath hitched, and she felt a commanding nudge between her legs. Hot arousal throbbed in her pussy, knowing his cock was mere inches away.

"I was tested after the last time I was with someone and that was…" he hesitated. "A very long time ago."

"So, we're doing this?" she asked, gently rolling her hips over him.

His eyes shuttered and he nodded.

"Anything off limits?" she asked.

"Nothing too crazy, but let's go with the flow."

"Done."

Mina then took his face in her hands, then she was kissing him. Her mouth melded with his, his lips parting for her as their tongues flicked and tasted. The mint chocolate chip ice cream lingered between them as teeth nibbled on lips, and lips captured tongues.

Graham's hands went to her waist, pushing up the sheer blouse, feeling the strip of bare skin between the bustier and her jeans. His fingertips glided along the waistband, tucking into them and pulling her closer. Hastily, she pushed his flannel off his shoulders, hands all over his taut biceps, tracing the sexy veins in his forearms.

"You're so gorgeous, baby," he murmured as his teeth grazed her throat. "So fucking hot."

Mina's desire surged, turning her core molten. She leaned back and tugged off his shirt, tossing it to the side. That's when she saw.

"Holy fucking shit," she gasped.

Her hands roamed his entire abdomen. An abdomen that was cut like a Greek god and covered in tattoos. Sprigs of flowers and leaves climbed from the V of his pelvis, over his navel, around his ribs, and onto his pecs. It was all black and gray with white highlights. She couldn't tell exactly what they were—maybe cherry blossoms?

"I'll take that as a compliment?"

"Uh, fuck yeah."

"Good," he said, then grabbed her roughly by the nape of her neck and devoured her mouth. His kisses were hot and needy and he let out that sound again—that fucking sound of near pain, of pleasure so bright it burned.

While his hands were busy, hers were free and they went directly for his belt buckle. She flicked it open with ease and before she knew it, he'd switched up what he was doing and her sheer blouse was gone. His palms went to her breasts, cupping them, squeezing them. Graham applied expert pressure that had her moaning into his mouth.

She was shoving his pants down and he was inching hers down. She wouldn't admit it, but she wore matching panties to the bustier. It was the same creamy beige lace—the silky kind, not scratchy—and Graham's fingers slid over the center of them, a single finger tapping her swollen clit.

Mina cried out and Graham took it in, smiling against her lips.

The March breeze was a balm against her flushed skin, and well needed judging by how hot this was about to be.

"Jasmina, did you wear a matching set just for me?" he teased, finger sliding beneath the waistband and over the hair she kept meticulously short and groomed.

"You wish," she retorted, the words falling into a moan as he slipped that questing finger against her wetness, teasing her entrance.

He switched their positions so now Mina was the one nestled in the blankets, cushioned like a queen, a ceiling of stars and butterfly lights above them. Graham's weight above her was a comforting presence and—

Graham's finger plunged inside her and curled.

Mina arched with a gasp.

God—DAMN.

Pleasure rang in her bones; fingers turned to claws as they scrabbled on his still jean-clad thighs. They were slung low, exposing that sexy V and the base of his—*holy fuck*—thick cock. She shoved his pants down, exposing him further as he continued pumping that digit inside her. A fine trail of hair went from his navel to his shaft, but as his pants came off, it appeared that aside from that, he was bare.

"Fuck, you're so wet already, baby," Graham murmured.

"I know," she moaned.

"Who are you wet for, baby?"

Mina groaned. "You."

His thumb grazed her clit and stars burst behind her eyes, an orgasm already building, pulling her taut.

"How bad do you want me?"

Mina had had no idea Graham would be like this in bed—the dirty talking, the teasing, the coaxing, the near begging. But it drove her wild. It turned her on and seared her blood, wetness surging between her thighs.

"So bad."

"Oh, yeah?"

"So fucking bad, babe."

Graham's breath hitched and then he added a second finger and pressed his thumb to her clit, rubbing firm circles.

Mina keened a breathy sound as bliss roared through her. Already, her orgasm was on the edge. With one hand he was going to make her come.

Fuck, she was so screwed.

Her inner muscles fluttered around his fingers, a climax only a breath away.

"Are you going to come already, Jasmina?"

"Yes!" she panted, rolling her hips.

Graham pulled his fingers out of her and she let out a sound of deranged frustration as her core squeezed around nothing, suddenly achingly empty.

"*Graham!*" she nearly shrieked.

Graham kissed her hard.

She wanted to bite him.

"That's right, baby," he whispered, breaking the kiss. "Scream my name just like that when you come."

The prospect of that alone turned the dial up inside her, her pussy craving him, ready to do anything to have him touch her again. She was so hollow, and she needed him inside her.

Graham reached behind her, and pinched the four clasps open on her bustier, tossing it aside. Her breasts were heavy and full, nipples brown and painfully hard.

"You're so beautiful."

She let out a dark chuckle. "You don't need to compliment me, big boy. You're already getting in my pants."

"I like complimenting you." He licked her nipple—just a flick, but she gasped. He grinned. "And I'm not complaining about you calling me big boy."

"Have you seen the size of that thing?" she asked, brow raised as she pointed to his considerable size. He was long and thick, likely the biggest dick she'd let near her.

"You can take it," he told her, all smug, taking a nipple into his mouth and grazing his teeth over the peak.

She let out a breathless, *'fuck'* as he tormented her with pleasure.

"Oh, I know I can," she managed. "But can you handle me?"

"Are you challenging me, Jasmina?"

"Always."

Before Mina could process it, Graham's face was between her legs, her thighs over his shoulders as he licked her needy clit. Her hands immediately fisted in his hair, pushing him harder against her pussy. He licked and sucked, pulling that bundle of nerves between his lips, applying divine suction.

That wave that had dwindled without his touch came roaring back like a tsunami, and suddenly that wave crested and broke. Mina's orgasm shattered through her, and she began uttering nonsensible sounds, mixes of *'fuck'* and *'oh'* and *'Graham'* spilling from her lips. He continued licking and feasting through her climax as she rode his face, grinding, making a mess. She didn't know how hard she was pulling his hair, but it wasn't hard enough.

She needed him.

She needed more.

Mina collapsed against the truck bed as the pleasure abated, the stars spinning above her as her chest heaved.

"I didn't…I wasn't expecting that."

"Surpassed your expectations?"

"Something like that."

Challenge lit within her and she rose up on her knees, holding Graham's gaze. His blue eyes blazed with amusement. And then she pushed him down, straddled him, and sank down onto his huge cock.

"*Fucking Christ, Jasmina,*" Graham hissed, his hands digging into her hips. Squeezing, hopefully leaving marks.

The stretch was a slight burn, but it was satisfying. Her core soft from the orgasm he'd just given her, ready to take him easily.

Mina met his gaze and the realization struck her.

Holy fuck.

Graham Starling's cock was inside her.

And she was about to fuck him.

"You still think you can handle me?" she asked coyly.

And then began riding him into oblivion.

Mina bounced on his length, soaking them both in her wetness. Her hands were on his back, scraping and clawing, his fingers digging into her thighs, grinding her down. As Mina's breasts bounced, they grazed against his chest, adding to the stimulation.

A second climax was already creeping up on her and she thought she'd see nirvana. Her pussy clenched and Graham groaned, his mouth buried in her throat.

"Baby, I'm not going to last much longer."

"Come inside me, Graham. I want you to know it's me who makes you feel like this."

"Only you," he groaned as he came.

She felt his cum spurt inside her, the flex of his cock as he pumped every last drop into her pussy. As Graham ducked his head and sucked on her nipple she came too, crying out and breaking.

Pleasure rocked through her as she shuddered through the mind-numbing ecstasy.

They collapsed together among the blankets as The Waterboys sang about the moon. Sweat like glitter clung to their skin, breaths sawing out of their chests, Mina was still on top of him, his cock slick on their thighs. She could feel the trickle of his release inside her as he brushed her hair off her shoulder.

Post sex clarity hit her.

Oh. My. God.

What have I done? She thought.

But it wasn't in horror, like she expected. Unexpectedly, it was surprise. And wonderment. It didn't make sense. They didn't like each other, but this…sex, they made sense.

"Are you okay?" Graham asked, sensing her inner turmoil.

"I am," she said with conviction and cheer. "You?"

"Never been better," he replied, tossing an arm over his eyes. "Fuck, Jasmina. That was…it's never been like that."

"Same here. Or neither. For me. It's never been like this for me either."

Suddenly, just once wasn't going to be enough.

CHAPTER TWENTY
Graham

He had finally had sex with Jasmina Coulter.

Graham had been pining after her for years—in a pathetically unrequited fashion—and it had finally happened. And it was even better than his imagination. Better than all of his fantasies.

God, he felt like a teenager.

Like it was the first time he'd ever fucked—despite the fact losing his virginity was many moons ago. Nothing, no one, had ever felt like this before.

He was replaying it all. The sounds she made, the way she rode him, the way she was so wet and tight. Graham was getting hard again just thinking about it.

Jasmina was still on top of him, her hot skin juxtaposed with the chill night air made for the most tantalizing of feelings.

He couldn't resist touching her, his fingertips dancing across the soft expanse of her form. Jasmina's hands were roaming too, grazing his abdomen, over his tattoos.

Her fingers stilled over a scar.

He stiffened.

"What is that from?" she asked tentatively. She barked out a laugh. "Sorry, I don't mean to do that whole asking about scars after sex trope, it's just…" Her fingers wandered again, finding another. And another. And another. And the last one. "Did someone…?"

"It was surgical," he answered.

He sighed. It was a point of insecurity for him, but nonetheless, he soldiered on.

"I had really bad acid reflux. To the point that it was damaging my esophagus. Various mediations didn't work and after a scope they discovered that my epiglottis didn't work properly. It would stay open and the stomach acid would climb up, then eventually close, locking in all the acid that rose. I was at a high risk of cancer, so they removed parts of my stomach and esophagus and twisted them over themselves. The procedure has a long and scientific name that I didn't care to learn.

"But the scars that were left…they made me insecure. So, I tattooed over them. And as much of my abdomen as possible to really hide them."

"Were you worried about what people would think?"

"A bit. I mostly didn't like it myself."

"Well," she said, propping herself up on an elbow. "If it's any consolation, I think you're hot. Scars, no scars, tattoos, no tattoos."

"Who are you and what have you done with Jasmina Coulter?"

"Oh, shush," she replied, laughing and shifting to his side. "I'm your fake girlfriend. I may as well properly act the part."

The words fake girlfriend were like a bucket of ice water, dousing his warmth and teasing air. He shivered and pulled some blankets up around them. From a corner of the truck bed, he reached back and grabbed a familiar package.

"Care for some peanut butter cups?" he asked, shaking the orange bag.

"Absolutely."

For the next hour, they cuddled in the back of the truck, naked, save for the blankets. Munching on peanut butter cups, talking, and listening to the 80s playlist he'd put on earlier—just for her. The sounds of the night rang around them, the distant croak of frogs, the shush of waves, the odd cricket, a whispering breeze through the tree boughs.

He imagined no better night.

Eventually, they retired to his house.

On his couch, they talked—about nothing in particular, until it, as it was fated to, circled to sex.

"Why did you clarify about boundaries?" he asked.

Jasmina didn't even act surprised. "You never know what people are into. I like to be a little rough, but nothing weird—if you're into golden showers, I'm out."

Graham laughed. "Don't worry, I definitely don't have a piss kink."

"Fabulous news. Praise? Degradation?"

"A little praise. Degradation is debatable," he admitted. "I like teasing the most, drawing it out and taking it away, only to give it back."

"I noticed that," she said darkly.

"You enjoyed it though."

"That's beside the point," she said dismissively.

"Butt stuff?"

Jasmina hesitated.

"You don't have to answer if you don't want to. It's obviously a very personal question."

"No, it's not that," she said. She drew in a deep breath. "To be totally honest, I really enjoy it, but I don't usually tell my partners about it because they get a big ego or big head about it, and they see it as attaining some goal—like they're just checking a box—and it just feels…I don't know, disingenuous?" she laughed a little awkwardly. "I like it, I just don't do it often unless I trust a person."

"That's fair," Graham offered. "I enjoy it too. Both ways."

Jasmina cocked a brow. "I've never pegged a guy."

Graham shrugged. "There's a first for everything."

A fire lit in her hazel eyes, and he recognized it—arousal.

"Speaking of firsts…" she drew in a deep breath. "Us having sex. What if that was just the first time? Why don't we just…keep doing it? We both clearly enjoyed it and it would help solidify the ruse."

"Is that something you want?" he asked, trying to keep the hope hidden. His heart was racing, excitement screaming through him. He wanted nothing more than to keep having sex with Jasmina.

Okay, the only thing he wanted more was to be with her. In full. With a future together. In whatever form that took.

"Yeah, I do. We can keep doing this until our contract ends."

Graham swallowed the revulsion at the thought of this ending. He wanted May 22nd to stay as far from them as possible. He wanted to exist in this temporary bubble. Delusion or no. An alternate reality or whatever. He had gotten a taste of Jasmina, and he didn't want to let her go.

Jasmina's leg was extended toward him and he took the opportunity. He began caressing her calf, gliding his palm up her leg until he tucked it into the curve of her knee and tugged. He climbed atop her as she slid down the couch cushions, giggling.

"Are you going for a round two, Mr. Starling?"

"And maybe a third."

"I think you're overestimating your capabilities."

Graham cocked a brow. "I think I'm going to make you regret saying that."

"Oh? How so?"

He was on top of her now, pinning her to the couch, watching the playful light in her green-gold eyes.

"You like games, don't you, Jasmina?"

Jasmina's brows narrowed. "I do."

"Then let's play a little game," he said, fingers popping open the buttons on her blouse again. "We can play either; *How Many Times Can I Make Jasmina Come in One Session?* or *How Long Can I Edge Jasmina Until She's Begging For It?*"

"You wouldn't dare," she retorted, promised violence in her eyes.

"I would. I would get you so close," he whispered, hand drifting to her waistband. "I would get you making those breathy little sounds, arching your back…and then I'd take it away, letting it fade out of reach before I worked you back up again." He kissed her neck as his fingertips slipped into her panties. "Over. And over again."

Jasmina shivered and moaned lightly, her fingertips digging into his shoulders.

He pushed her pants off, underwear falling away with them as she tugged on his shirt and divested him of his pants. Her bra disappeared as he kept taunting her with that touch that didn't quite sate her need.

Graham was hard as a rock, already leaking pre-cum onto Jasmina's thigh as he kissed her collarbones, her shoulders, her pulse, never fully giving her what she wanted between her thighs. She rolled her hips against his delicate movements, seeking the friction he wasn't giving her.

"Please, I need it," Jasmina whined, stroking his cock.

Stars burst with violet color behind his eyes.

"You're impatient, baby. I'm trying to win a game."

"Your game sucks. I want to start a different one. What would you say to that?" she pushed in frustration as his index finger slowly rubbed her clit. She bucked in response.

"I would tell you a new term I learned—" He took his cock in hand and slid it against her soaked pussy. *"Shut the fuck up and take this dick like a good girl."* And then he slammed inside her.

"Oh, fuck, yes," Jasmina hissed, arching off the couch just like he'd hoped she would.

Graham began a relentless rhythm, pumping in and out of her with hard thrusts, each one of them bumping that little ring inside her pussy. The ring that kept them protected while he fucked her raw.

It was hot.

He'd never forgone protection with anyone, but Jasmina wasn't just anyone.

Jasmina's nails scratched at his back, and he hoped they carved lines. He wanted every proof that he'd been inside her. That he'd made her so wild with pleasure that she'd left her mark on him.

In and out he rolled his hips, making sure he delivered delicious friction on her needy clit. Her gorgeous tits bounced with every undulation and he couldn't resist plying them with kisses and taking those pretty dark nipples in his mouth.

Already her pussy was fluttering around his cock and his entire worldview pinpointed sensation. But, unfortunately, as incredible as it felt, he was a man of his word.

"Graham, I'm so close."

He pulled out of her completely.

"No!" she cried out at his loss. "You fucking asshole!"

"You remember what I said?"

"You're the worst," she growled.

"No," he replied, taking her by the hips and flipping her onto her belly. "I'm the best you've ever had."

Then he lifted that pretty ass and slid back into her pussy.

Jasmina threw her head back, golden brown curls spilling down her back. Her fingers gripped the edge of the couch cushion as he railed her.

"More," she whined.

"More what?"

"Touch me more."

His hand went to her back. "Here?"

"Lower."

His dick throbbed in excitement. "Here?"

"Lower."

He slid his finger down her backside. "Jasmina, do you want something in here?"

"Fuck me how you want to, Graham," she moaned.

Lightly, he slapped her ass and rubbed away the sting. With his opposite hand, he coasted down her belly and toyed with her clit—giving her what he knew she liked. Still rubbing her clit, he took his other thumb and stuck it in his mouth.

In lieu of lube, spit would have to do—for this specific thing at least.

With his thumb wet, he rubbed her tight hole, giving her a hint of what he was planning, giving her plenty of time to say no. He rubbed her asshole gently and after a few more moments he slid in.

Jasmina let out a high-pitched keening sound, like pleasure strung so tight. He was fucking her with his cock, rubbing her clit, and fingering her ass. Fuck, he hadn't imagined it would be so good with her—it was better than any imagination.

"It feels so good," she rasped, face buried in a pillow. "Fuck, yes. Please let me come, babe."

How could he say no when she called him that?

"Only because you asked so nicely," he told her, kissing down her spine.

This time, when he felt her orgasm clenching his dick, he let it take her. He pushed her over the edge with the stimulation he delivered and she cried out as she came, squeezing his cock so hard that the orgasm that was building at the base of his spine exploded into his cock in blinding light. He throbbed and spilled inside her as her contractions still rippled around him, still working her through it.

Breaths later, their climaxes dissipated and they disentangled, cleaned up, and entangled again—this time clothed and in his bed.

No more guest room stays.

He couldn't beat that grin off his face with a stick.

The next few weeks passed in that manner, banging, sleepovers, veiled reasons ala the contract to allow so much coupling activity, Graham being painfully aware of the ruse's end date, and the guilt that was eating at them both.

Sometimes they debated coming clean, but the conversations devolved into nothing and they remained locked in their contract as initially agreed. Graham felt bad lying to the boys. They were so close, it felt wrong. And he knew that Jasmina was struggling with not telling Illiana and Madeline, but she, of course, understood more than he did. This was her idea in the first place.

Early April, Graham got a phone call from Illiana's cousin, Leo—with whom he was becoming steadily closer, courtesy of Tuesdays at Blue's and wedding planning.

"Do you know about this path of cherry blossom trees down by DuPont Ave?" Leo asked once the niceties were out of the way.

"Yeah, there's like twenty of them that back onto the vineyard."

"I want to get some pictures of you and Mina in them so I can show the ideas to Emmett and Illiana for the wedding. You down?"

"Yeah, sure," Graham said, scribbling down some client notes he was getting ready to dictate. "When?"

"I'm free virtually whenever, so that depends on yours and Mina's schedules."

Graham wracked his brain for ideal times and told Leo their availability. Leo was humming in contemplation.

"Let's do Saturday afternoon," Leo decided. "It's supposed to be nice that day, and hopefully the afternoon light will best reflect the wedding day."

Graham wrote it down on a blue sticky note. "Done, you're booked in, man. I'll let Mina know."

"Awesome, you're the best! Talk later."

They hung up, and with plans in the works, he texted Jasmina and anxiously waited for Saturday to arrive, hoping against hope that maybe Leo would give them copies of the photos and just maybe it could help convince her that they could be real and they could be so good together.

Saturday afternoon arrived, bright and sunny. It was one of those near cloudless days uncommon in April, warm enough to forgo a jacket, but not quite enough to not have a spare in the car.

Graham pulled into Jasmina's apartment parking lot and found his fake girlfriend in a short, sage green dress with sheer short sleeves. She walked to his truck in a pair of Birkenstocks and a canvas tote slung over her shoulder, proclaiming something about reading.

It was very on brand for his girl.

"Afternoon," he greeted warmly, handing her the chai latte he'd picked up from Cupid Café on the way. "For you."

Appreciation shone in her eyes. "Thank you."

"No problem," he told her, driving out of the lot and heading to Cherry Blossom Lane—not its official name, but Graham thought it should be.

Jasmina sipped her chai latte delicately, the interior of his truck filled with the scent of her cinnamon-y drink and her peach perfume—a scent he'd never get sick of. He watched her lips close over the hole on the to-go cup, trying very hard not to picture her lips wrapped around his cock.

Graham cleared his throat and sipped his French Vanilla to keep the sexually intrusive thoughts at bay. He prayed his jeans were containing his betraying dick.

The windows were down half-way, tossing Jasmina's silky curls about, letting in cool air touched with the ocean. Their drive was only a few minutes longer before they pulled onto the shoulder of the road and found Leo standing against his black Jeep, camera around his neck.

He was engrossed in his phone, sandy blond waves covering his face. He looked up when their doors shut and he greeted them with a smile.

Graham imagined him looking like the sort of guy you'd meet in Australia, but Leo definitely didn't have an accent, and he had no idea if the man surfed. It wasn't totally out of the realm of possibility, though. Tofino—just a few hours north on the wild west coast—had a strong surfing scene, and Graham knew from his photography career that he *did* travel a lot. Therefore, it wasn't ludicrous to imagine.

"You two ready for this?" Leo asked cheerily.

"You bet," Jasmina responded.

The three of them began walking towards Cherry Blossom Lane, the twenty-plus trees sprawling thirty feet over them. Soft pink blooms erupted all over the canopy, dangling like a curtain of blush around them. The trees themselves were slender with gray-brown bark and smooth trunks. Between the trees wound a gravel pathway, and at the very end you could see the bright green stretch of the vineyard and clear blue sky.

It was a marvel of nature, made even prettier because it was all temporary.

Like his fake dating contract.

No.

He had to stop thinking like that. It was not conducive to his mental health, nor did it make Jasmina fall for him.

"So," Leo began, stopping their pace and framing the scene with his hands. "I want you two right here—" he indicated a spot by the trees. "And we'll work our way around the positions and see which one captures the light best. We'll also work on different poses to give them examples and maybe work on some movement and candids. Does that work for you two?"

Graham made a sound of confirmation.

Jasmina shrugged. "Yeah, works for me." She took another sip of her chai, set it on the ground near Leo, and walked over to where he'd pointed.

Graham did the same.

"All right, start by looking at each other, arms around each other's waists—yeah, just like that."

They were wrapped in each other's arms, the warmth of her skin like sunlight, the electricity between them like a livewire. She was gorgeous. All warm and golden: golden brown hair, golden green eyes, golden dark skin. She was a Midas-touched treasure made human. He couldn't believe he was the one who had the privilege of touching her like this.

He squeezed her in affection and grinned down at her.

The sounds of the camera shutter clicked around them.

"Okay, Mina look up and part your lips slightly—good. Graham, loosen your grip a bit, turn your face a bit to me…okay perfect. Now I want Graham's hand on Mina's jaw, your thumb resting gently on her chin, the rest of your fingers soft—that's it exactly. Mina, please place your hands on his chest."

On and on it went.

Hands in hair, eyes closed, eyes open, lips parted, lips smiling, turning into and against the light. They posed with Graham behind her, arms wrapping. They posed with Mina's back to the camera and Graham facing it, then switched. There was hand-holding, laughing, playing, and even kissing.

"I want this one to be lingering," Leo told them. "Keep everything light and longing. Barely touch your lips together, eyes nearly closed but not quite, hands soft, yet desperate—yes, perfect. You two are naturals."

It was thrilling. Graham was captivated by the idea that there would be photographic evidence of him and Jasmina— even if it was during their agreement. There was the hope, and maybe promise, that it would, or *could* be more.

After they finished with the cherry blossoms, they took to the beach and got some pictures—including some of them running barefoot on the sand—and then some in a provincial park that had golden light made warmer by the rich reddish brown of the cedar trees around them. They tried so many poses, so many ideas, went over lighting and a bunch of terms Graham didn't know or understand, but he saw how pretty the pictures were turning out.

Nearing the end of their trip around Rose Point, Leo suggested photos outside of Illiana's ballet studio—between the red brick, large glass windows, and the emotion attached to it, it would be perfect for them. Graham knew Illiana's studio was a huge facet of her mental health and he was so glad for his best friend's fiancée for having that outlet.

Outside the studio, the reflections from the windows proved difficult to photograph without capturing Leo as well, but being the professional he was, he figured it out. Leo urged them to try out a few different poses under strict direction and then they were finished.

"Are you two going to Emmett and Illiana's tonight?" Leo asked, smiling.

Graham had the wild association of Leo's likeness being a golden retriever. He was all floppy blond hair and smiles. It was nice, honestly, and he was grateful he'd come to Illiana's corner—fuck, she had so few others.

"Yeah, we're going around seven. You?" Jasmina asked, leaning close to him to look at the pictures he was scanning through on his camera.

A wild surge of jealousy flared through him.

Unwarranted.

Unwanted.

Un-fucking-believable.

He wasn't allowed to be jealous. He had no claim on her, even then, she wasn't doing anything wrong. She was just *talking* to the guy, for fuck's sake.

But it was the threat of it.

The idea of him losing her so completely to him.

And the worst part was, Leo seemed like a genuinely great guy.

"Yeah, I'm going to be there. Madeline was saying something about karaoke?"

Jasmina's brow lifted, an amused smile gracing her lips. "You and Mads talking much?"

It didn't take a genius to figure out that Jasmina was hoping her other best friend and Leo would hit it off. Graham was honestly hoping for the same thing—for virtuous and non-virtuous reasons. But Madeline was kind, and if Leo was what she wanted, he hoped it worked out. The question, though, was Leo interested?

"A bit, yeah," Leo said distractedly. "She's really cool. We've watched a bunch of movies together—she has such an eye for explaining filming techniques and cinematography. And noticing that sort of stuff has always distracted me when watching movies, so it's fun to share that with someone. You two are close, right?"

"Since high school."

"That's amazing. I haven't kept in touch with anyone from high school. But I've met so many people in the years since, though I don't really know them. I'm looking forward to staying in one place."

"Do you get to see your girlfriend much?" Jasmina inquired, not so subtly.

"Ah, we actually split up a couple weeks ago. It just wasn't working out and right now I don't think I'm ready for a relationship—I've got way too much to figure out first. I want to get settled before I consider anything."

Graham got the indication that while Leo admired Madeline, there didn't seem to be attraction there—at least yet. He wasn't ready to shut that door and call that book read yet.

"You and the guys have been friends since high school, right?" Leo asked, directing this question to Graham.

"High school and college. Nate, Kieran, and I went to Rose Point High, whereas Emmett and Chase went to high school in Victoria."

Then the three of them lapsed into easy conversation about school, life in Rose Point, small things, big things—it was easy, pleasant.

When they parted ways, Graham and Jasmina returned to his house, seeing the familiar 1816 at the end of his drive as he pulled in had him imagining what little touches and changes Jasmina would add to his house if they became an official couple.

Would she paint the front door blush pink like Illiana had done to Emmett's? Would she add a seasonal wreath to the door? Add her fantasy books to his floor-to-ceiling bookshelves? Toss her clothes all over his floor?

His cock began to grow hard and he shifted uncomfortably to contain it beneath his fly.

Inside the house, they freshened up. Jasmina changed into a black band shirt, which she tied with a knot and a dark, flowy, floral skirt paired with white ruffled socks and white sneakers. Graham added a flannel over his charcoal tee and styled his hair with a bit of pomade.

While he was at the kitchen counter preparing some sandwiches for them, Jasmina entered the room with a coy smirk.

"I don't trust that look," he said, putting the bacon on the lettuce. "You're up to something devious."

"You should learn to wait before passing judgment," she retorted.

Then she slid between him and the counter, dropped to her knees, and began undoing his zipper.

Oh god.

She wasn't about to—

Was she?

Jasmina took his cock out of his boxers and with a devilish smile, took the head of him in her mouth. The warm, wet heat was almost too much to bear, and he wrapped his fingers around the counter's edge, trying to hold onto his sanity while she tried to suck it out of him.

She took him in, hazel eyes seductive as she gazed up at him, her glossy lips moving over his shaft, taking him deeper and deeper. Her tongue laved the underside of him as her cheeks hollowed, and he swore he saw stars. It was only minutes, but he already felt his climax coiling at the base of his spine, his balls tightening in anticipation.

He knew he wasn't going to last long, so he leaned back and stared at the ceiling for—help? Salvation? She was already delivering him heaven in her mouth.

"Jasmina," he rasped. "I'm going to come."

She hummed a pleasant sound.

"If you don't want me to come in your mouth you need to start using your hand."

She just looked up at him with determination and began sucking in earnest.

He groaned as his orgasm blazed through him. His cock pulsed in her mouth as he spilled his release down her throat. Jasmina swallowed every drop, and when the waves ceased, she didn't stop.

His knees weakened.

Finally, she took mercy on him and his dick popped from her mouth. She wiped the excess saliva away with her thumb, watching him all the while, and it was the hottest thing she could do. As Jasmina stood, she shook out her hair and nodded toward the plates.

"Is one of those for me?"

CHAPTER TWENTY-ONE

Mina

Emmett and Illiana's house was full of light and laughter. There were a couple of people Mina didn't recognize, but many she did. Music played at an appropriate volume, pumping out a today's hit list, while the open concept kitchen, living, and dining room hummed with overlapping chatter. Snacks were spread over the kitchen island, and drinks were overflowing from the fridge, while blue coolers sat on the deck.

In front of the TV was a karaoke machine that Mina would go no where near unless she was very tipsy. She wondered what Graham was like at karaoke. Did he have a terrible singing voice? Would he refuse to even try? Was he a secret karaoke aficionado?

"Want something to drink?" Graham asked with a hand on the small of her back.

"Something non-alcoholic, please! Maybe sparkling water?"

"Coming right up!" Graham kissed her cheek and slipped into the kitchen.

Mina scanned for familiar faces and was surprised to see the owner of Cupid Café, Harlowe, in the corner of the dining room. She was reading something intently on her phone, a disconcerted look on her face. Concerned, she walked over to her.

"It's Harlowe, right?"

Harlowe looked up, her light hazel eyes surprised behind her cat eye glasses. Recognition lit her face. She wore a burgundy bodycon dress and Doc Martens with thigh high socks. A thick, plastic barrette shaped like a butterfly pulled her silver curtain bangs aside.

"Yeah! You're Mina?"

"Correct," she said, leaning against the wall. "You doing okay over here? You looked a little off."

"Oh." Harlowe blushed, the color spreading beneath the tattooed moth on her throat. "Um…kinda. This is my first time out since my separation, and I'm just checking in with my babysitter."

"Oh, you have a little one?" Mina inquired.

"I do," Harlowe said with a soft, almost private smile. "She just turned two."

The other girl scrolled on her phone and flipped it to show Mina. On the screen a little girl appeared with the same light hazel eyes as her mother, and fine, dark brown curls. She was grinning with only five teeth in her mouth, tongue pressed between them. She was dressed in a lavender sleeper with a big white bow on her head.

"Oh, she's precious," Mina cooed, her ovaries tingling. "What's her name?"

She had to remind herself that while this baby was very cute, she was not ready for one of her own yet. She still had a whole lot of shit to figure out first.

"Odette," Harlowe revealed, swiping to show Mina more pictures of this adorable, rosy-cheeked tot. "She's my everything."

"What is she like?"

"Sensitive. Sassy. Particular. It's still early, but she's such a little empath. She can pick up on emotional cues better than a fully regulated adult."

"She sounds incredible."

"She is."

The two girls lapsed into other conversations, Harlowe revealing that she and Ana had been chatting more outside of wedding planning and it became evident that they had a lot in common—including reading books. They'd been swapping titles and Mina added a few new ones to Harlowe's TBR while Mina gained an unfamiliar one herself.

"You know," Mina said, tapping her lip. "If Ana hasn't mentioned it, you should talk to Delilah. She should be around here somewhere, but she's an author and writes spicy romance books."

"No way. You guys are friends with an author?" Harlowe's eyes were round with shock.

"Yeah, it's a whole long and complicated story, but Del has become one of our really good friends since last summer."

Just then, Graham returned to Mina's side. Mina made quick introductions between Harlowe and Graham, then gratefully accepted the can he handed her. Peach sparkling water.

"Thank you, babe."

"You're so welcome, baby," Graham replied, kissing her forehead.

"I can't believe you two ever hated each other," a voice said behind them.

Mina turned and found Mads grinning from ear to ear, a blended margarita in her hand, her matching heart necklace which was twin to Mina's around her neck. They didn't wear them every day, but they did wear them often as a staple piece in their wardrobe.

Madeline was dressed in a light, long-sleeved shirt with lace edging the neckline and a pair of straight leg jeans where periwinkle painted nails peeked from the hems. Her auburn hair was left down, save for two pieces from the sides pinned to the back.

"Honestly," Madeline continued. "You two are like freakin' soulmates."

Panic thundered through Mina. Her thoughts became a vignette, hazed by the fear as the prospect pushed down on her. It bumped a staccato rhythm, injecting her blood with alternate shots of fire and ice. Her head felt floaty and a cold sweat beaded on her brow.

Soulmates?

She knew Graham believed in such things, but did she?

She didn't know.

She'd read about them in books—loved them in books, in fact; fated mates was her favorite trope—but the idea they existed in actuality? Ludicrous.

"They hated each other?" Harlowe asked in disbelief.

"Oh, yeah," Madeline confirmed. "Their animosity was legendary. Everyone knew they disliked each other within seconds of meeting them. But I guess one day that hateful passion turned into something else—" Mads elbowed her. "Scorching sexual tension, perhaps? Am I right, Jas?"

"Jas?" Harlowe asked, confused.

"Jasmina. That's my full name, but I go by Mina. Back in high school I went by Jas. No one calls me Jasmina."

"No one but me," Graham interrupted, pulling her tighter to his side.

"That's right, no one but you."

"Oh, that's so romantic. Do you have anything cutesy you call him?"

"She did once drunkenly call me Teddy Graham. And once said I reminded her of a s'more—cause of Graham Cracker."

"That was told to you in confidence!" Mina complained, gently swatting his arm and rolling her eyes.

Feeback from the microphone shrieked through the house.

"Sorry! Sorry!" Illiana called from in front of the machine dressed in a sparkly pink dress. "Does anyone want to go first for karaoke?"

Mina was not about to volunteer for that shit show.

"I'll do it!" Harlowe announced, raising a hand.

In front of the karaoke machine, Harlowe's fingers white from clenching, her full lips parted, she selected a song quickly from the roster and settled in.

Within seconds, *I Want It That Way* by the Backstreet Boys began playing—minus the vocals. Harlowe closed her eyes and counted the beats. And then she began.

And she could sing.

Her voice was like an angel.

Seraphic.

Cherubic.

It was so magical, she couldn't believe it was happening before her eyes, let alone at karaoke during a house party. Singing Backstreet Boys. Harlowe managed all the emotion without it being overdone or like a pick-me. She just seemed like she was genuinely having a good time—being fun, playful, goofy.

Once Harlowe was done, Chase went next with Carly Rae Jepson's *Call Me Maybe*—which was hilarious and humorously provocative. After Chase, Madeline and Leo sang a duet of *Just Give Me a Reason* by P!nk and Nate Ruess.

Graham squeezed her side.

"Do you want to do a duet next?" he asked.

"Are you crazy or just drunk?"

"I'm still in the middle of my first drink," Graham defended. "I mean it, though. Try new things, all that jazz."

"What's your singing like?"

"Like a Disney Prince. You?"

"Let's not talk about it, just try to drown me out."

Once Mads and Leo wrapped up, it was their turn and Illiana handed them the mics, her straight white teeth on display in a beaming smile.

"I love you, but try not to pierce our eardrums," Ana whispered conspiratorially.

"Only if you promise not to heckle me like a banshee."

Illiana laughed hysterically and walked away, shaking her head, her curtain of long, golden waves swinging.

Mina let Graham select the song and she nearly lost her shit laughing.

"All right then," she said as the opening notes of David Bowie's and Queen's *Under Pressure* began.

Her favorite song.

And he knew.

And he'd remembered.

Graham's voice was unfairly charming and the entire time he was grinning, animated, and enthusiastic. And the worst part was, he did have a nice voice—one he enjoyed using to sing even the parts that weren't lyrics.

When it was Mina's turn she tried not to cringe at her own voice, but luckily, eagerness won out and she sang with horrendous gusto.

They sang face to face, playfully wiggling as a form of dancing—even with Graham messing up a few lyrics, but Mina nailed them like the faithful 80s fan she was.

They were flushed with energy when the song ended and Mina found herself still staring at Graham, still grinning, and her heart beating fast.

Something clearer struck her through.

She wasn't just happy to see him.

She wasn't just having fun.

She was falling in love.

"Girl," Mads said, bumping into her and knocking her out of her reverie. "You have it so bad for that boy."

She had to face the facts.

She did.

The party passed in a haze after that, the realization having knocked her off balance, unsettled her to her core.

She was in love with Graham Starling.

As much as the inner turmoil had her in shambles, she kept it together, unbeknownst to anyone there. Anyone aside from Graham—because he was *Graham*. He knew these things—he saw these things.

And because he knew her so damn well.

Conversation ebbed in and out and she only had the most basic comprehensions of them—especially something about how Illiana had befriended Harlowe, who was now invited to the bachelorette party and the wedding as a guest. There was also a point where Illiana was thanking her for coming wedding dress and bridesmaid shopping with her last week—where they'd successfully found all the dresses. Mina nodded appropriately and enthusiastically, selling her mood like she'd been selling the charade of her and Graham dating.

And she did a damn good job, because those fake feelings turned real, real fast.

When Graham suggested they call it a night, Mina was all too eager to accept and head back to his house. There were things she wanted to say, but first, and more importantly, there were things she wanted to do with that man. Dirty things. Filthy things.

She hoped it conveyed what she meant, because despite her realizing this was real for her, she didn't know if he felt the same way, and she wasn't willing to risk Emmett and Illiana's wedding just because. This whole thing was for them to begin with. Talks could happen the day after they married. It was only a few more weeks.

The car ride home was pleasant. The heat filled the cab and made her feel languid and dreamy, despite the fact that she hadn't consumed any alcohol during the night. She'd stuck to sparkling water, courtesy of Graham, and—

Hold on.

Had she mentally referred to Graham's house as home?

Shock struck her as she realized she most certainly had.

Oh, she was so fucked.

In the driveway, the numbers 1816 reflected back at them, the golden digits shining in the headlights. When Graham opened her door, she attacked him.

Her kisses were fierce, hungry, devouring, confirming. By kissing him, she was affirming that what she felt for him was real. Their tongues danced and fought as they stumbled all the way up the stairs and into the front door. Graham fumbled with the lock and when the door gave way, they went with it.

Tumbling to the floor, Mina tore off his shirt.

"Fuck, Jasmina," he groaned, palming her ass. "What has gotten into you?"

"I'm horny," she whined, nibbling on his lips.

"I'm gathering that," he retorted sarcastically.

"Then do something about it."

Graham did.

He picked her up, closed and locked the door, kissed her breathlessly against it, then crashed up the stairs together in that sexy way they did in the movies that Mina had never thought was feasible.

News flash: it was very much feasible.

Mina and Graham tripped into bed together, leaving a trail of clothes strewn in their wake. By the time they fell atop the blankets, they were naked.

"Do you remember what I said before about liking anal but not doing it as much because guys felt like it was a goal?" she whispered between kisses.

"I recall this," Graham answered softly, mouthing her collarbone. "Are you asking me something, baby?"

Mina's nails dug into the firm curve of his backside. "I want you to fuck me in the ass tonight."

Graham's cock stirred at her words and she got a thrill right through her pussy about it.

"If that's what you want," he told her, mouth going to her breasts. "Then I'm going to do pre-care on you."

"What are you—? Oh!" she gasped as Graham's lips closed over her nipple and his fingers found her clit.

He began working her up in the way he'd learned her body, playing a tune strummed just for her. Graham's talented fingertips danced along her pussy, his tongue singing silent songs against her hardened nipples.

Mina's hands were coasting all over him—digging into the strong muscles of his back, diving into his hair, scrabbling at his arms.

She couldn't get enough.

Just then, his face slipped from her breasts and buried between her legs. Graham's first lick against the seam of her had her toes curling. Bliss began winding through her as he created the perfect tempo.

When he slipped a finger inside her core while still eating her out, Mina surged off the bed. Her hips began an involuntary undulation, rolling with the movements. Desperate for him.

Her climax was building. She felt the throbs of it growing as he curled his finger inside her and licked and sucked. His other hand was busying itself pinching and tweaking her nipples, rolling the tight buds between his index and forefinger. All the stimulation was coming together in an orchestra of pleasure, and this time when she cried out that she was close, Graham let her come.

The orgasm shattered through her in blinding light and Graham licked and fingered her through it. As the waves bathed her in angelic vibrance, she panted, buoyed by the bliss.

When she came to after the mind-numbing awe, she found Graham trailing his fingers on her inner thigh, spreading the wetness from her pussy on her skin.

"You're so wet, baby," he told her. "That's good. You did so good."

Her pussy clenched at his praise.

"I think you're close to ready, aren't you?"

She nodded enthusiastically.

Graham took her by the waist and maneuvered her onto her belly. Kissing both globes of her ass, he lifted her rear into the air and rubbed her cheeks.

"You still want this, Jasmina?"

"I do."

"Good."

Mina heard the sound of the nightstand drawer opening and the crack of a bottle. Cold lube dripped down her ass and she shivered as she heard Graham covering his cock with it as well.

"I think your pussy has been a little neglected tonight," Graham told her, rubbing the head of his cock against her slit. "I think we should fix that first."

Graham slid into her pussy in one smooth, long, thrust. She opened eagerly for him, her core stretching perfectly to take him. He groaned as he thrust into her, in and out. Slow and torturous. But when he pulled out, she ached for him.

"Ready, baby?"

"I'm ready. Just start slow."

"Of course," he said, kissing the back of her neck. "I won't do anything you aren't okay with."

And then he was rubbing the head of his dick on her tight hole. More lube was added and then he pushed. The head of him breached her with a slight sting and burn, but the discomfort passed quickly as his fingers went to her front and toyed with her clit. He paused, letting her adjust, and when she pushed back against him, he inched in deeper, still rubbing small circles on that bundle of nerves.

It was so full, so tight. The process was slow to begin, but he worked himself in, and when he was fully seated within her, he waited for her go ahead.

She gave it.

Slowly, he pumped in and out once and the pressure was so intense, she cried out.

"Oh, fuck. Oh, fuck. Why does it feel so good?" she moaned.

Graham hooked two fingers into her pussy as he fucked her ass, rubbing her clit with the heel of his hand. He was slamming into her and she was loving it, the pleasure crackling through her so intensely that tears sprung to her eyes. She was speaking gibberish while he fucked, an orgasm building low and deep in her belly.

"Your ass is perfect, Jasmina. You take me so well," Graham praised her. "You're doing so good, baby girl."

Mina let out a keening sound mixed with various expletives, most of them being 'fuck'.

It was then the climax tore through her, soaking Graham's hand, clenching around him as she shattered and nearly screamed. Her words were breathless and unintelligible. She felt as if she were being torn apart at the seams in the best way.

Graham came right after, bowing over her, spilling cum inside her. She felt each throb of his cock in her tight channel, triggering aftershocks of pleasure within her.

Both spent, Graham withdrew from her carefully, and rather than letting her waddle, he carried her to the shower. They cleaned off in the mint-tiled room, the hot water glorious against her skin. Graham was careful not to wet her hair, and controlled the spray so she could rinse the lube and aftermath of lovemaking from her body.

Once they were both clean, Graham noticed a few globs of lube of the top blanket and swapped it out for a new one. Still naked, they crawled into the bed together, cuddling. Mina's head was cradled in the crook of his shoulder where his scent was most potent—timber, magnolia, and spice—and let her fingers dance over his tattoos.

"What kind of flowers are these?" she asked.

He hesitated a moment, but then spoke. "They're jasmine flowers."

"Do you just like them?" she asked, hope hammering her heart.

"Something like that."

Before she could press further, Graham's phone went off on the nightstand. The fine hairs along Mina's body rose. Who was calling at this hour? And, if they were calling right now, something was going on, right?

The call displayed the name of his sister, Willow. He picked up and put the phone to his ear immediately.

"Will?" he asked, concern etched across his face,

Mina couldn't hear what was said on the other line, but she heard Willow's voice, and it was distraught, tears choking the clarity of the syllables. But whatever she was saying, Graham was understanding it because his shoulders slumped, and all the air seemed to have slipped from his body.

"When?" he asked, voice lifeless.

Mina's hackles went up in a protective manner.

"Okay, we'll figure it out tomorrow morning." A pause. "Yes, I will." Pause. "Okay, love you, too."

Graham hung up and looked down at his phone, seemingly staring through it. Mina held her breath, not willing to break the fragile air they held. Her hand was on him silently, her body still pressed to his. She was there for him, but not pushing. Slowly, he turned to face her, and his blue eyes were decimated.

She broke.

"Oh, love," she said softly, tears in her eyes, her hands going to his cheeks.

"My grandpa just died," he whispered.

And then his crystalline eyes overflowed with tears, streaking down his face as sobs wracked his spine.

CHAPTER TWENTY-TWO
Graham

Graham cried against Jasmina's chest, his body shaking with grief.

His grandfather, who'd taught him how to fish, who'd imparted on him the wisdom of keen observation, and always snuck him chocolates, was gone.

As a child, his grandpa had been bigger than life. Ready with a rumbly laugh and an encouraging hand. As he'd gotten older, he'd drifted more. With Grandpa living in the interior and Graham busy with life, school and work and such, it had been hard to see him much outside of holidays.

But as Graham had gotten older, so did grandpa.

And eventually age-related illness caught up to him and a heart attack had struck him down.

Willow's words echoed in his head, the sounds of her choked sobbing hitching on the line. She'd hiccupped her way through the news and told him that the family was going to the mainland to help with Grandma in lieu of Easter weekend.

Grandma was now a widow.

Grandma and Grandpa had been married for fifty-eight years.

Since they were eighteen.

And now she was alone.

Graham rubbed a hand over his chest as if he could scrub away the crack that had formed there. The pain was a dull throb, pulsing with loss.

Grandma and Grandpa Starling were one of the reasons why he believed in soulmates. He wanted to show them Jasmina, so they could see that he'd finally found the other half of his heart—his person.

But Grandpa was gone.

Graham sobbed while Jasmina brushed his hair with her hand, uttering sweet nothings and comforts while he broke and cracked. Her lips moved over his forehead, alternating kisses and words.

How had they gone from fucking, to this?

To having fun, to requiring emotional stability?

It was fucked.

It wasn't fair.

It was cruel.

The tears burned his cheeks and he wiped them away, sniffling.

"I'm so sorry, Jasmina."

"Don't apologize to me. Not for this," she told him. "I'm here for you."

He nodded and silently broke again.

It was some time later when he finally got the energy to speak. He explained everything Willow had said on the phone, including Easter weekend.

"Do you want me to come with you?" she asked.

"What?"

"My family doesn't really do Easter. Not right now at least, maybe if I had kids, but there won't be any egg hunts or bunny for us. I can be there for you."

"I can't ask that of you."

"Sure, you can," she argued back.

"What about work?"

"I can book off extra days. I get Good Friday and Easter Monday off. I'm not worried. Say the word and I'll be there."

Graham allowed himself the thought of selfishness. Imagining her being by his side, a steady emotional support. It was appealing, no doubt, but he felt like that could be crossing a line in their contract.

He tried to remember if there were any rule or clause indicated for the case of bereavement or traveling to see family. He didn't think there was, ergo, it was not breaking any rules.

He let selfishness win and accepted.

That night, Graham cried himself to sleep in Jasmina's arms, warm and close with the woman he loved.

Sunlight filtered in the window and across the empty bed. Jasmina was nowhere to be found, but when he went to the kitchen, a hot pot of coffee was ready for him. He poured himself a cup and then sat at the island. There, he found a note.

Just went for a run, be back soon. Have some coffee and water—crying dehydrates you.

Jasmina

P.S. Tylenol doesn't hurt, either.

Graham grinned while he readied his coffee and drank some water. That one spot of brightness—Jasmina's consideration—was the only thing that kept him from fully becoming an automaton. The movements of transferring milk and two spoons of sugar were mechanical, just as mechanical as he felt without the one touch of her.

He couldn't believe Grandpa was gone.

During the night his sisters had texted in their group chat, planning for the weekend. More details related to Grandpa's health were included, but there were other things too.

Busying himself making toast, he just finished spreading the peanut butter and jam when Jasmina came in, wearing a magenta zip up and black spandex leggings. She pulled off her headphones, breath huffing out of her.

"How're you feeling this morning?" she asked.

He shrugged. "Kinda to be expected."

"That's not surprising. Can I do anything to help?"

"The coffee is plenty, but if it's not too much to ask, maybe you could spend the day with me?"

Jasmina approached him slowly and then slowly ran her hands through his hair.

"Of course." Then she gave him a peck on the lips and made for the hallway. "I'm going to have a shower first. Want to do a movie day and order food?"

"That sounds great."

Once Jasmina disappeared into the shower, he ate, put on a load of laundry, folded what was in the dryer, and did a quick vacuum of the downstairs common areas. He tried his hardest to keep himself busy. In her absence, the grief came crushing down. She was the only balm to his pain, and he wasn't ready to admit it in this way, but he needed her.

Willow would probably call him once she woke up, and knowing his sister, he knew she wouldn't appreciate anything disrupting her rest, even under these circumstances. But with his phone in hand, he decided to let the boys know. He made it clear he didn't want to talk about it, but that he wasn't ignoring them. It was that the grief was too sharp, but Jasmina was with him.

A flood of texts came in once he sent it, all some variation of I'm sorry and other condolences. There were offers of company, shoulders to cry on, going out for a beer, whatever he needed they were there. He felt extremely grateful that he had these guys in his life.

Jasmina's shower ended and she came out wearing a pair of boxer shorts and one of his t-shirts, padding barefoot over to his couch. She sat down and pulled her feet up, digging them under a throw blanket.

"What's the first movie?" she asked. "Want to start with our favorites?"

Graham didn't feel keen on watching a movie where a beloved grandfather died, no matter how much he loved that film.

"Can we watch yours? I don't think I've ever seen Stardust."

"It's incredible," Jasmina cooed, stealing the remote from the table and queueing it up. "You're in for a treat."

They cuddled up on the couch and tuned in to her favorite movie, her head cradled on his chest, her scent of peach a comforting presence.

Part-way through, Willow called and they finalized the plans for leaving Thursday morning and staying until Monday. Both his parents had been in contact with Grandma and luckily, she wasn't alone as his aunt and uncle lived nearby.

The rest of the day passed in a fugue, and he let Jasmina take the reins. She guided him through his day as the tenderness in his heart wavered with excruciating pain and a dull ache. She was soft and patient with him, catering to his needs, offering soft words. It was so unlike their typical dynamic, but it was a nice change.

Sometime during their movie marathon, he'd fallen asleep, drained by the sheer toll of emotional pain. He napped on and off throughout the day, and this sort of behavior continued for the rest of the week. When Thursday morning blared its alarm, Graham and Jasmina climbed out of bed, dressed, and then hit the road. They'd packed the night before, so that they could optimize as much time as possible. The hit the first coffee shop they could find on the way to the ferry for some much-needed caffeine to begin the long journey.

Drinking the coffee, they waited to be let onto the ferry. They'd reserved their tickets during their movie day so they didn't need to worry about the crowds traveling for Easter—especially since this trip was not meant to be overly enjoyable.

Jasmina was sitting on the tailgate of his truck, knees tucked up as she stared at the early morning light over the ocean. It was that soft and downy dawn that spoke of blue baby blankets and quiet words. Spring was fully in bloom on the island now.

"Are you sure you want to come with me?" Graham asked.

Jasmina turned her gaze to him, her curls gently tossing in the breeze, thin golden lines tracing her from the backlit sky.

"I wouldn't have offered if I didn't want to."

He nodded, accepting this. He leaned against the tailgate beside her and she ran her fingers through his hair, gently scraping those pearl painted ovals over his scalp. His eyes shuttered as he enjoyed the affection, cozying up to her further.

Just then, the sound of a car door closing met their ears. Graham looked up and found his entire family standing there, watching them.

His mother and father were walking towards them, arms around each other's waists. His father, Pete, was a slowly aging man with dark brown hair like his; and the same oval face as all his sisters. All of Pete's daughters had also inherited his green eyes, whereas Graham had Samantha's blue. And all of her features. Looking at his mother was like looking in a mirror.

Graham straightened as they made their way over, taking Jasmina's hand. His mom and dad did not miss the touch and despite the grief in their eyes, a flash of warmth entered them.

"Jasmina," his mother said, "It's so nice to officially meet you."

"You too," Jasmina said, slipping off the tailgate and embracing his mom. "I wish it were under happier circumstances, though." She pulled away after a quick squeeze. "And it's just Mina."

"Oh, right, I did know that," his mom said with a wink, nudging her husband.

His dad introduced himself to Jasmina and then there was another car door slamming, and then another, and then the three Starling sisters poured out.

The three of them joined their little group and made their introductions, all of them dressed for comfort during the long commute in yoga pants, sweatpants, and pullovers, faces free of makeup. His sisters, too, made Jasmina's acquaintance, and Sabrina sidled up to him and nudged him.

"Nice thinking being all touchy-romantic with her before we came along. It really sells it," Sabrina commended.

Guilt chewed at him. He knew he was lying, but at this point he didn't know who he was lying to and exactly what about. Certain stories were no longer true, while other ones that started as artifice were now reality.

"Yeah, I thought so, too," he said distractedly.

When Graham looked over at Jasmina, surrounded by his family, all he wanted was for her to really be part of them. To go for family dinners, holidays, game nights, and to share the future they could grow together.

Jasmina looked back at him and smiled, and even though everything was not okay, it felt all right in the world.

They'd eaten and slept some on the ferry, grabbed coffee and chai again when they got on the mainland, and began the long drive to the interior, and the small town of Silverwood Pines. Graham was more than comfortable doing all the driving, but Jasmina had offered to trade off if he needed it. Behind them was the rest of the Starling family, their SUV fully loaded.

"Did Evan and Drew not want to come?" Jasmina asked an hour into their mainland drive.

"I suppose not," he replied.

Willow and Sabrina hadn't said anything about their partners not making it, and he didn't know if they didn't want to or they didn't ask. He would say that the relationships were newer, however, the same could be said of his and Jasmina's, and she was right here.

The 80s music was playing softly on the radio when the phone call came through. Graham used hands-free to answer.

"Bad news," Sabrina began. "The inn we all booked had a water leak overnight and there's no available rentals within a ninety-minute drive because of Easter weekend."

"Well, fuck."

"I know," Sabrina said with a sigh. "So, that means we have to stay at the farmhouse."

The farmhouse that Grandma and Grandpa Starling had lived in was a large, rustic structure, lovingly maintained by his aunt and uncle, where his grandparents hadn't been able to. The whole reason they'd booked the inn though, was to not impose during Grandma's time of grief. The farmhouse had plenty of room for them—if there was sharing involved—but that was besides the point.

"Willow is already talking to Grams, she's over the moon that we're coming to stay at the farmhouse instead. Says the house is too quiet."

Guilt and fear panged at him. He couldn't imagine how his grandma was feeling. He couldn't imagine how it would feel to lose Jasmina like that. The thought was nearly a physical pain.

"Okay, well that settles it."

Graham could hear someone conversing in the background on the other line, and Sabrina was relaying all the communication. Apparently, the disaster was thwarted immediately and new plans had been set. They were now all driving to the farmhouse.

It was just before dark when they pulled into Silverwood Pines. The farmhouse was just on the fringes of it, a loose sprawl into fields and pastures that backed onto quaint streets and buildings that had hung onto a vintage western feel. They drove through the center of town where their pride and joy was a brightly lit, red painted cinema with classic black letters proclaiming the showings against a white backdrop. Velvet ropes lined the front of it, and stars, like a memento to the Hollywood Walk of Fame lined up on the pavement.

Fatigue drew on him as they drove past the grocery store, a bakery, two pubs, a boutique, and a diner. He knew there was only another ten minutes left until the house but he was so damned tired.

"Pull over," Jasmina commanded.

He was too tired to argue and acquiesced.

They swapped spots, Jasmina adjusted the seat and mirrors, and they were off again. Graham fell asleep the second he rested his head against the side panel.

When he awoke, they were parking on the long gravel drive of his grandparent's farmhouse, his parents and sisters parked in front of them.

Steeling himself, he got out with the aid of his fake girlfriend, and then went inside.

The house was full of aunts, uncles, and cousins, chatter filling the space, not lending any idea of quiet. People milled about, food was spread out, and drinks were in hand.

And there, on a purple, highbacked living chair, was Grandma Starling.

Her long silver hair was tied up in a neat bun and her blue eyes, while tired and filled with pain, still sparkled. Deep lines carved into her face now, etching her mouth in a downward turn, but that didn't stop her from applying hot pink lipstick to her lips. She wore a pair of slacks and one of grandpa's cable-knit sweaters.

The sight had Graham's heart aching.

Was this the future he was looking forward to?

Wearing the clothes of his lost spouse just to be closer one last time? Utterly alone in a house full of people?

Anxiety crawled up his throat, and he felt like he'd choke on it.

Jasmina's nails dug into his arm.

"Graham, are you all right?" she inquired softly.

"I think I'm having a panic attack," he replied under his breath.

"Okay, breathe. Stay with me."

Jasmina pulled him over to one of his sisters—he wasn't sure which one, Willow or Piper?—and they held a low conversation while he focused on his breathing and not falling apart. But how could he not fall apart when life could upend itself so completely?

Words passed between the two women and then there was a lull. Jasmina's hand was in his, locked around his arm.

"I'm here, love," she whispered. "Listen to my voice. Breathe in through your nose and slowly out your mouth."

The sister who'd been conversing with Jasmina returned and more words were exchanged. He didn't hear them; all he heard was ringing. But he could feel Jasmina and he hung onto that knowledge.

When Jasmina nodded, she began tugging him away from the crowd and up the stairs. She guided him along the wooden steps, careful on the worn runner that ascended with them. The world tilted on its axis but the one constant was her.

She led him into a room—it was tiny, little more than a cell—and prodded him to the bed. He sat, and she sat with him, rubbing his arms.

"Can you tell me what happened?" Jasmina asked.

Graham shook his head.

"Because you're not ready or don't want to?"

"Not ready," he managed, grabbing her hand.

They sat in silence a bit longer before he regained breath control. When he finally felt ready, he squeezed her fingers.

"I was afraid of losing you."

"I'm right here," she told him.

"Not like that. Of how Grams is right now. Wearing Grandpa's sweater because she can't feel him. The idea terrified me. I've grown quite…attached to you," he confessed and held his breath.

Jasmina leaned into him. "Though I'm loathe to admit it, I've become attached to you too. And I'm not going anywhere."

"Not until our agreement is finished."

Jasmina flinched. "Yeah," she deadpanned. "Not until then. But in the meantime, let's not think about that."

Those words ended up hanging over them the entire weekend, and what he'd expected to be reconnecting with family, coming together for Grams, and not being alone, was not the case.

The entire weekend in Silverwood Pines was a blur of comforting Grams—with her rejection of the attempts, saying Grandpa would've wanted her to be happy around family, so she would be—and helping around the house—chores, cooking, repairs, etcetera.

The nights were spent sharing a twin bed with Jasmina, and while the mattress was surprisingly comfortable, it was a very tight fit, and the walls were very thin. He and Jasmina shared a room and a bed, while Sabrina and Piper shared the room over, and his parents the one across the hall. Willow was staying at their aunt and uncle's five minutes down the road on their pullout couch.

On Sunday, Graham found himself walking the property alone with his thoughts while Jasmina bonded with his family. There was an odd air between them after his panic attack, but he couldn't pinpoint it. It was full of words unsaid and untruths, but he didn't know where the threads of them began.

Beneath an oak tree, he paused in the shade, watching the gold dappled light turn the green leaves into petals of peridot. It was there that Sabrina found him.

She leaned against the bark of the tree and stared at him.

"What?" he asked.

Her emerald eyes narrowed. "You said what was between you and Mina was fake."

"It is."

"It sure as fuck isn't. I see the way you look at each other."

"Like what?" he pressed.

"Holy fuck, are you blind? The second either of you enter a room you gravitate to each other and at the very least you look at each other. You laugh, and you make sure she's laughing too. You're like…connected."

"That doesn't mean anything."

"Oh yeah?" she countered, popping a hand on her hip. "And what about how you look at her like she hung the moon and is the reason the sun rises every day?"

Graham grumbled.

"All right," she began, shifting uncomfortably, and putting a hand up. "I don't want details, just a yes or no. Have you two had sex?"

"Yes."

A breath left Sabrina's lungs. "More than once?"

"Yes."

"Oh, my god. You're in love! You're practically dating for real!"

"Sex and love are not synonymous," he argued.

"Yeah, well in this case, it is."

"It's not that simple."

"Sure, it is."

"No, it's not." He explained the reasons he had, about not wanting to ruin the plan right before the wedding, about not having the whole contract blow up in his face before it was due. "My feelings for her are real, but hers for me aren't."

"I beg to differ," Sabrina scoffed, flipping her pastel pink, bubble-gum hair.

"Well, I don't. And I'm not willing to risk it."

"Fine! Suffer in silence. But don't be mad when the truth comes out and I say, '*I told you so.*'"

And with that, Sabrina left him alone under the oak with his thoughts, retreating back to the farmhouse without once turning around.

It was a while before he made his way back and when he did, he ran into his grandma—alone, as she had been lately—taking a breather on the back deck, leaning over the graying railing. He hadn't actually had any time with her one-on-one during this trip, and it seemed this was his chance.

"Grams?" he asked tentatively.

Grams turned with a small smile. "Yes?"

"How are you doing it? How are you carrying on like…like you don't want to fall apart every moment?"

Her eyes dimmed a little, pain etching the wrinkles in her face.

Yesterday was Grandpa's celebration of life. He hadn't wanted a funeral, and he hadn't wanted to be on display. He was cremated and there was a small party where people told the crowd their favorite memories of him, played his favorite music, and shared his favorite food. For a moment, it had felt like he was really there.

"I do, my boy," she admitted, pulling Graham back to the present. "I wish I were with my Arthur every day. But I see the life we made together in this home, and through the people in it right now. Every single one of you carries a piece of our life and our love within them—even your Mina, especially your Mina. Knowing all that, he's not really gone—not completely."

Tears pricked his eyes. "What did you mean about my Mina?"

Her name softened something in grams. "I talked to her earlier. She told me about what you said to her—that your grandfather and I made you believe in soulmates." Her hand reached for his. "If I believed in them, then you and Mina have made *me* believe."

A single tear slipped down his cheek. "I miss him."

"I miss him, too," she confessed, voice cracking.

He turned away to hide his tears and found himself peering into the window of the farmhouse. There he saw where Jasmina was bonding with his family, chatting animatedly with Piper, and then turning to laugh at something his dad said.

In that moment, he felt, not whole, but healing, and she was the reason for it.

CHAPTER TWENTY-THREE
Mina

It had been a couple of weeks since their trip to Silverwood Pines and they were back at Graham's house. There had been a notable lack of discussion about the surrounding facts of the trip, namely that fact that a fake girlfriend didn't typically join the family for an out-of-town celebration of life. But she had, and what was odder still was that neither of Willow's nor Sabrina's partners had joined—despite being real.

Even so, she felt it was deeper than that. There was a line they'd crossed with this trip. In being there for Graham and his grief. It was a different line than the sex, but it was no less messy and tangled.

Speaking of tangled…

Graham's legs were twined with hers while they lounged on his bed in nothing but underwear and t-shirts, trying vainly to write their Best Man and Maid of Honor speeches.

"This makes it sound too much about you," Graham said, holding her notes and indicating a line with the end of his pen. "Try rewording it."

They'd been passing their notes and drafts back and forth to get an idea if they were on track—if it was the right one or needed to be scrapped.

She took the pages back and scanned them. "Ugh, but if I adjust that part then I need to remove this part. And if I do that then the flow is just—ugh, no."

Mina tore the sheet out of the notebook, crumpled it, and tossed it aside. The bed and floor were strewn with various discarded page, the room was littered with an air of frustration.

"I'm not cut out for this," Mina despaired. "Maybe I should ask Delilah for help—she's an author and good with words."

"She's also Emmett's ex."

"Oh, good point." She flopped back and covered her eyes with a crooked arm. "I give up. Ana's getting a 'thank you for choosing me to be your Maid of Honor, you look beautiful, I love you, now let's eat cake.' Or something like that."

"Eloquent," Graham said, setting his papers aside on the night stand and then moved over her. "I think you need some stress release, baby."

He plucked at the waistband of her panties and dipped his fingers below them. She parted her thighs in response, eager for more, as he teased the edges of her sex.

Graham did just that—teasing. He traced the edges of her pussy, but not sinking inside her, and deliberately avoided her throbbing clit. He just skimmed over her sensitized nerves. Taunting.

"This is doing the opposite of stress release," she pouted as her hands dug into his back, urging him closer.

"I'm getting there, baby," he murmured, kissing her neck.

Graham nipped the juncture between her neck and shoulder, sucking her flushed skin between his lips as he carved a path down to her breasts. He pushed down the very loose collar of her shirt for ease of access, his mouth following the trail as his fingers simultaneously slid lower. Her breast popped out of her shirt and his mouth closed on her taut nipple as his fingertip rubbed circles on her clit.

Mina moaned. "That's right, just like that."

"I know, baby. I know," Graham coaxed. "Give me more."

"You want me to give you more, you're going to have to work for it," she taunted back, hips undulating.

"Another game, Jasmina?"

"Mmhmm. This one is called *Let's See How Fast We Can Make Mina Come.*"

"Well, that sounds fun, but I like delayed gratification."

"I think you're saying no because you can't do it."

As she knew he would, he rose to the challenge. He could never resist her in that, their history had always been games and arguments, and fights and retorts.

Graham dove between her legs, spreading her wide and devouring her. He lashed her with feverish licks, flicking her clit with his tongue, and alternating with suction.

"You taste so good," he murmured against her, plunging a finger inside and curling as he went back to feasting.

Graham's other hand went to her backside and palmed her ass, lifting her pussy up to his mouth to absolutely ruin her. Her orgasm coiled low and tight, and she thrusted her hips against his mouth, riding his face. His finger notched her up, her climax clicking like a gear, each of his ministrations tugging her closer to the edge.

"You're so close, baby. I can taste it. Come for me, Jasmina."

"I know," she wailed in pleasure.

"Come," he commanded.

She did. She shattered on his tongue, coming over and over again in waves. Pure bliss spread through her like fireworks; ecstasy was too weak a word for what Graham had given her.

Then, as she was limp and sated, Graham took her leg, hoisted her ankle on his shoulder and then sank his thick cock into her soaked pussy. She felt like she was being split in half in the best way, his length driving into her at a punishing pace that spun her wild. She scrabbled at him, needing more, needing to touch him.

Mina clambered for him and he hitched her knee on his hip, still fucking her. Her fingers clawed at his back, pressing into his ass cheeks. She felt his muscles flex there as he pummeled her into another budding orgasm. The sounds she was making would rival a pornstar's, and she couldn't get enough. Her hips were chasing him as his pelvis crashed into her over and over.

"Graham, fuck. You feel so good."

"You're unbelievable," he murmured into her hair. "Fucking amazing."

Her finger drifted between his cheeks, and carefully, she pressed against that puckered hole. He groaned and shivered when she touched him, so she kept doing it and his rhythm began to falter.

He was close now.

Mina grinned and applied more pressure.

"Fuck, baby. Just like that."

"More?" she asked.

"More," he consented.

She pushed and her finger slipped into his ass and he groaned. His hips ground against her and that budding orgasm bloomed. She came, and seconds later he followed her over the edge. Graham spilled into her, long, slow, thrusts sinking deep as he rode out his climax. She felt warm and wet from his cum, filled so tight by his big cock.

No longer did she feel the frustration from the speeches. No longer did she rail against sexual frustration. She was pleasantly sated and languid.

Getting fucked was exactly what she needed.

After she'd peed and they cleaned themselves up, they tidied the papers and then packed for the upcoming bachelor and bachelorette parties.

"You boys are still camping?" she asked as she tossed a crumpled paper in the recycling bin.

"Yeah, we're not really the strip club type of guys and Em doesn't want to do the whole 'last time as a bachelor' because he's already so committed to Illiana. He just wants a fun boy's weekend to fill out that prerequisite of wedding traditions." He straightened from zipping his suitcase. "You ladies still going to Van?"

"Yeah," Mina confirmed, counting underwear for the trip—six pairs was enough for a weekend, right? "We're going to do a little club hopping and spa days."

Ana was the same way as Emmett. Strip clubs weren't her scene either and she didn't need a getaway before marriage. It was just a fun event that was all part of the wedding fun.

"Think you'll meet anyone there?" he asked in a nonchalant way that was completely not nonchalant.

"No one that could compare to you."

"That's not reassuring."

"Don't worry," she said, chucking him under the chin. "I remember the terms of our contract. I'm not planning on jumping into bed with anyone else—even if they know their way around a vagina."

"Those are bold words coming from someone who just had the best sex of her life."

"Oh, is that what you thought it was?" she stood up straight and laughed. "Maybe for you. Maybe it was just all right for me."

"It sounds like you need a refresher," he teased, gathering her in his arms. "I think I need to remind you that no one can fuck you like I can."

"Well?" she asked, baring her neck, letting her fall of golden-brown hair cascade down her back. "What are you waiting for?"

Suddenly, he was waiting for nothing.

They arrived in their hotel room and promptly dropped their bags. Mina, Ana, Mads, Sloane, Delilah, and Harlowe all rolled in with an air of travel fatigue.

The bachelorette party had begun, the same time as the boys went on their bachelor party campout. They—the boys—had stuck their tents in the middle of nowhere by a pretty lake and set out with beers and rowboats. Wherever they were, somewhere north of Rose Point, they didn't have cell service. If they wanted to call or text, they had to drive thirty minutes out on the logging roads. Even then, it depended on their phone provider.

The girls, meanwhile, were comfortable in a plush, white hotel room, with all the complimentary cell service they could ask for. Which Sloane was more than taking advantage of as she collapsed on one of the three beds—they were double bunking—and scrolled on her phone. Mina and Ana were sharing, then Delilah and Mads, and in the third was Sloane and Harlowe.

Mina wandered over to the floor to ceiling windows that overlooked downtown Vancouver. The sight was dizzying, but yet so similar to Toronto. The traffic was congested down below and soaring above them were skyscrapers. Cranes and buildings dotted the skyline below a gray-blue sky, the street below a sad gray filled with the life of milling people whose destinations were as varied as their personalities.

Pulling herself away from the pane of glass, Mina kicked off her shoes and sank into an armchair.

"We decided it was sparkles tonight for our going out theme, right?" Mina asked.

"Yes, of course," Mads replied, pulling out a short, red, glittery number with skinny straps, draping fabric, and a golden thigh chain. "And if it wasn't the theme, I was wearing this anyway."

"And I brought this," Delilah announced, pulling out two bottles of spray-on body glitter. "To add to the vibe."

For the duration of the afternoon, they just settled into their suite and slowly got ready—doing their makeup and hair with technical precision, hydrating, and narrowing down dress selections. Delilah was on a bit of a writing deadline so she was holed up on one of the beds, headphones on, tapping away at her laptop in the few spare moments she had. Harlowe was nervous, frequently texting with her mother who was babysitting her daughter for the weekend—the first time she'd left her this long, she'd admitted. Sloane was napping on her bed, sprawled across it starfish style, while Mina, Ana, and Mads were helping each other get ready.

In addition to body glitter, Delilah had also brought temporary tattoos in a bridal theme. Illiana had a giant, cartoonish engagement ring with curly script proclaiming Bride on her wrist, while Mads had a #teambride along her forearm. Mina took the one that said Maid of Honor.

Mina had been meticulous with her hair today, trying to keep it as smooth as possible. She'd had her hair wash day the day before yesterday so she still had plenty of sleek, bouncy curls. A stubborn coil fell over her brow and into her eye and another one kept brushing her throat in a way that reminded her of Graham. Which just made her miss him.

All the girls had their dresses hanging up, and even though they weren't on yet, Mina had to say that they were fucking gorgeous and they would look stunning in them all.

Mina shimmied into her sparkly dress, the pastel pink fabric clinging to all her curves. She applied an obscene amount of sparkle to her makeup, while Harlowe, clad in black, doused her with body glitter.

When they all left the suite, buzzing from a little pre-drinking, they definitely drew eyes to them. As they crossed the lobby, a guy even boldly sauntered up to their resident author.

Delilah's dress was a svelte blue, the sparkles bringing out the shine in her equally sapphire eyes. It emphasized all her lush curves and hugged her large breasts, making them look more fantastic than usual.

Which was probably exactly why gold-chain dude bro here was shooting his shot with a preconceived notion about what he thought Delilah was based on her size and weight alone.

He was sorely mistaken.

Mina didn't hear what dude bro said, but he did hear Delilah's cackling response.

"You really singled me out from all these ladies, thinking I'd be an easy lay cause I'm fat, right? That I'd be so dependent on your desire for validation?" Delilah let out an unkind laugh. "Boy, you couldn't handle me if you were six feet making six figures. Your inherent misogyny and compensating ego will always hold you back. Have the night you deserve."

And with that evisceration, Delilah left him behind, swishing her thick hips with every step back to their group.

Dude bro's eyes lingered on the rest of the girls and without even turning around or missing a step, Delilah called out: "Don't even think about it, bitch boy, they're not interested."

Mina's jaw dropped.

Delilah Rose was a force to be reckoned with.

"What did he say?" Ana asked, appalled.

Delilah rejoined them and linked arms with Ana, shaking her fire engine red hair out over her shoulders.

"He said that I was pretty for a big girl and that he bet I didn't see the dating scene much, so he'd be willing to show me around." Delilah practically gagged.

"What a pig!" Ana gasped.

"He's definitely a piece of work, but not the first one I've encountered."

"Was that negging?" Harlowe asked, concern etched in her eyes behind her cat eye glasses.

"No fucking clue," Delilah responded. "But whatever it was has a certified 100% failure rate."

The girls laughed and left the hotel behind. Once on the street, Mina stopped Ana with a hand.

"Before I forget!" Mina fished the baby pink sash out of her silver clutch. When the sash unraveled it displayed a golden BRIDE in calligraphy. "And there's this," Mina said, retrieving the tiara from Mads.

They crowned and sashed Illiana, the pink and gold offset beautifully against her glittery white minidress. With perfect pearly pink oval nails, Illiana carefully shifted the plastic on her head and grinned.

"This is amazing," Ana proclaimed.

Linking arms, the girls went on their way to the first bar. Immediately, a group of guys saw the sash and ordered the girls a round of lemon drop shots—Sloane refused hers, while Madeline happily made sure it didn't go to waste.

The first bar was full of flashy disco balls and cheap light shows—the kind you always saw at bowling alleys after dark. It smelled of spilled beer and over sweet perfume, the sort of sickly sweet that turned your stomach. The music was loud and the speakers were painfully crackly. It was a bit of a dive, but honestly, it was pretty fun.

They stayed at that first bar for less than an hour before moving onto one a block down when Ana kept getting hit on. The second destination was called Elevate, and it was sleek and chrome. All blacks and silvers with hot electronic music, abstract drinks, and severe lines. It felt like something out of a lite sci-fi film. That bar they managed less than a half hour—especially since the drinks were exorbitantly priced.

As they walked to the third bar—their high heels clicking in near unison—they encountered wolf-whistles and cat calls. All of which they ignored. Especially when Sloane gave them cutting looks that tucked their tails between their legs. Mina was realizing so many of the dynamics of the city no longer held the appeal it once did. The people were not small town friendly. There came a certain amount of audacity that a crowd anonymity provided, one that let certain actions eclipse all the people walking on the street. Not to mention the air quality was subpar—her lungs felt tighter than they had in Rose Point.

Not to mention, who was in Rose Point.

Throughout the day, Mina had been checking her phone, used to the intermittent texts from Graham, but his lack of service rendered her phone useless with regard to him. Even so, she hadn't stopped picking it up. Just to see. Just in case.

Third time's the charm was the hope when they entered Fair Folk's. The lights were dim, but dancing on the walls were projections of flowers and butterflies. The flashing lights were purple, pink, and blue, oscillating in a slow, pulsing gradient. The air was filled with scents of perfume, like berries and liquor. They found a table with a faux marbled top and violet booth cushions, and once settled, a server came by in a little black dress and tiny fairy wings to grab them drinks.

A tequila sunrise, bellini, sangria, margarita, mojito, and a fancy mocktail appeared before them minutes later. The girls sipped as Sabrina Carpenter played on the club speakers, voices around them singing, screaming, and yell-talking over the masses.

This vibe was exactly what Mina expected a modern version of her romantasy books to look like in club form. The book girlies would love it here.

Suddenly, Madeline said the one word that Mina dreaded. The one that would give her a skull-crushing headache tomorrow.

"Tequila!"

CHAPTER TWENTY-FOUR
Graham

Around the crackling fire, a beer to his lips, and music pumping from a portable speaker, Graham should have been happy. And to a degree he was, but he was sorely missing his fake girlfriend. If Jasmina were here, she'd be beside him, or maybe even on his lap, her golden-brown curls tickling his cheek as she leaned against him to whisper something dirty. Something that had that floral peach scent of hers driving him more wild than usual—

Yeah.

Yeah, that would be nice. That would make him happy.

The tents were set up in an arc, two giant things that slept ten people with room to spare, which backed their camping chairs, butting up against the treeline. In the daytime, you could see the snow-tipped mountains and the sunlight glittering on the lake below, just a three-minute walk down the trail.

They'd spent most of the day at the lake after setting up, but unfortunately, sunscreen hadn't been too much of a concern in early May—even though it should have been. Chase's pale skin was already sporting an angry red sunburn, while his husband had a tomato red nose from neglecting application there. Graham, fortuitously, had spent enough time in the shade to be protected by the sun's wrath.

Graham took another swig of his beer and sighed.

"What's wrong, babe?" Kieran asked, seated next to him.

Graham glanced over at him, catching the softness of his dark eyes in the firelight. Graham shrugged.

"You remember those unresolved things I mentioned about me and Jasmina?"

"Yeah? You talk to her about it?"

"Nope," Graham said, popping the P. "And it's just gotten more complex.

"Why haven't you said anything? It's been weeks."

"Remember what you said about status quo?" he asked as Kieran grumbled something he took as confirmation. "Same thing. I don't want to rock the boat. Not before the wedding."

"So, you're waiting until…?"

"The day after."

"Jesus. So, until then…"

"I'm just riding the boat."

The fire snapped and crackled as a hoot of laughter from the woods reached them. Leo came darting out, stoned harder than a rock, naked save for his boxers which allowed strategically placed ferns to adorn his hips like a loincloth. He giggled as he hopped over to a fallen log and sat upon it, like Pan—or a forest deity.

From the same spot Leo materialised, both Emmett and Riley joined the group. Riley was Emmett's older half-brother, a man they hadn't known existed until ten years ago. Like Emmett, Riley had black hair, but unlike his younger brother, he kept his short. Riley also had brown eyes lacking the amber hue of Em's, but the shape was the same. Riley had broader features and was an inch or two shorter, but it was clear they were related. But only by their looks, not mannerisms. They'd been raised by completely different people.

Emmett and Riley both had that stoned softness to them, that light, carefree, 'life is good' kind of way. Graham and the guys didn't partake in weed very often—some of them not at all—but if there was a time to partake, a boys camping trip would be it.

Riley also had originally been a groomsman, but after some family concerns, he'd been forced to ask Em to step down. Luckily, Emmett took it with grace and had also saved Illiana from having to add someone to her bridal party to even the numbers.

Flopping into the chair next to him, Emmett looked at Graham with a mushy adoration.

"I can't wait to marry my wife, bro," Em whispered. "I love her so much."

"I know," Graham responded, a small smile on his lips. But it held a touch of sadness.

"I also can't wait for you to marry Mina."

Graham jolted. "Where did that come from?"

"Illiana and I have talked about it a bit. How fun it would be, best friends marrying best friends. She has these dreams of her and Mina being pregnant together, baby playdates, calling each other aunties of our babies…it's infectious."

Suddenly, Graham felt ill.

How fucking bad he wanted that too.

How close, and yet so far away it was.

The idea slipped through his fingers like mist, the water vapor only tangible enough to see, not firm enough to feel.

"Do you think you'll pop the question?" Emmett asked, staring into the firelight.

"One day I'd like to," Graham managed, swallowing.

"I like the sound of that."

Graham did too.

CHAPTER TWENTY-FIVE

Mina

"Okay, Jas, bebe. Please," Mads begged, more than six drinks deep and who knew how many tequila shots—she couldn't resist them. "You have to tell us how freaky you and Graham get. I'm dying to know."

They were still at Fair Folk's and the drinks had flowed freely. The establishment had gotten busier, but they maintained their seats. It had been a unanimous decision to stay, and so, several hours into the night, Mina was on her third sangria, trying to avoid Mads's question.

"I've been sex deprived for so long," Mads pouted. "It's been six months."

"Oh, you poor thing," Mina playfully mocked. "How will you survive?"

"I won't. Not without those juicy details."

"Why am I being grilled here?" Mina deflected. "It's *her* wedding," she said, indicating Illiana with a pointed finger. "Ask her.

Illiana shook her head from behind her bellini. "Mm, no. We're not discussing my sex life with my sister-in-law right there—" Ana pointed to Sloane, who nodded stoically. "Sloane doesn't want to hear about that."

"I appreciate you not divulging the details about my brother's penis," Sloane affirmed.

"Right," Mads piped up. "We're talking about Graham's penis."

"Can we stop saying penis?" Mina muttered.

"We could say cock?" Delilah suggested, sipping her mojito.

"Leave it to the romance author to say cock," Mina quipped, laughing.

"Well, we could just come up with other words." Delilah tapped her lip. "Like man meat."

"Man meat?" Mina choked.

"Schlong?" Ana added.

"Pleasure lever," Sloane offered.

"Disco stick!"

"Flesh wand!"

"Satin swathed sword!"

On and on it went, more and more ludicrous names for dicks jumping into the fray until they were laughing so hard tears watered down their face at the stupidest suggestions. Mina was wheezing, not having expected the wild prompts from Harlowe, but the ones from Ana and Delilah checked out— heathen smut readers they were. Herself included in that assessment.

Drinks were consumed in record quantity, the only one of them abstaining was Sloane. To put it simply, the girls were drunk. Very.

"Okay, okay," Mina relented, liquor turning her tongue loose. "You all wanted to know about my sex life with Graham?"

Madeline, who'd been standing on the dais nearby meant for dancing, popped down at the sign of Mina's weakness. She perched on the empty chair next to Mina.

"Oh, yes, darling. Please tell," Mads trilled, staring with the laser focus of a drunk person who couldn't actually focus.

"He has this thing he likes to do…" Mina began. "Where he gets me almost there, then stops. And he does it over and over. And when I finally get there, it's so intense." Mina sipped her drink. "We also really enjoy butt stuff."

"You mean…he does?" Ana asked, almost awed.

"Mmhmm."

"Have you pegged him?" Sloane asked.

"Not yet."

"This is enlightening information," Delilah practically purred.

"But it's been discussed?" Sloane pressed.

"It has—a little."

Sloane leaned back with a devilish smile. "Right on, girl. You got lucky with that one."

"I've never pegged a guy so I have no idea where I'd even start."

"Oh, I have," Delilah interjected, crossing her legs and leaning back. "It's very fun."

"I might have to ask you for some tips later."

"You know where to find me, Sweet Love."

"Wow, you're wearing that sash like you're doing it a favor," a male voice came from behind them. "I wouldn't mind taking it off, though."

"Ew," Harlowe muttered.

Mina discovered a man probably many years older than the oldest of them standing behind them, dark hair slicked back in a way she was sure made him look like Henry Cavill, but instead aged him by revealing his receding hairline. He wasn't unattractive—physically per se—but his personality took him down several notches into gross.

Illiana turned with her lip curled in distaste. "I'm going to quite enthusiastically pass on that."

"Come on, sugar—you look so sweet. I'd love a taste."

"Holy fuck, no," Sloane stood, getting between the guy and Ana. "She's not interested. You see what that sash says? Or are you illiterate in addition to being a reptile?"

"Ooh, a bit of a watchdog, this one, eh?" he chortled, his dry lips curved in an ugly sneer.

"Yep, and this bitch is her soon to be sister-in-law, so back the fuck off." Sloane sat and waved her fingers in a shooing gesture. "Off you pop."

His eyes slid to Ana again.

Ana shook her head. "Nope. Like she said—off you pop."

The guy turned and took a couple of steps, then tossed back. "Whatever, you're probably just a skank anyway."

"Oh, *hell*, no," Sloane snarled.

Sloane got up from her seat and marched over to fuck face in her sparkly purple dress and grasped him by the back collar of his shirt and forced him down onto a table while *Call Me Maybe* blared. She hovered over him, a clawed hand hovering over his head.

"Apologize," she hissed in his face.

His eyes went round, the whites showing, while his mouth flopped open like a fish.

"I'm sorry," he rasped.

"Not to me," Sloane practically growled. "To her." She nodded to Ana.

He turned his face to Ana, who had her jaw similarly dropped. "I'm sorry."

"Weak, but fine." Sloane shoved him away. "Don't bother us again."

Sloane returned to their table, snatched waist and thick thighs displayed in her confident walk and skin-tight dress. She retook her seat, crossed her legs, and picked up her mocktail.

"That was so hot. If I were gay, I'd fuck you," Harlowe said, awed.

Sloane winked at her. "Back 'atcha, babe."

Luckily, things calmed down after that and they were able to return to drinks and conversation. Meanwhile, Mina's gut twisted with longing and insecurity. She missed Graham, and the fact that she was so attached to him had her very concerned. They were just fake dating for twenty more days.

That was it.

Emmett and Illiana were getting married in nineteen days.

And in twenty her fake dating arrangement was going to be over.

But she didn't want it to end. She wanted it to keep going. She wanted to keep hanging out with Graham, kissing him, fucking him. She wanted to keep going on dates, have homemade dinners, and sleepovers together. She wanted to keep their joking up, to keep challenging each other, to keep dancing in his living room. She wanted to put her books on his shelf, to have her toothbrush next to his, her favorite mug at his coffee bar station.

She wanted it all.

And she wanted it with him.

But she was terrified he didn't feel the same way.

"Do we want to call it a night out here and head back to the hotel?" Ana asked. "Its just after one."

"Can we get McDonalds on our way back?" Mads asked.

"Oh, my gosh, yes," Mina agreed, practically salivating.

After finishing their drinks, settling their bill, and stepping outside in the cool night air, Mina looked up the closest McDonalds. Alcohol imbued blood kept them warm, while Sloane sidled up to Delilah for heat. Del put an arm around her, perhaps as much for heat conservation as it was to keep her steady. Her heels were tall and she was quite tipsy.

Ana and Mads got distracted by the butterflies on the Fair Folk's sign, watching the colors morph from pink to purple to blue, and then fade in reverse. Harlowe was immersed in her phone, furiously texting, and Mina was a few steps away, leaning against the building's exterior.

"Is this the bitch that put hands on you?"

They all turned at the voice—Sloane forcefully so.

A woman, somewhere between forty and fifty, grabbed Sloane by her long black hair and pulled. Sloane yowled and pushed at the woman.

"What the fuck is wrong with you?" she yelled, trying to pry the woman's hand from her head.

Delilah immediately intervened, digging her nails into the woman's forearm and hand, forcing her to let go. The rest of the girls moved in, but it seemed Del had it under control. Just as she freed Sloane's long tresses, fuck face from earlier came sidling up to the woman.

"Did you really go bitch to your mommy about getting rejected?" Delilah scoffed. "Wow. Just fucking wow."

"My man would never!" the woman snarled, stinking of cigarettes.

Oh.

Awkward.

"Sounds like you and your *man*—" Sloane made it seem like a dirty word. "Need to have a chat. Because he propositioned the bride here and insulted her when she—well, all of us, truthfully—said no."

"You—"

The woman lunged.

Delilah caught her and wrapped her arms around her. "Nope, Baby Cakes, we're all done here. This is not happening. Go sort out your toxic relationship elsewhere."

They were drawing attention from the loiterers outside. Either the woman gained sense and listened to Delilah, or didn't want to cause more of a scene than she already had. She stomped off, taking the arm of her guy and muttered expletives all the way.

Delilah swept a hand over her brow. "Well, how about that McDonalds now?"

Tensions had run high, but now, coming down from those cortisol levels, hunger was evident. The six of them made their way to the nearest McDonalds—four blocks away—and devoured their meals. They'd all gotten ice cream in addition to their food because, one, they were drunk and it was tradition, and two, you only live once—how often are you going to go to your best friend's bachelorette party?

"I have a confession, and I need y'all to hold me accountable for it," Harlowe said, swirling her chicken nugget in sweet and sour sauce. "I was texting my ex tonight."

"Oh, Honey Bun, no," Delilah despaired. "What did you say?"

Harlowe shrugged. "It was mostly me ripping him a new one. That he made so many promises he couldn't keep and that I was angry at him for abandoning us. He just woke up one day and decided this life was too hard—being a husband and a father and he just…fucked off. He doesn't even see Odette anymore. Do you know how hard it is to explain to a two-year-old why daddy isn't around? He's such a fucking prick and I hate him for that."

"Oh, Harlowe…" Mina said, voice soft. "I'm so sorry, that's so fucking shitty."

She drew in a shuddering breath. "It is. And now look at me. I'm crying drunk in a McDonalds at two in the fucking morning." She let out an ugly laugh. "I can't believe my life has come to this."

"Well, if it helps any," Mads said, gesturing with a long fry. "We're all drunk in McDonalds at two a.m. and while we're not crying, the night is still young. Take it from a psychologist."

"One time I got so drunk off Smirnoff Ice I ended up crying about shelter dogs and Graham had to comfort me," Mina revealed in an attempt to commiserate. "And this was back when we hated each other, so the vulnerability made me hate myself more—and him in turn."

"I really can't believe you two hated each other," Harlowe said, repeating earlier sentiments.

"Honestly, same," Ana added. "And I saw you two interact during that time."

"Same here," Mads said.

Mina shrugged, trying to play it off. "Guess there's a thin line between love and hate."

Ana gasped. "Mina, do you *love* him?"

Mina opened her mouth. Closed it. Opened it again. Eyes widening. That really just came out.

"Yeah," Mina admitted. "I…I do."

The girls all squealed in response, and while Mina was simultaneously reveling in the feeling, she was also dreading it. Because it wasn't supposed to be real, and she was breaking their last rule.

Back in their hotel, they were trying their damnedest to play games—Werewolf and cards—but the girls were painfully drunk and had the attention spans of a goldfish. Not to mention Mads was currently hunched over the toilet talking to dinosaurs, while Sloane, mother hen that she was, was holding her hair back.

"I'm so glad I don't drink," she quipped.

"I think I'm dying," Mads moaned.

"You're not dying, you're just suffering with regret."

"I think it's the same thing."

"You should've been an actress. Your flair for dramatics is unparalleled."

"I know," Madeline groaned just as another wave of sick took her over.

Mina, meanwhile, was pretending to not be the werewolf she was, but failing miserably due to the alcohol and the racing thoughts in her head.

That she loved Graham.

Not only that, that she was *in love* with him.

She was so absolutely fucked.

CHAPTER TWENTY-SIX
Graham

It was Sunday morning and Graham had packed up everything he could as soon as he woke. He was chomping at the bit to get back to Rose Point.

To get back to Jasmina.

The smell of campfire smoke clung to his clothes like mud, permeated his nostrils in a way that made him wonder if the scent would ever come out.

Graham's blankets, sleeping bag, cot, and clothes were already packed up and stored away in his truck. His personal cooler full of his food and drinks—that weren't shared by the community of guys—was also loaded into the box. The box where he'd first had sex with Jasmina.

His cock twitched in his pants and he sighed heartily. Facing the early morning sunshine on the hillside, with a coffee in hand, Graham looked over the glittering lake washed with golden dawn. The trees were gilded by the early light, each pine needle traced by the sun, battling the shadows. The mountains were carvings against the sky, the same blue shade as if a giant had worked a chisel against the horizon.

It was a matter of manners that he hadn't left already. He knew they were doing this for Emmett, but he truly wanted nothing more than to be at his house with Jasmina.

Wandering around their campsite, gathering up any missed litter, Graham cleaned up the spot, and tied up the garbage bags that held the empty bottles and cans. Aside from the other guys' stuff and the tents, there wasn't much else for Graham to do.

Drawing in the smoke-tinged air, he filled his lungs the scent of timber and outdoors—sun-warmed skin, trees, soil. In doing so Graham resisted the urge to cough—even though he thought it might wake the guys, which he supposed, wouldn't be the worst thing. That meant they could leave sooner.

He was being so dramatic.

When all the guys woke up, some were ready to pack up and go—namely Emmett, Riley, and Graham—while the others were nursing hangovers or fatigue.

It was all said and done within the hour and Graham was on the road minutes later. The gravel dust puffed beneath his tires and he knew every rotation brought him closer to the life he wanted to lead.

At home, he immediately texted Jasmina good morning, unpacked everything necessary, aired out the tent in the backyard, shoved all the clothes and blankets in the wash, and stuffed the fridge full of the remaining groceries. Jasmina finally texted back sometime during his tidying, echoing the good morning and telling him they would be on the 2:00 p.m. ferry. He checked the clock—Jasmina wouldn't even be on the boat yet—and hopped in the shower to wash off the camping smell.

The hot water mixed with thoughts of Jasmina had his cock hardening, and he couldn't resist it—it had been days since he'd had any contact with her, he missed her peach scent, the way her nose scrunched in frustration, her laugh, her voice, her body—and suddenly his hand was wrapped around his shaft.

Graham spent the rest of the day cleaning the house—deep cleaning, he may add—to pass the time. He texted Jasmina intermittently, asking how the bachelorette party went, with her responses of "tell you in person", and other nonsensical things. He was just trying to get his fill of her.

He was so unbearably obsessed with her.

Not in a weird way.

When he took his garbage outside, he noticed the cherry blossom tree in his yard had shed its pink flowers, and now greenery had taken its place.

Hold on.

The cherry blossoms weren't pink anymore.

Which means Cherry Blossom Lane was for nothing.

Emmett and Illiana couldn't get the pretty pink pictures they were imagining.

He made a mental note to text Leo about it and see if he'd had the same realization. It was a shame all those photo ideas had to be trashed now. He did have the thought of asking Leo for their versions, though.

It was nearly five p.m. when he heard Jasmina's tires crunch on his drive. He wasn't afraid to admit that he raced to the door, but nonchalantly opened it, and leaned against the frame in a very book boyfriend way—he also wasn't ashamed to admit that he'd researched that.

Jasmina utterly stole his breath. She sauntered up from her car in a pair of tight jeans and a white t-shirt that slipped deliciously off her shoulder. Her brown skin held remnants of glitter, more of which was caught up in her curls. She grinned at him and he felt his heart flutter away in his chest, his breath catching—much as he tried to hide it.

"Hey there, stranger," she announced.

"Hey baby, you come here often?" he returned flirtatiously.

"Mm, just the last couple of months."

Jasmina ascended the steps and he swept her up in his arms. Brushing her curls back from her face, he cupped her cheek and gazed down at her.

"It's good to see you, gorgeous."

"Back at you, love."

Graham leaned down and pressed his lips to hers, a deep, lingering kiss that spoke of "I missed you's" and "I'm so glad you're home", all feelings he poured into her and prayed she reciprocated.

Right on the front step of his refurbished Victorian, he wondered if he should just throw caution to the wind and make it all known. To have the chance to make it all real.

But fear, the cruel nightmare it was, prohibited him from doing so. At least yet.

"You hungry?" he asked, pulling away just enough to brush his lips over hers as he spoke.

"Starved," she responded in like fashion.

Graham grinned and tugged her into the house where he'd already prepared dinner. Steak, loaded baked potatoes, corn on the cob, and garlic buttered broccoli.

"Damn," Jasmina said practically drooling. "You sure know how to treat a lady."

"I live to serve."

The two of them dove into dinner, exchanging tales of their bachelor and bachelorette party trips, the wild night out Jasmina endured, the drunken hide and go seek the boys had entertained, among all the other shenanigans. After they ate, Graham washed the dishes while Jasmina perched on her chair, enjoying a cup of chai. She was regaling him with the misfortunes of men who'd hit on Illiana and Delilah, and how both Delilah and Sloane had fended them off.

"Do you think we've had enough practice with our dance?" he asked suddenly.

They'd only practiced a handful of times, but nothing compared to the first time. When they'd had their first real kiss, and he pressed her against the window. He always got hard thinking of that moment, no matter how many times, it never got old, and this time was no different.

"You know what they say—practice makes perfect."

Graham took her by the hand and led her to the living room where he once again took her in his arms and put on the song. They began the routine they'd unanimously and somehow wordlessly developed together. They dipped and spun, feet moving in sync as Ed Sheeran's vocals guided them on.

Jasmina's peach scent stole his breath; it was everything—it consumed him. He tucked his cheek against her golden-brown hair, slowly swaying through the words. As the song came to a close, it didn't repeat as it always had, but instead drifted into Edwin McCain's *I'll Be*.

His favorite song.

With the new song, Graham guided them into a new dance, and something shifted between them. Something deep and intimate. It was threaded with a low hum of passion, twisted with yearning.

Slowly, Jasmina's nose skimmed up his throat, and in silent answer, Graham tilted his face downward until his lips slanted over hers. Their lips molded carefully against each other, gently building to something more intense as their tongues danced.

And then suddenly, the crescendo struck and he picked Jasmina up, wrapped her thighs around his waist and carried her to the bookshelves behind them. He swept the shelf free of anything that could poke her.

She gasped at the sacrilege he displayed to his books.

"Don't worry," he murmured between kisses. "Those were all old stuffy non-fiction and self-help. I'm just making room for your fairy porn."

Jasmina laughed and twisted her fingers into his hair, letting prickles of pain intensify the pleasure. Her hands were busy with his waves while his worked the buttons of her jeans free. They shimmied off their pants as fast as they shucked off their shirts—he swore he heard a tear—before their undergarments followed suit.

"No foreplay," she gasped as her hard nipples brushed against his chest. "I just want your cock right now. I want you. I need you."

Graham's dick grew painfully hard at that.

"Fine by me. But just know I'm licking your sweet pussy later."

"Deal."

Immediately, Graham sank into her wet heat—fuck, she was so soaked—and slammed fully into her. He thrust in and out in a punishing rhythm, her pussy squeezing him with every roll of his hips. Jasmina tossed her head back and moaned in pleasure, every upward stroke of his cock brushing her clit.

"Harder," she rasped.

Graham complied, the slap of flesh on flesh growing louder as he delivered just what she wanted. Their lips crashed together, teeth biting, tongues tangling. His orgasm started building at the base of his spine, tightening his balls, making his pace falter.

"You getting close, babe?" she taunted.

"Only after you," he replied through his teeth as he nibbled on her neck.

Her pussy began fluttering around him and his control was slipping in earnest.

"That's right, baby," he coaxed. "Come on my cock. Come for me."

She shuddered as she came, waves of bliss forcing her hips to undulate, chasing those dregs of pleasure as he carried her through it. He kept fucking her until it was his turn to come, and when he did, he swore he saw the universe explode into creation—is that what the Big Bang really meant? He came and came, pushing every last drop inside of her. The possessiveness he felt for her had him wanting to claim her on every instinctual level.

Still inside her, he settled his forehead against hers.

"I missed you."

She laughed softly. "I missed you, too."

His heart took off, excitement turning it into a jackhammer.

Was there a chance this was already real?

CHAPTER TWENTY-SEVEN
Mina

The rest of the month passed in a blur. Mina was so busy between work, seeing Graham, and helping Illiana with wedding preparations that she hadn't realized how fast the night before the wedding snuck up on them. Even when they were at the rehearsal dinner earlier in the evening. Even when she and Graham had practiced walking down, arm in arm, taking their places on opposite sides of the bride and groom. It was really real. It was happening.

Mina and Graham were tangled up in his sheets, post sex, his fingers roaming over her bare shoulder. She was luxuriating in his touch, but even then, she couldn't completely hide the tension running through her.

"What's wrong?" he asked.

"Tomorrow's the wedding," she said flatly.

"I know."

"And the day after, this is over."

His fingers stilled. "I know."

"I just…I kinda got used to it. I know it's not real, and it's just for them, but I got comfortable. With us. This dynamic." She heaved in a breath. "It's just sad that an era is coming to an end. We'll go our separate ways after this and find our own people."

The words as they left her mouth burned her tongue. She didn't want anyone else after Graham. She just wanted him. But she couldn't just say that. Especially not post sex. Especially *especially* not post fake sex.

"Isn't that what you want?" Graham asked, a hard edge to his voice.

She immediately felt like she'd overstepped with her words and put him in an uncomfortable position. To repair it, she began backtracking, but not in such an obvious way.

"Well, yeah. That's what we agreed on. I mean, maybe we don't have to go back to hating each other, friends works for me, but we did sign a contract."

"Right. Yeah, the contract."

Mina's brow furrowed. "Are you all right?"

"Yeah, just peachy."

Mina knew he was lying but she wasn't going to push it. Not right now. Not when they had to get a good night's rest. Not when the wedding was tomorrow. Not when it was the last day that she got to enjoy this.

This was it.

One last time.

She pounced on him again.

Hair dryers were going and a happy buzz suffused the salon. Mina was sitting next to Illiana getting her makeup done, while the bride was receiving the finishing touches on her hairstyle. Ana's hair was half up and half down, waves cascading down her back in a golden fall, baby's breath threaded through her hair.

Around them, the rest of the bridesmaids were getting hair or makeup done, all of them having had their nails painted the day before. Illiana hadn't been too strict on the colors, just as long as they didn't clash with the sage green bridesmaid dresses. Most of the girls had opted for pink or pearl, while Mina had chosen a brushed gold that matched her hoop earrings and chain bracelet.

Sloane and Delilah were chatting animatedly with each other while Madeline was getting her long, dark auburn hair curled. As Mina finished getting her lips painted, she glanced over at Ana.

"You nervous?" she asked her best friend.

"In a good way," Ana whispered, breath shaky. "It's my wedding day. I'm actually getting married. It feels unreal."

"When did it feel right? Being with Emmett. When did you know he was the one?"

Illiana smiled a small, private smile. "On our first date. I think I fell in love with him right away. No one's ever made me feel the way he does." Ana's eyes turned dreamy. "Why do you ask?"

"No reason."

Oh, there was a reason.

A big fucking reason.

And she was going to confess it tonight.

The Ellis family lake house was bustling with activity. Caterers, decorators, and people milling around to set up were wandering the property. A party shop was hired to set up and take down all the chairs and such for the ceremony, then prep the rest of the yard for the reception. Entertainment was set up while Emmett and Illiana were to take pictures in the form of yard games—washers, ladder ball, lawn Jenga, and the like—with snacks and beverages. However, the bride and groom's parties were not going to take part of that pre-reception fun, as they were meant to be involved in a bunch of the photos.

Illiana and all her bridesmaids were ensconced in the pool house to await their cues. Leo was walking Illiana down the aisle in lieu of her father, both because she was no contact with her father, and he wasn't in attendance. Also, because he held the title in name only, not in any action.

Guests were already taking their seats, and quiet instrumental music was playing over the speakers—a Bridgerton soundtrack, as per Ana's request. Conversation could be heard over the music through the open windows, burbling excitement in voices included. Familiar voices sounded far closer to them and Mina remembered the boys were outside the pool house in a white, three-sided, windowed tent, awaiting their cues.

Like the rest of the bridesmaids, Mina jittered with nerves. It wasn't even her wedding, but she knew for a brief moment all eyes would be on her.

On her and Graham.

And for more than one reason. So many people present knew their history of loathing, knew how much they'd bit back at each other, and suddenly they were together? Mina knew they'd be scrutinized.

Uncle Walt popped his head in the pool house.

"Ladies, you look incredible. It's time for the bridesmaids to start walking down the aisle," her uncle announced.

Mina swallowed her nerves, took her bouquet of white and pink peonies—inspired by Emmett's backyard garden—and stepped outside the pool house.

There, standing in caramel suspenders with gold clips, gray suit pants, a white button down, and a matching gray tie, was Graham. His hair was carefully styled with pomade and he looked like a fucking treat. Her eyes were only for him, so much so that she didn't even notice the rest of the guys until she heard a few snickers.

Mina blinked rapidly, shaking herself free of the fugue.

"You look amazing," she said.

It wasn't until she spoke that she realized Graham had been just as taken as she was. She watched him reorient himself to the wedding and the present matter. It made her tummy do somersaults.

"You're breathtaking."

Mina blushed and mumbled a thank you as she took Graham's proffered arm. He was warm and solid beside her, a steadying heat she so desperately needed.

Her dress was a light sage green, made from satin material, the straps thread-thin with a dipping neckline. It wasn't tight but it did fall all along her curves. A thigh slit allowed for ease of walking.

At their cue, they began descending the steps from the deck to the lawn.

The lawn before the lake had been transformed. White chairs with pink satin bows lined an aisle made from white and pink flower petals. Strung above were globes of fairy lights, hung from posts framing the scene and nearby trees. At the end of the aisle was an arch, crafted from cedar and florals, framed by willow boughs. Off to the side was a pergola mapped with hanging wisteria and more lights, round tables covered in white cloths scattered beneath it, while the chairs were crossed back, dark wood. To the other side was a dancefloor set up beneath a willow tree, lights dangling among the branches to create a private setting—perfect for first dance photos. On the rest of the grass were the yard games, while on the deck were coolers, covered platters of food, and signs indicating where to go in a loose, handwritten script.

Mina and Graham walked down the aisle to the instrumental version of *I Get to Love You* by Ruelle, each step cushioned on the grass, all eyes on them. Her heart raced, and if not for Graham holding her, she might've fallen over. They walked down the long stretch, meeting eyes, giving smiles. When it was time to part at the arch, she gave him a lingering look and took her position. Graham did the same.

Sloane and Nate followed them, effortlessly smiling and striding. The sage green dress shimmered with every step in the sunlight, the slightly shiny fabric a gorgeous compliment to all their figures.

Once Sloane and Nate took their places, it was then Kieran and Delilah, and then Madeline and Chase. In the front row were Riley and his wife sitting with their children. Beside them were two empty spots off the aisle for Emmett's moms.

Once the groomsmen and bridesmaids were lined up, then came the flower girl and ringbearer. Leia, with a basket tied to her collar was shaking petals around the aisle, a big sage bow tied to her neck. Gimli, clad in a matching bowtie, carried two rings tied to a pink pillow down the way. Both of them elicited delighted laughs from the guests, a few even let out happy squeals—namely the children in attendance.

Leia took her seat at Mina's feet, panting happily—she'd practiced so well with Emmett and Illiana—while Gimli was carefully contained by Graham on the other side.

And then it was Emmett's turn.

He traversed the aisle with Ashley and Danika on either side of him, both of them wearing sage green a few shades darker than the bridesmaids. Their dresses were off-the-shoulder lace, just longer than their knees. Long hair was pinned up with light makeup.

Emmett, meanwhile, wore a matching suit and suspenders combo to his groomsmen, his shoulder-length black hair tied in a topknot on top of his head. His warm brown eyes were glowing and Mina could see the love he had for her best friend in them.

At the end of the aisle, he kissed both his mothers' on the cheek, and took his place. Danika and Ashley found their seats next to Riley and his family.

As the song reached the bridge, Illiana made her appearance.

Illiana's white dress was covered in delicate, glittery floral appliques. It had a sweetheart neckline and drop sleeves, the corset snug around her breasts and waist where it then flowed down from her hips in a beautiful A-line.

On her arm was Leo, his golden hair slightly darker than hers, dressed in a charcoal suit, sans tie. Proudly, he walked her down the aisle, having taken a place that Ana had so desperately needed.

Leo had called in a favor from one of his photography friends who was present to take pictures of the ceremony so he could walk Ana down the aisle. After the ceremony, Leo would take over.

Illiana's face was glowing with love. So much brightness and happiness utterly poured out of her.

When Mina glanced over at Emmett, his eyes were full of emotion, tears softly dripping down his cheeks. There, too, was so much love.

Mina's heart gave a flip at seeing the love between the two of them, and for some reason, she couldn't stop her gaze from wandering to Graham.

Who was already looking at her.

Graham's blue eyes were trained on her in a way that made her feel like she was the only person in the universe. It was their best friends' wedding, yet all he could look at was her. And all she could take in was him.

Emmett and Illiana took each other's hands.

Mina and Graham just kept looking at each other.

Emmett and Illiana began reciting their vows.

Mina and Graham couldn't pull themselves from each other.

Their vows were heartfelt and emotional, personal and written themselves, yet Mina couldn't focus, because all she could see was Graham. And all she could wish was their future.

Tears pricked at her eyes and she prayed everyone thought they were because of Emmett and Illiana. Not that she was sad her fake dating agreement with the man she was actually in love with was ending tomorrow. She had mere hours of it left.

If not that, maybe they'd think it was the sun in her eyes. Which it wasn't—but a girl could hope.

Mina finally tuned in as both Emmett and Illiana said: I do.

Cheers erupted as the groom kissed the bride and Emmett and Illiana were pronounced married. White butterflies flew across the aisle and danced around them, capturing a perfect scene. Mina clapped along with everyone else, tucking her bouquet into the crook of her elbow.

The husband and wife duo hooked arms and made their way back down the aisle, then all the bridesmaids and groomsmen followed suit. They all made their way back to the deck, where they signed the official marriage certificate with Graham and Mina as the witnesses.

With the ceremony completed, they were all swept away to do pictures while everyone else around them was enjoying the Ellis lake house property—including two of Mina and Ana's friends from university, Juliette and Holly. It was all a blur of posing and smiling, so many of Leo's words blending together. Mina felt like she was only able to complete basic functions and commands because her head was so full of anxiety.

There were only hours left. And she was squandering them with these tumultuous thoughts. Forcing herself to box up her fears, she threw herself properly into the wedding mindset.

By the time Mina had a chance to sit down and take a breather it was dinner time. She ate like she was starved, downing it with two glasses of water and a generous amount of white wine.

The sun was beginning to set, twilight over the lake a beautiful violet and gold. Mina took a moment, watching the fading light play over the water. Just a moment for herself and the feelings that felt too big.

When Mina was summoned to give her Maid of Honor speech, she'd had two glasses of wine that had significantly calmed her nerves. Taking the mic and her place in front of the crowd, Mina cleared her throat.

"For those of you who don't know, I'm Mina, best friend of the bride and Maid of Honor. I would first like to start by welcoming you all here tonight and thanking you for celebrating my beautiful friend and her new husband." Cheers and clinking glasses erupted. "With that said, I just wanted to say a few words. Ana, you are such a gift to the world and I am so unbelievably glad that you have found someone as good as you. Someone who makes you glow brighter each day, who treasures you like the angel you are, and constantly uplifts you. It is such a rarity to find a best friend within your partner, but you have found not only that, but your soulmate in Emmett and I am so honored I got to witness that journey.

"Emmett, you are quite possibly the kindest man I've had the privilege of meeting, and I am so happy that you love Illiana as much as I do—more possibly—which I cannot thank you enough for. You two complete each other and all of us can only hope to find the same kind of love that you two have built together.

"Now, could you all please give it up for my best friend Illiana King and her husband, Emmett King!"

Mina whooped and clinked her glass while everyone else did the same, chanting, "kiss, kiss, kiss, kiss" over and over. Emmett and Illiana obliged, placing a tender and romantic kiss on each others' lips.

Graham was then prompted to give his speech.

"It's going to be hard to top my incredible girlfriend's speech, but I'm going to try—and we totally didn't write these together." He pressed a finger to his lips in a secretive manner. "While everything Jasmina said was true, what she failed to mention is that while Em and Illiana were meant to be, he was mine first." He laughed. Graham was bright, charismatic, and utterly happy delivering his speech. He was the kind of joyous that was contagious, and Mina wanted to bottle it up and keep it for herself. "I'm totally joking, but he is one of my dearest friends and I would be doing them, and their love a disservice by undermining it with cheap jokes. What I can say is that Emmett has stayed true to himself in all the years I've known him, and Illiana has just made him a better, happier version of himself. I wish you both an eternity of love. Give it up for the soulmates!"

After that, the other speeches and cake cutting flew by. It was only when the bouquet toss was scheduled and all the unmarried women were summoned—Harlowe excused herself from that one—that Mina woke from her haze by catching the bouquet.

Of course, she immediately found Graham's gaze, which was already locked on her, and she blushed furiously. The blush turned more furious when Emmett ducked beneath Ana's dress and tore off her garter with his teeth, because when he threw it, Graham caught it.

Everyone who knew Mina and Graham were "together" cheered and were already planning their wedding. Mina's stomach twisted at the guilt and the want of it all.

As Emmett and Illiana stepped beneath the willow tree for their first dance as husband and wife, Mina stepped to the back of the crowd to confine her feelings as much as possible. She swiped beneath her eyes as they began dancing to *Belong Together* by Mark Ambrose.

It was beautiful and emotional and happy. But Mina knew what was coming next. Her's and Graham's dance.

As if she were disassociating, she met Graham on the dancefloor when it was time and took his hands. They moved through the practiced movements like second nature, the familiar song thrumming through the air.

She'd barely gotten a moment to speak to Graham today, let alone touch him, but here she was, dancing with him in front of everyone. She tried to soak it all in. To immerse herself in his touch, his scent, all of it. To try to imprint it in her memory. To make it last as long as possible.

Graham dipped her and spun her, both of them sure on their feet. Even knowing that everyone had eyes on them, she only paid attention to him.

As the final notes in the song hit, they broke apart and then the dancefloor came alive. Mina excused herself from the throng and plucked up a glass of champagne, drinking it on the way to the lake.

Alone on the shore, she let out a shuddering breath as tears slowly coasted down her cheeks. It was all blue-dark and glittering moonlight before her, while everything behind her was golden-green and warm fairy lights.

"Jasmina?"

Mina stiffened at the voice. Only one person called her Jasmina, but even if he hadn't said her name, she'd have recognized his voice anywhere.

She turned slowly and found Graham standing behind her, concern etched across his face. That concern grew into outright alarm when he saw her tear-tracked face.

"Baby, why are you crying?"

CHAPTER TWENTY-EIGHT
Graham

Jasmina's chin quivered after he asked her the question, moonlit tears shimmering on her dark cheeks.

Graham took a step toward her, cupping her face in his hands. Worry soured in his stomach at seeing her so upset.

"Baby, talk to me," he whispered.

"I can't," she managed in a quaking voice.

"Why not?"

"Because this is it. The end of our contract."

"Well, technically, we have until tomorrow—if you want to be a stickler for those pesky terms we signed."

Jasmina's laugh was sad and watery, filled with pain. She swiped at her face, the tears disappearing with the action as she cleared her throat.

"What's going on?" he pressed as his heart raced.

"Can we renegotiate the terms?"

Graham's heart hammered so hard he swore it would break free of his ribcage.

"As in, extend the timeline so it doesn't look suspicious we end it as soon as our Best Man and Maid of Honor duties are fulfilled tomorrow?"

An odd smile twisted her lips. "I was thinking more along the lines of making this permanent."

Shock flooded through Graham and he swore he must've heard wrong. There was no way that Jasmina was the one proposing this to be real. There was no chance that it wasn't him trying to convince her to give them a shot. In no universe had he expected her to make the choice first—to suggest them being together for real. Graham couldn't believe it. He shook his head free of the words in shock.

Graham took her by the hand and guided her to one of the tables at the edge of the reception. It was empty, everyone either crowded near the dancefloor, on the dancefloor, busy with lawn games, or on the deck. Graham lifted Jasmina onto the tabletop and stood between her legs.

"But…you hate me," he finally managed, his voice small.

Jasmina barked a laugh. "Graham, I haven't hated you for a long time—if I ever did." She drew in a big breath. "But that leaves the matter of you hating me."

"Jasmina, I've never hated you. I love you. I always have."

"You—you love me?" she choked out.

"Yes, Jasmina," he replied, cupping her cheeks. "I have been unbearably in love with you for years, falling harder every time I look at you. Everything about you has been everything I've always wanted. When I said I believed in soulmates, you were what embodied it all. You challenge me in the best ways, you are my dearest friend, and I adore everything about you. I dream of making my house, our home. I dream of the life we could build together. All I've wanted for so long was you, but I never knew how I could get you to see me as anything but an adversary. So, I took the scraps of what you could give me, just so I could be close to you."

"But…" Confusion colored her face. "You hated me first."

"I promise you I didn't."

Jasmina shook her head. "I overheard you. Right after graduation. Right after I'd broken up with Corey. You were talking with Kieran at the bottom of Lisa Cunningham's staircase and I was above you. You were kind of drunk and telling him that you couldn't stand to be near me. That talking to me was almost painful. You were telling him all this and he wasn't even defending me." She shook her head again, as if trying to remember the falsely recollected context. "You…you said I drove you crazy and that you didn't know how to handle it."

"Jasmina," he said in a half relieved, half chastising tone. All this time.

All this time this rivalry was based on an wrongly overheard conversation with misunderstood context. Their whole enemies thing was based on miscommunication—and the lack thereof.

"Jasmina. I couldn't stand to be near you because all I wanted to do was kiss you now that you were single. Talking to you was almost painful because all I wanted to do was confess that I wanted to be with you. You drove me crazy and I couldn't handle it because I wanted you so badly, but you'd literally just broken up with Corey after being with him for four years." He cleared his throat. "I didn't want to be a rebound. I wanted you to be ready for the real thing, because you were it for me. You still are."

Tears slipped from her eyes.

"All this time you never hated me?" she croaked.

"Never."

Jasmina let out a choked sob. "All this time I was wrong. I was so completely wrong."

"You were," he said softly. "But the truth is out now, baby. And I love you. I am so pathetically in love with you."

"I'm in love with you, too," she whispered.

Graham's heart blossomed in his chest, like a flower unfurling all its petals at once. Like fireworks. It filling his chest as a repeated, "she loves me, she loves me," chanted through his head—his soul.

Overcome, Graham kissed her.

A real kiss.

Tears mixed between their fingers as their lips crushed against each other, tongues battling for the confession of love.

"So, this is it?" she asked. "We're going to be together? For real."

"Yes," he said, grinning against her lips. "This is real. Very real."

Happy tears brimmed her eyes and she kissed him again, consuming him with all she tried to convey. He did the same, pouring all his love and devotion into her.

Graham's hands went to her thighs, tugging her closer to him, letting her pelvis bump up against his.

Jasmina paused and looked down pointedly. "Babe, I think you have an issue."

"Yeah, my issue is that I really want to fuck my real girlfriend."

"Then we should take care of that."

"Just one last time?" she teased.

"Fuck that. This is the first time of many real times."

And with that, he scooped her up and hurried her to his truck while she laughed delightedly the whole way.

They clambered into the back of Graham's truck, giggling. It was luckily parked off to the side least populated, tucked near a tree.

Graham, grinning like a fiend, helped her in. Jasmina fell against the black leather seats, laughing with delight as she tugged him in atop her.

Somehow, he managed to get the door closed and locked as she pulled him in by his tie. She didn't let go when his lips crashed upon hers, she just wrapped it around her fist to keep him close while her other hand palmed his hard cock through his dress pants.

Hitching her leg up on his hip, he spread her thighs as wide as possible in the cramped space, revealing her lace panties. He bit his lip as he took her in, her pretty pussy covered by a mere scrap of black lace.

And it was all his.

She was all his.

He kissed her again, hard. Their tongues battled, homage to the loathing identities they'd shed.

No longer were they enemies.

They were lovers.

Boyfriend and girlfriend.

Soulmates.

It was real. They were real. She was real.

Graham tugged the crotch of her panties aside, revealing her glistening sex. He slid a finger in and curled, pumping while the heel of his hand ground against her clit.

"Oh, just like that—don't stop," she moaned.

The windows were getting fogged up as she planted one foot on the ceiling of the cab and the other on the door. She was thrusting her hips up, chasing the friction. She was too beautiful. Too sensual. He had to have her.

Leaning back, he undid his belt and freed his cock, while simultaneously, Jasmina undid the buttons of his shirt, her fingers exploring his abs. She tugged him by his open pants, urging him inside her. He chuckled, and slowly rolled his hard shaft against her slit, the ridge of him pressing her clit.

Jasmina moaned, and lightning shot through him. Yanking down the neckline of her dress, letting her tits pop out, Graham pulled a peaked nipple into his mouth and flicked his tongue against it. He delivered the same teasing to the other one, and after a keening sound of begging from his girlfriend, he pushed his cock inside her.

His hips rolled, grinding into her clit with every thrust, working her up. As much as he wanted to fuck her senseless, this was their first time for real, and he wanted it to be lovemaking. He wanted to savor it.

Jasmina was making the most delightful of noises—desperate pants, cries of his name, muted moans as she bit into his shoulder—and he couldn't imagine a more beautiful sound.

Graham had never been so happy as Jasmina had made him.

They were real, and he was having sex with her for real.

Graham's climax began curling inside him as Jasmina's pussy clenched around him. He felt her getting close and he was determined not to finish before her. He kept chasing her, building her into her orgasm. When she shattered, she raked her nails down his back, his dress shirt having slid mostly off in the process. She mewled as she squeezed him and then he was coming too, waves of ecstasy swallowing him beneath the tsunami of pleasure.

He groaned her name, kissing her throat as his thrusts slowed. As their orgasms waned, a quick series of knocks sounded at the window—too fogged and tinted to see into—as a few whoops and hollers of "ooh get it, buddy" and "hell yeah, brother" sounded from a few drunk hooligans passing by.

"Oh my god," Jasmina said, covering her face and laughing.

"Think they enjoyed the show?"

"I don't care if they did, because I did."

He kissed her again out of pure joy then helped her clean his release from her thighs with some napkins and restaurant wet wipes from the glove compartment. After straightening themselves out, they used the peach hand sanitizer he kept in the center console and rejoined the party.

"Did I mention I love you?" he asked, holding hands.

"You, did—but I don't mind hearing it."

He stopped and brushed her golden-brown curls from her face. "I love you, Jasmina Coulter."

"And I love you, Graham Starling."

The next day was the gift opening and many people were horribly hungover, Graham and Jasmina, not included. No, instead of indulging in liquor, they'd indulged in each other all night long. They were certainly tired, but there was a certain revitalization to waking up to the love of your life sucking your cock.

They were at the Ellis family lake house once again; remnants of the night still scattered across the lawn. After their confessions together, they'd rejoined the party in earnest, danced, socialized, and congratulated Emmett and Illiana, all while holding hands and stealing kisses. At some point, Jace had even told off some rowdy guests and then they overheard him apologizing to Illiana for his behavior last summer, and that he was actively trying to change and not be an asshole. It was shocking.

After everything had come out, though, it had become one of the best nights of his life—and he hoped Jasmina's, too.

Graham and Jasmina were early to arrive, the only other people present on the deck were Emmett and Illiana, Madeline, Kieran, Leo, Sloane, Nate, Delilah, and Chase. They joined the group with a silent agreement and while holding hands, cleared their throats.

"We have something to confess," Jasmina began.

All eyes turned to them with varying degrees of concern.

"We didn't want to make things awkward as the Best Man and Maid of Honor for you guys, so we agreed to fake date until your wedding," Graham managed.

"*What?*" Illiana gasped, blue eyes round as saucers.

"But don't worry," Jasmina interjected with an awkward laugh. "We uh, we actually fell in love—or realized we were in love the whole time—in the process. So, we're actually together now."

"For real," Graham added.

"What the fuck, babe?" Emmett asked in shock.

"I'm so sorry," Jasmina said. "I just wanted your day to be perfect and I overheard you and Emmett talking about picking us, but knowing our feelings, so I came up with the idea and dragged him into it. If you're going to be mad at anyone, please be mad at me."

Emmett and Illiana blinked. Graham tugged Jasmina closer.

"Did anyone know?" Illiana asked.

"Only my sister, Sabrina—but that's because she found our fake dating contract."

"You had a fake dating contract?" Illiana asked, shock hollowing her words.

"Yeah," Jasmina confirmed sheepishly.

"Girl, you went straight into build-your-own-romance-book territory. Did you not expect this?"

"I kinda kept telling myself this wasn't one of my romance books. You know, that it was just for you and to keep the peace."

"And now?"

"Um…it's definitely like one of my romance books."

Illiana gave a whoop of delight. "At this point, I don't care that you lied because one, it worked out, and two, you came clean before getting caught."

"And seriously, no one found out?" Emmett asked.

"I mean…technically, I knew," Kieran inserted.

"And you didn't tell me?"

"Hey," Kieran defended. "I didn't rat you out when you were sneaking around with Illiana, did I?"

"Touche," Emmett allowed.

"I can't believe you two pulled this off," Madeline said in shock. "I was so convinced you two had your Valentines Day moment and everything—that was just a story?"

"Oh, um, actually…" Jasmina's face flushed. "That ended up coming true. That whole date and everything. Just not on Valentines Day."

"Okay, tell me everything," Madeline said, grabbing Jasmina by the arm and pulling her away.

"Me too!" Illiana added, kissing Emmett quickly and taking off after the two.

"Oh, fuck it, I want to know, too," Sloane said. "Del, you coming?"

"Uh, fuck yeah."

The girls all took off to be regaled by the tale of Graham's very successful date with Jasmina. He wondered if she would stand by the "best she'd ever" had statement. Judging by the tittering laughs and coy looks he was being shot, he guessed things were being spoken of in a positive light.

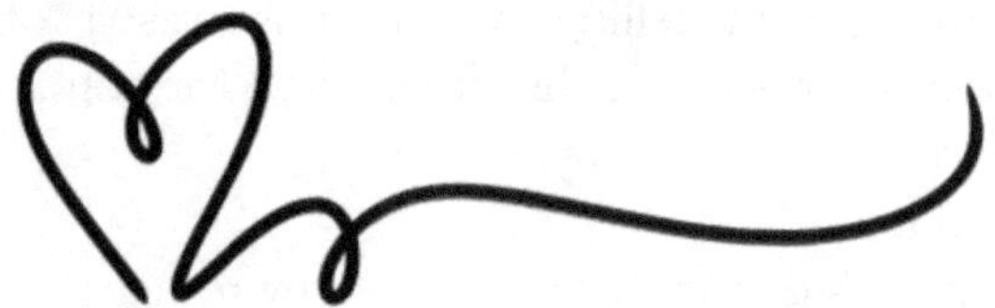

Once the gift opening ended, Graham and Jasmina were curled up on his couch at home, flipping through the fake dating manuals in a nostalgic fashion.

"You know, I never did figure out your middle name," she said casually.

"Oh, it's David."

"Oh, no. That's my ex's name. I don't know if this can work after all."

He laughed. "Sounds like I need to get rid of it."

"He didn't traumatize me too badly, just unapologetically cheated on me."

"Well, when we get married, we'll have to change my name, too. To whatever you want. We could even take Coulter as our surname."

Jasmina crawled over him. "I appreciate that," she purred. "But I'm quite fond of Starling. Makes me feel like I'm in a fantasy book."

"Giving you a contemporary love story wasn't enough?" he teased.

"No way," she murmured against his lips.

"Well, don't worry. We've got plenty of time to try."

"And that we do."

Two pink lines stared up at her.

Mina covered her mouth in shock. She knew she'd been a little late changing her birth control ring, and she knew she'd felt a little off, especially when she'd taken it out and her period hadn't come, but this…

This was unexpected.

Her hand shook as she beheld the stick of plastic that very confidently announced she was pregnant.

She set the test on the bathroom counter, and placed a hand on her still flat lower belly, her rock of an engagement ring glittering on her left hand.

It had been two years since she and Graham had made things official and nearly a year since he'd proposed. They'd discussed children, knew they'd be in the future one day, but Mina hadn't imagined it'd be right now.

She was scared shitless, but simultaneously, she was over the moon. She was pregnant. Her and Graham were having a baby. Unless…

Anxiety tore through her.

"Baby, are you ready?" Graham asked from just outside the bathroom.

Her fiancé walked through the door, and she never got sick of seeing him. Tall, dark, and handsome as fuck. But he was a tall, dark, handsome fuck who'd gotten her pregnant.

He stopped in his tracks when he saw Mina's hand on her belly and the white test on the counter. His blue eyes went round and he raced over to the pregnancy test to confirm. He stared at her, joy painted across his face.

"We're having a baby?" he asked, so much hope and restrained happiness in his voice.

Mina burst into tears.

"Jasmina, baby, what's wrong?"

Graham pulled her into his arms as she sobbed.

"It's going to be twins!" she wailed.

Her fiancé froze, but his hand still rested on her back.

"We don't know that."

"Of course, we do!" she cried. "Your sisters are twins, and my mom is a twin. Oh my god, we're going to have two babies."

"Jasmina," he lifted her face to his. "We're going to have two babies. This is incredible."

She sniffled. "It is. I'm so happy. But I'm really scared."

"Oh, hell, baby. I am, too. But we've got this." Graham placed a hand on her belly. "Whoever this is—or these are—will be so loved. I can't imagine a better mom than you."

Mina sniffled again and nodded, a watery sort of nod that was on the cusp of breaking.

Graham paused. "We do want this, right? Are we happy about this?"

"We're very happy about this," she whispered. "It's just a lot."

"One step at a time. But, maybe we should start reading up. Maybe put some non-fiction back on those shelves downstairs. We might need to move some of your books for What to Expect When You're Expecting—I hear there's a whole collection now."

"You wouldn't dare do that to a pregnant lady."

"I would never," he replied, kissing her forehead, then dropping down to kiss her belly. "You better be nice to your mom in there, she's a lovely person and deserves nice things."

Mina's eyes watered again.

Graham stood and hugged her. "Oh my god."

"I know."

"Do you still want to go to Emmett and Illiana's?"

She nodded. "Yeah, I've been looking forward to game night. This explains why I've been so fucking tired, though."

"All right, I'll go get Juno loaded up in the truck."

He kissed her forehead again, just as she heard the familiar pad of puppy footsteps from the bedroom.

Juno popped in the bathroom, all fifty pounds of blue nose staffy affection scooting in. Juno wound herself between Mina's legs and panted happily up at her.

"Hey, baby girl," Mina stroked her. "Are you going to be the best big sister?"

Mina and Graham had adopted Juno from the SPCA shortly after she'd moved in. Which was virtually right after Emmett and Illiana's wedding. She'd been an abandoned puppy—dumped for her breed and the horrible stigma—and Graham and Mina had taken to her instantly. They treated her like the queen she was, and she ruled the house. Now she spent her days in the lap of luxury and regularly got to see her best friends, Leia and Gimli.

Graham whistled and Juno darted from the bathroom. Mina could hear her thundering down the stairs as she finished getting ready. Downstairs, Mina grabbed her tote bag, slipped her sandals on, while admiring their cherry blossom tree. The leaves were once again green, having shed its pink flowers for the season.

She glanced at the canvas that hung in the living room—a photo of her and Graham down Cherry Blossom Lane, looking like two idiots in love. It was one of her favorite things ever. Leo had gifted it to them shortly after they'd announced their real relationship. He'd told them that even if it had once been fake to them, it was never fake to him.

She smiled and locked the door behind her. Gingerly, she climbed into the truck and Graham took pains to make sure she was safely buckled in.

"Is it too tight?"

"Babe, it's a seatbelt. It's supposed to be tight."

"I'm just worried about them."

"Whoever they are, are fine. They're the size of an orange seed or something."

"That little?" he asked in shock as he pulled out of their driveway.

"Yeah, I think so."

"Oh my god."

They continued driving through Rose Point, making their way to Emmett and Illiana's. At least once a month they aimed for a regular game night. It was their standing date just in case the days were too busy, at least they had this one thing—just like the boys had beers at Blue's.

When they pulled in the driveway, Mina paused, placing a hand on Graham's forearm.

"Do we want to tell them?"

"Do you?"

She hesitated. "Kind of. Yeah."

"Then let's tell them."

The three of them poured out of the truck and went inside. Juno immediately raced to the backyard to play with Gimli and Leia, the three of them chasing each other to their heart's content.

As soon as Mina walked through the door, Ana wrapped her up in a hug. She smelled, as usual, like strawberries and cream, but something about it was more intense than usual. She supposed that's what happened with scents when you were pregnant.

"Hi hon!" Ana greeted as she pulled her inside. "You hungry? Thirsty? I don't have any wine to offer but I have a bunch of sparkling waters and tea."

"Oh, well that works anyway, because I can't drink."

Illiana froze, eyes roving down Mina's frame, settling on her belly and rising again.

"Are you—?" Ana asked, emotion in her voice.

Mina nodded. "I am."

Illiana squealed and hugged her tight. "So am I."

Mina pulled her back and stared at her. "You're what?"

"I'm pregnant, too. Nine weeks."

Mina started crying.

"Graham!" she wailed, her fiancé having wandered to the backyard with Emmett to supervise the dogs.

Graham poked his head in, Emmett following suit as Mina and Illiana wrapped their arms around each other.

"She's pregnant, too!" they both said in unison.

It took a second, but then it clicked for both the guys and Graham and Emmett let out whoops of delight and embraced roughly.

"We're going to be dads!" Emmett proclaimed.

"We're going to be fuckin' dads!" Graham echoed.

Emotions ran high, but eventually all the congratulations were ordered and they settled in for game night. Happiness was thick in the air, and everything was just so good. Life was so good.

The two of them discussed pregnancy symptoms and signs before they knew, in addition to things they were looking forward to, hopes for what they'd have, names, and everything of that sort. The boys also chimed in, as well as conversed between themselves, discussing dad park dates and milestones.

The energy was so infections and Mina noticed both her and Ana would unconsciously touch their bellies, hands drifting there protectively.

They were going to be moms.

As the rest of the night passed, a few games were played, but unfortunately, due to the first trimester fatigue, they had to call it an early night. Illiana claimed she was sleeping close to sixteen hours a day some days, but that exhaustion hadn't struck until almost six weeks along. Mina didn't even know if she was there yet. She was probably closer to five.

Once they got home, Mina collapsed in bed in a comfy shirt and shorts, tracing shapes on her soft belly. Graham crawled in next to her and began kissing a belt across her tummy before that trail drifted north. He met her lips with a sweet, decadent kiss.

"I love you," he murmured into her mouth.

God, she never got sick of hearing that.

"I love you, too," she returned, kissing him deeply.

"Should we start picking baby names?"

"It's never too early."

"Well, in that case. I have a few suggestions."

Mina yawned, sleepiness beginning to pull her under. "How about tomorrow, love?"

"Tomorrow sounds good," he whispered. "Tomorrow sounds very good."

Graham placed his hand on her tummy, over their baby—or babies—and curled into her.

"I'm so glad you said we should fake date."

She laughed sleepily.

"I'm so glad you agreed."

"It was all part of my secret master plan. All I needed was a chance to show you."

"Show me what?"

"That we're soulmates."

She smiled softly.

"Yes, we are."

AUTHOR'S NOTE

Please be advised that I am a white woman author who has written a half Black FMC. I want it known that I am aware of my privilege and that I am not trying to take the place of POCs stories. Mina's experience will not give an in-depth reflection of what it is to be POC as that is not my place to tell that story. If I have inadvertently used racial stereotypes or other offensive terms or scenarios, please let me know. I have tried with diligence to give respect to the character while not imposing myself in spaces that are not mine to be in.

ACKNOWLEDGEMENTS

My seventh book and this is still surreal. This one especially, since Romance Thy Enemy was the first book I've written since so much of my life turned upside down. I went through so much and I came out of it changed. I am not the same person who wrote Love & Other Tropes, but I am a better, stronger, happier version of myself.

As always, thank you to my husband, Michael. We've been through so much and it was hard, but it only proves that we really are soulmates. Thank you for believing in me, encouraging me, supporting me, and giving me the time to write this book. I love you so much.

To Tess, my god, I love you. This book would not exist if not for you. You have been a constant in my life when things were so uncertain. Thank you for being so excited about my books, the art I show you, and being one of my dearest friends. I appreciate you more than you know, and I hope everyone finds someone like you in their life.

Indigo, babes, you are incredible. Thank you so much for the endless fan art and the gorgeous piece of Mina and Graham in this book. Thank you for always listening to me and being so excited for every book and art idea I have. Thank you for being you. I adore you so much.

Sam, this STUNNING cover. Thank you for knowing exactly what I wanted yet again. Thank you for being so enthusiastic. I can't wait for more.

Ashley, the art of Graham's house is absolutely, fucking stunning and I can't get over how perfectly you brought his home to life. Thank you so much for your enthusiasm and I can't wait to work on future projects with you.

Ali, thank you once again for editing my dumpster fire manuscripts and for your hilarious commentary. I appreciate you so much.

My babies, Vivienne and Rosalie, thank you so much for playing outside so mommy could sit on the deck write this. And for sleeping 13 hours through the night so I could stay up late working on this without fear of a 5 a.m. start to the day. Thank you for being you. Thank you for being so curious about mommy's work. Thank you for cuddling me while I edit. You two are my world.

Leah, there are no words for the way you helped me. I wish you knew what an angel you are. Just…thank you for everything.

To my Safe Space. I have no words for how special you all are to me. Thank you truly for everything—writing and non-writing related. You all listened to me and empathized with me during the hardest time of my life. Especially, KP, thank you for checking in with me every day last summer. I needed it and you are a fucking saint.

To all my readers who show so much enthusiasm for my books, thank you, you truly keep me going. I hope to share many more books with you. Thank you eternally.

ABOUT THE AUTHOR

Kayla McGrath has been writing since the age of thirteen out of spite, having read a book with a love triangle that didn't go her way. After that, it became a passion. If she's not writing, then she's reading, or drinking endless cups of chai. Kayla lives on Vancouver Island with her husband, two daughters, and two dogs.

She is the author of the Cold as Iron trilogy, the Infernal Curses series, A Deathless Empire series, and the inter-connected standalone Love and Other Tropes novels. Romance Thy Enemy is her seventh book.

You can find her mostly wasting time on Instagram and Threads (@kaylamcgrathbooks) and TikTok (@kaylamcgrath_).

THE COLD AS IRON TRILOGY
This Broken Memory
These Ruined Dreams
Our Shattered Fates

INFERNAL CURSES
The Nightmare Curse
The Hallow Curse (Summer 2025)

A DEATHLESS EMPIRE
A Deathless Empire

LOVE AND OTHER TROPES
Love & Other Tropes (Emmett & Illiana)
Romance Thy Enemy (Mina & Graham)

CHAPTER ONE
Illiana

Illiana was willowy grace and lithe muscles. Her face was serene and her blonde hair was pulled back tight in a bun, not a wisp out of place. She was careful with her plié—softly swooping her arms in the sun-dappled studio. The red brick, gleaming cherry floor, and walls upon walls of mirrors was the epitome of stereo-type. It was in one of these many mirrors that Illiana watched her once flawless form buckle beneath her weight, her surgically re-paired foot crippling her poise—and soul.

She caught herself on the bar at her side before she could crash to the wooden planks. And although physically she remained upright, emotionally she was in a million shattered pieces on that floor.

The pain was real, but it wasn't new. Two metal plates, six titanium screws, an ugly scar and you had a triple fusion. It was the name of the surgery that saved her foot and ended her career.

"You held on much longer this time, Ana," Mina, her physiotherapist and best friend, reassured her gently. "Maybe next week we can try out the pointe shoes."

Illiana ducked her head, staring down at her slipper clad feet, the edge of a glaring white scar creeping out from the right one. She knew it was futile to even try—the bones of her foot were fused for fuck's sake—but she didn't know how to be anything other than what she was told she would be—great. It didn't matter that the arch of her foot couldn't curve like it used to. It didn't matter that she'd lost a large percentage of mobility in her ankle. It didn't matter that standing on her toes was like shoving iron pokers in her bones. All that mattered was that she defied the doctors and their odds and returned to her world.

"You're being generous," Illiana admonished, unwrapping her ribbons and yanking off her yellowing slippers. These had lasted her the longest in her life—four months—and they showed little sign of requiring replacement. "I can't plié for shit and you know it. Besides, I'm still missing muscle-tone in this leg. I'm sure once it's up to par again things will be different." It's what she had to say, even if it wasn't the truth.

Mina crossed the room and Illiana watched her reflection approach, her spandex-clad legs flexing as she sat next to her, crossing her umber arms over her knees. The sunlight caught gold specks in Mina's hazel eyes and slanted across her face, casting her high cheekbones and full lips in an unfairly glowing light. She looked like a goddess, meanwhile, Illiana looked like a failure.

"It's been a year, hon," Mina whispered, the solemn words echoing vacantly in the empty studio.

Illiana tightened her jaw, staring hard at the spacers between her toes and the cotton covering them.

"I know, how could I forget?" Hot tears burned in her eyes, and Illiana refused to let them fall. "Why do you think I've been pushing myself so hard these last few weeks? I need to see progress, I can't stay—" she swallowed past the lump in her throat. "I just need to keep at it. Mind over matter, you know?"

"I know," Mina answered softly. "It's just…I don't mean to push, but maybe it'll be a good idea to get out of the city. Before, you know, the anniversary. Without the constant reminders."

"What do you mean? Like I should go on a weekend get-away? A spa trip? Camping? None of those seem particularly appealing considering I have no one to go with. And I'm not discounting you, I just know you're going to the west coast this summer."

"Well, see that's exactly what I was thinking. What if you joined me? You haven't been to BC since Christmastime our first year of college and instead of doing your sessions remotely, I can continue doing them in person. It's beautiful and maybe it can help you find some peace, or clarity, or solace, or whatever the hell you want to call it."

Illiana's mouth popped open. A summer vacation. With her best friend. In their twenties. Nothing could have prepared her for the serotonin and dopamine rush she was experiencing at the prospect. She thought that opportunity had passed her by in the final summer of high school, the definitive line that demarcated adolescence and adulthood. The wonder of a summer, un-hindered by work, and a relationship that had turned to complacency. Was it possible Illiana could do this and get out of the ditch her life had turned into?

"But where would I stay?" Illiana had savings and a comfortable sum in her bank account, but her finances were being sparingly fed by Disability Insurance every two weeks but it was a laughable amount. She couldn't afford to fund a hotel room for the entire summer. Maybe if her settlement came in, but she wasn't holding her breath on that one.

"With me, of course! The pool house has plenty of room and my aunt has been harassing me for months to bring some-one home with me. I'm sure she meant a new boyfriend and not my best friend, but you know she loves you."

Illiana hesitated, removing all her shoe prep and slipping on fresh cotton socks. "I really don't want to impose. Maybe I should just stay here and practice."

Mina grasped Illiana's hand, squeezing. "Please? I want you to come with me." A devilish smile spread across Mina's face. "If not for you, then for me! This way Aunt Lacey can harp on you for being single, too. I can't handle her reminiscing about Marcus anymore, it was five years ago and she had no idea how bad in bed he was. Please, Ana, I need you."

Mina wasn't single but things with David were so new they were hardly out of infancy. Much too soon to bring home, especially across the country.

"I bet that's something Marcus never heard."

Mina snorted with laughter but doubled down. "Come on, it'll be fun! And maybe you can forget about that douchebag, and find someone new." Mina gasped. "Ana, imagine having a whirlwind summer romance!" Mina fell to the floor in a dramatic swoon. "I'm picturing you being swept off your feet by some country boy. No, definitely a brooding hipster in an eclectic coffee shop. Ooh, actually—"

"Okay, okay, I get the picture." And she did. She hadn't wanted to imagine it, but what if she did? What if she saw herself sparking up a summer fling? Starry nights around the campfire, beaches with golden sand, barbecues on a sprawling green lawn, all of it accompanied by a handsome, nameless someone that gave her butterflies and made her heart race. Just like in the movies. Could she do it? Was she ready? It had been almost a year since Adrian left her.

"So, will you come with me?" Mina prodded eagerly. Illiana inhaled slowly and then exhaled. "Yeah, I'll come."

Mina squealed with delight and threw her arms around Illiana's shoulders, rocking her nearly to the floor.

"We leave Friday," Mina announced. "I can't wait! This will be the best trip ever."

The pavement was baking beneath the hot Toronto sun. Despite the fact that the heatwave was only just beginning, people were already cranky in the evening light—wiping sweaty brows and fanning shirts. Illiana herself was uncomfortable in the heat as well, but she was good at hiding her discomfort after most of her life was spent on a stage. Ballet was where beauty demanded pain and serenity was granted on blistered toes. Her black bodysuit was tucked into a pair of grey sweat-shorts while white tennis shoes replaced the slippers that now resided in her dusty rose gym bag.

Her apartment was only six blocks from the studio her and Mina practiced at so she walked there three days a week, rain or shine—and in Canada that weather could depend on the hour. Popping in her AirPods to drown out the drone of traffic, buskers, and people yelling into their phones, Illiana began the trek home.

She limped ever so slightly while shards of pain radiated through her foot and up her leg. She'd really overworked herself today. Maybe she should have listened to Mina when she suggested water aerobics that afternoon, but Illiana was determined.

Mina called it stubborn.

Skyscrapers towered above her while the male singer crooned in her ears about being good to you. The landmark of the city, the CN tower, was crowned by wispy clouds far on the horizon. Illiana took a swig of water from her white insulated water bottle as she waited for the streetlight to change. It was moments like this, in the hustle and bustle of the city that she could pretend like she belonged. That she was just like the business man behind her, or the Cottage Core girl to her right. When she was among the people of the world's most diverse city, she didn't feel like her parents had disowned her or her boyfriend had dumped her for her understudy.

The light changed and WALK appeared above her head. With the suited man and the girl in a mushroom patterned dress with her, she smiled mildly to the music's vocals and crossed. She ignored the coffee shop the girl slipped into, suffocating the craving for a chocolate croissant, and she gritted her teeth when the man entered the hole in the wall Italian restaurant, her stomach rumbling for seafood fettuccine. She'd already gained six pounds since this time last year; she couldn't afford any more. The music switched over to Harry Styles and she quickened her pace with thoughts of roasted vegetables and lemon salmon to distract her.

As her building came into view, a brick and glass façade, the first beads of uncomfortable sweat were slipping down her spine. When she input her code, she was greeted with a rush of AC upon entry. The walls were cream and the floors an inoffensive shade of gray, the faux wood doing nothing for the arbitrary canvases of landscapes shot in black and white. She debated the stairs but the splints in her foot begged for the elevator. So, she rode the six floors up to her apartment quashing the regret.

The door pinged and she fished her keys out, a second Harry Styles song cresting the first chorus as she unlocked her door. As she removed her earbuds and was welcomed to an emp-ty home, the magic of the city drained away.

When Adrian had left her a year ago, he hadn't just broken up with her, he had *abandoned* her. She was in the hospital being told that her dream of becoming a prima ballerina was as crushed as her foot. Upon hearing her career was over, Adrian promptly left, skating out with the poise only a ballerino could summon. Illiana thought he just needed time to digest the news, not an excuse to replace her with her own understudy. Within hours Adrian had packed his things from their shared apartment and moved in with Violet, taking the cat with him.

To add insult to injury, her parents—a set of two who hated each other and should never had been married in the first place—were devastated to hear about the accident. Not because their only daughter had gotten hurt and had to undergo surgery, but because their prized star that they had sunk thousands into was a now damaged thing and they weren't getting their money's worth. No celebrity and no accolades. Just burdened with a depressed child they had no interest in supporting beyond a guilt that lent them to pay the exorbitant rent on her one bedroom apartment in the heart of downtown Toronto.
So, in one fell swoop she was single, unofficially orphaned, and utterly alone. Mina became her emergency contact after dozens of phone calls from the hospital staff to Adrian and her parents went unanswered. The only response she got from Adrian was a voicemail ending their relationship and a text from her mother offering kind, hollow words and the promise to pay for whatever therapy she needed and that was all.

Illiana sighed as she dropped her bag and keys by the island counter and made her sad dinner of leftover fish and vegetables. After she finished the necessary meal satisfying the hunger and none of the craving, she headed for the bathroom for a cool shower. She placed her phone on the sink, prepared to hit her shower playlist but picked it up again.

I'm a glutton for punishment, aren't I? She thought as she stared at her lock screen, a non-descript floral thing she used to replace what was a photo of her and Adrian. Summoning her courage, she entered in her passcode and then texted her mom.

Hey mom I just wanted to let you know I'm heading to BC on Friday with Mina for the summer. I'll be back some time in September, I just wanted to let you know in case you decided to visit and I wasn't home.

She paused before adding more, glancing in the mirror at her tired blue eyes and the purple rings below them.

I've been practicing a lot and I think I'm making progress.

Illiana exhaled sharply, not knowing what else to type. She ended the message with an XO and sent it, then turned on her playlist and set down the phone.

In the shower Illiana washed away the days fatigue and wear, refreshing herself with new purpose and optimism. After, dressed in a set of blue bamboo pajamas she checked her phone. No message. She brushed her teeth. No message. She French braided her hair in two. No message. She sighed and climbed into bed, putting on Bridgerton for the third rewatch and envied the smoldering glances Anthony kept passing Kate.

No message.